KALEIDOSCOPE

ALSO BY CECILY WONG

Diamond Head
Gastro Obscura

KALEIDOSCOPE

A Novel

Cecily Wong

DUTTON

DUTTON

An imprint of Penguin Random House LLC
penguinrandomhouse.com

LIBRARY OF CONGRESS CATALOGING-IN-PUBLICATION DATA

Names: Wong, Cecily, author.
Title: Kaleidoscope : a novel / Cecily Wong.
Description: New York : Dutton, an imprint of Penguin Random House LLC, [2022]
Identifiers: LCCN 2021046792 (print) | LCCN 2021046793 (ebook) |
ISBN 9780593184455 (hardcover) | ISBN 9780593184479 (ebook)
Subjects: LCSH: Chinese American families—Fiction. |
Sisters—Death—Fiction. | Bereavement—Fiction. |
LCGFT: Psychological fiction. | Novels.
Classification: LCC PS3623.O59749 K35 2022 (print) | LCC PS3623.O59749 (ebook) |
DDC 813/.6—dc23/eng/20211213
LC record available at https://lccn.loc.gov/2021046792
LC ebook record available at https://lccn.loc.gov/2021046793

Printed in the United States of America
1st Printing

BOOK DESIGN BY TIFFANY ESTREICHER

For Read

Kaleidoscope, *noun*

    a. a diverse collection

    b. a scene, situation, or experience that keeps changing and has many aspects

    c. an instrument for optical illusion

KALEIDOSCOPE

PART ONE

No Special Occasion: August 2006, New York City

The clinic was on Bleecker and Mott, just south of Union Square where Riley had booked the hotel room, paid for it with the collection of money they called the Fund: partly hers, partly her sister's, partly cash taken from their parents' house, the knickknack drawer by the kitchen phone, the silver box on their mother's vanity, the pockets of her father's cast-off pants. A week before, when she first found out, Riley had called to book the room she saw online—with a king bed and soaking tub—and to request a high and quiet floor. The receptionist asked how many guests, and when Riley said she'd be with her sister, the woman wondered if there was any special occasion. Riley had laughed, unexpectedly, paused for a minute too long imagining the flowers by the bed, the bottle of champagne they might receive, and if her sister would find it funny, or if this would be the thing to finally freak her out.

Miss Brighton, are you still there?

Yes, Riley said. Sorry. Just a regular weekend. No special occasion.

Of course, the receptionist said. No special occasion required.

It was late August when Morgan came to deliver the news, arriving at Riley's sophomore dorm with iced coffees and croissants. They hadn't seen each other in nearly three weeks. Morgan had been at a trade show in London, Riley assisting her sociology professor to prepare for a research trip to Lithuania. These stretches of time were becoming more familiar; a distance that was once intentional was by then simply natural, a byproduct of living in New York, their schools at opposite ends of the island. They tore immediately into three weeks of material, the things they'd been saving up to discuss, like how their father had recently discovered poking on Facebook and had been poking them both, along with god knew who else, with disconcerting frequency. They swept through the primary subjects, school and work and their mother's new "Sharon Stone" haircut, when Morgan announced she had something to say, and she was so calm, so perfectly nonchalant, it took Riley a minute to register that they had crossed into serious territory.

It was Kyle Webber, Morgan said. Her high school boyfriend had come to the city back in July and they'd stayed out late. One thing had led to another. As Morgan tried to make light of her condition—tried turning the spotlight of astonishment on Riley, at her concern, because she'd always hated Kyle, hated how hard he hammered for their parents, how he picked people up when he was drunk—Riley sat there, quiet and stunned.

"What am I missing here? Why aren't you more upset?"

Morgan took a bite of croissant, oblivious to the spray of flakes—another uncharacteristic lack of care. "Why should I be upset? I don't want it. The idea of keeping it is absurd."

"We agree on that, but Jesus. Morgan. You dated the guy for two years, not me."

"Am I supposed to want it, then?"

Riley leaned forward in her chair, examined her older sister.

"You're being really weird."

"Am I?"

Morgan sat crossed-legged on the bed, wearing one of her trademark designs, a gauzy marigold kaftan that draped her long limbs in her easy, frustratingly glamorous way. The fact that she was growing a tiny Kyle Webber was incomprehensible, made Riley's heart beat a little slower.

"I'm going to take care of it," Morgan said, slightly more serious, reprimanded.

"Have you looked? Have you made an appointment?"

"I will," Morgan said, and Riley reached for her laptop right there, opened it, and began to google. "Riley, come on, I'm more than capable of—" Riley lifted a hand, silenced her sister, whose stupid, stubborn glibness made Riley want to angrily google.

"I," Morgan said, and Riley could hear the tightness in her sister's throat, how hard she was trying to keep herself steady. "I need your help. I know it's serious. Please don't be mad."

For the next hour, Riley read, asking her sister questions without looking up. Morgan swept the pastry crumbs from the duvet and made the bed, answered Riley's questions, and sat quietly while she made phone calls—sometimes pretending to be Morgan, whose personal details she recited as easily as her own. At a certain point, Riley put on music and stood up to stretch, to jump in place, before plopping beside Morgan on the bed. Riley had made a to-do list in Excel, the cells turning slowly green as they were completed. The cover story was Morgan's only task—to find some event in DC or Boston to tell their parents—and now Morgan flipped through the tabs, showing her sister how seriously she'd done her job, presenting the options like they were actually going.

By the time they left the dorm, winding down the stairwell and spilling into the summer night, bleary from screens and sober with information, starving, crazy from being inside too long and softened into their regular selves—Morgan the calm, sensible one; Riley cursing Kyle Webber, that fucking fuck—they'd begun to refer to what they'd planned, the coming weekend, as their abortion vacation.

In the waiting room, Riley looked up each time the door opened and a person stepped out, until nearly two hours later, that person was her sister. Morgan looked fine, surprisingly civilian-like in her shorts and T-shirt, her hair hiked up in a ponytail. She checked out at the counter, paid the woman with cash from the Fund. In her hand, she held a small plastic bag.

"I'll get a cab," Riley said as they left the clinic.

"Perfect. Could we get a wheelchair too? Or did you bring a stretcher?"

Riley looked up to glare at her sister.

"I'm sorry." Morgan tried to smile, her wide, heart-shaped face jangling with nerves. She scratched at both her arms. "I'm sorry. I've been sitting too long. Can we please walk?"

"We have to stop at the pharmacy anyway. You got the pain prescription?"

Morgan lifted the plastic bag.

"Are you okay?"

"Fine," Morgan said. "I mean. I don't know." She looked at the inch of concrete in front of her feet. "I saw it on an ultrasound."

They stood on the sidewalk, August sun beaming hot and bright, Riley no good at this kind of thing. Asking what it looked like or how it made her feel, that was Morgan's territory. Beyond that, they were out of practice.

"Oh man," Riley said. She waited for her sister to say something more, whatever she needed to say, and when she didn't, just stood there atop her long, leggy shadow, Riley took the plastic bag from Morgan's hand, reached for the rolling bag she'd packed for the weekend, and led them forward.

The hotel room was smaller in real life—the bathroom door, when fully open, nearly touched the bed—but it was clean, reassuringly white, everything smelling briskly of eucalyptus. Riley checked the time. Morgan could take the codeine the next morning at eleven, the misoprostol at noon. Morgan swallowed the antibiotic and they lay on the bed, the air conditioner humming impatiently, frustrated that she couldn't drink.

Morgan flipped on her side. "Let's go see a movie."

"Really?" Riley sat up. "What do you want to see?"

They saw *Step Up*, Riley pretending not to notice when Morgan wept each time—at the one appropriate part, when Skinny dies and Mac vows to be a better person, but also when Channing Tatum and Jenna Dewan dance on that rooftop, when the violin starts to play and the curtain lifts for the year-end recital—chewing passionately on her Milk Duds. Feeling her sister's familiar warmth, Riley tried to remember the last time they'd done this, killed a whole weekend just the two of them, and found that she could not. It brought her world into strange perspective, sitting there in the freezing dark. She realized Morgan had kept her word, had granted her the space she'd promised back in Oregon.

Afterward they went for pizza, and when Morgan started to cramp, leaning over the table just slightly, eyes closed, they returned to their room so she could change her pad.

"What's going on?" Riley asked as her sister emerged from the bathroom. She handed her the dress she'd packed in the suitcase.

"You don't want to know." Morgan took off her T-shirt and shorts and pulled the dress over her head. Riley was already in hers, applying lipstick and fluffing her hair with her fingers. When Morgan stuck out her hand, Riley gave her a pair of big Kaleidoscope earrings. Then they took a picture for their parents, posing dumbly in the mirror, all teeth and cheeks, hands in the air like they were going to a concert.

11:00 a.m.: Two Tylenol #3, plus a biscotti they found by the coffee maker.

12:00 p.m.: Four misoprostol, placed between Morgan's gums and cheeks, dissolved in her mouth for thirty minutes.

12:30 p.m.: *House Hunters International*, a Michigan couple on the prowl for a centrally located turnkey condo (her) or a traditional Puerto Rican casita far from it all (him).

12:38 p.m.: Morgan in the bathroom, door closed, the unmistakable sound of liquid dropping into the toilet.

Riley turned up the volume for her sister's privacy, once, then again, until the Michigan couple was yelling about house number three, whether or not it was over budget, which it was. When they picked house number one, which satisfied neither of them, Riley mumbled, "Good fucking luck," and turned down the volume.

"Hey." She knocked. "Are you okay?" The bathroom door was frosted glass and Riley could see Morgan's darkened form, folded over her knees on the toilet. "Do you need anything?"

"Water," Morgan said, her breathing labored. Riley cracked open the door to pass her the bottle and glimpsed her sister's ponytail flipped over her head, shorts at her ankles.

Outside the door, Riley hesitated. "Are you okay?"

"Fine," Morgan exhaled. "Go watch."

During the next episode—an Australian family shitting on Cambodian housing—Riley crept periodically to the door, checked on her sister's silhouette, which remained on the toilet, head in her palms.

"Are you hungry?" Riley asked when it was nearly two.

"No," Morgan said. "I," she expelled with effort. "Pretend. I'm not here."

The *House Hunters* song played again. Riley found the heating pad at the bottom of the suitcase. She picked it up, held it a moment, knew she shouldn't go back just yet. Riley wasn't hungry either, but she eyed the bottle of wine she'd taken from her parents' cooler— something to pass the time—twisted off the top, and poured some into a glass. On the bed, she drank and watched the digital clock, waited impatiently for the commercial, when her sister turned down the heating pad.

Back on the bed, bottle on the nightstand, Riley tried to focus on the next episode—a long-distance couple moving in together, for the first time, in what would clearly end in disaster—taking determined interest in imagining their lives in each empty apartment. How he would find out she was bad at cooking. How she would discover he was dull. How they would eat her bad food to his bad conversation, sitting on the west-facing balcony. When the doorbell rang, three digital chimes, Riley leapt up, less sober than she imagined, to find the cleaning lady in the hall.

"No!" Riley said, too loud. "We're good. No, no cleaning. We're great."

She plopped back on the bed, confident the couple would choose the small apartment in the giant complex, drinking her wine. It took a minute to register the sound, the two syllables of her name, then just the one, the strangled Rii. When she finally looked to her left, the bathroom door was ajar and Morgan was on the floor, face pressed against the tile, arms and legs splayed like a movie corpse.

"Oh my god." Riley scrambled across the duvet and into the bathroom, put her palm against her sister's slick, hot forehead. "It's okay," she said, stroking Morgan's hair backward, bringing her head into her lap. Morgan closed her eyes, inhaling in long and exhaling in short, forceful bursts. Riley felt her panic beating slow and hot, the wine bringing unexpected composure to her thinking.

"How about a bath?"

Morgan grunted her approval and Riley gently returned her sister's head to the floor, came back with a bed pillow she slid beneath her cheek while the bath filled slowly, thunderously, with water. She told her sister it was going to be okay—that she was going to get into a cool bath—compulsively sticking her hand in the liquid every thirty seconds until the tub was full.

Morgan undressed. She leaned on Riley like a piece of furniture as she peeled off her shorts, her underwear and its bloody pad, getting tangled in her sweat-soaked tank top—Riley on tiptoe trying to help. As she lowered into the tub, Morgan let out an animal sound, the knot on her face loosening slightly as her body un-fisted in the lukewarm liquid.

"I," Morgan said, her voice pained. She put a hand on her face. "Sucks."

Riley laughed, a tear forming in her eye. "You don't sucks," she said.

"Life sucks," Morgan groaned.

"Don't say that. Today sucks. It will be over tomorrow." Morgan closed her eyes, unmoved. "Afterward, we'll put you in bed."

"I'll bleed."

"It's fine."

"It's horrible." She looked up and winced. "You didn't see."

Morgan shut her eyes again and Riley tried to look around, but what else was she supposed to do, sitting on the toilet lid? She hadn't seen Morgan naked in years. Her copper-blond hair was slicked to her head, making her eyes appear even larger, the curve of her eyelid wet and dramatic. Her nipples, floating pinkly at the surface, were the same color as her lips. Morgan was painfully beautiful, even like this, waterlogged and losing blood. For the first time in so long, the realization didn't sting Riley. It gave her an idea.

"I'll be back in ten minutes, okay? I'll be right back. Just. Stay right there."

"Uh," Morgan said.

Riley moved swiftly, down the elevator and tipsily around the block, dodging the pedestrians like she was in a video game. Inside the Duane Reade, the blast of icy air was like a respirator, her flip-flops still hot on her feet, her cheeks flushed, following the signs to the baby products, but they weren't there. She looped around the store, found them by the tampons. "Small," she whispered to herself, running her fingers along the puffy packaging, selecting what she needed. At the register, she grabbed a Kit Kat, a bag of cashews, pizza Combos, cheddar popcorn, adding items to the counter as the woman scanned.

Nearly breathless, Riley found her sister where she'd left her. "How we doing?" She leaned against the bathroom door. "Ready to evacuate?"

Morgan sat up slowly and the water shifted. A little splashed over the rim. Riley crouched at the tub, let Morgan put her hands on her shoulders. Together they stood slowly, Morgan lifting wetly from the water, when she doubled over with a cramp and reached frantically between her legs. She let out an anguished gasp, part pain and part horror, as something slid down her leg and into the water. "Don't look! Holy shit! Don't look."

But Riley had already looked, and now she couldn't look away, the two of them clutching each other, knees queasy. In the water was a gray mass the size of a kidney bean with a short, blood vessel tail, slowly leaking a cloud of pink. Morgan began to cry. "What the fuck."

"It's okay," Riley said, blinking hard. "It's fine," she said. "We read about this. It's supposed to happen. You're done now. You did it." Now Riley was crying too, cheering her sister and crying, coaxing her out of the tub and closing the curtain. Riley wrapped a towel around Morgan. "I got you something. Hang tight. We're going to put you in the bed.

"For you," Riley said, handing her the soft white wad. Morgan took it, began to cry again, harder and harder until she was laughing.

"Goddamn it," she said, leaning over to put on the diaper. Riley stretched a clean T-shirt over her sister's head. It was Morgan's favorite—soft and black with a thin gold star—and seeing that Riley had packed this item, Morgan wrapped her damp weight around her sister, tight with unwieldy gratitude. When Riley led her to the bed, Morgan crawled in.

"Take this," Riley said, two painkillers on her palm, "my little dumpling." She returned with water, found Morgan swallowing the pills with the wine she'd left on the nightstand. Riley opened her mouth to scold her, but instead she slid in beside her sister, took the bottle and filled her mouth, passed it back to Morgan. They spread out the three pillows, the fourth still on the bathroom floor, but ended up with their heads practically touching.

"I hate this concert," Morgan said. A minute later she was asleep.

OREGON MAGAZINE

September 8, 2007

EAST MEETS OREGON:
THE KINGDOM OF KALEIDOSCOPE

By James Greenly

The night Hank and Karen Brighton opened the doors of their first Kaleidoscope—the Eastern-inspired retailer that has since swept the country—the town of Eugene was hit with a party that has since been etched in local lore. The Brightons unveiled their new enterprise with spectacular mystique. Without a word, they boarded up their previous business, a humble but well-loved grocery store called Om Organics. Shortly after, an explanation arrived in the mail. The gold metallic envelope contained a heavy, bedizened card inviting 200 guests, my family included, to the grand opening of "Kaleidoscope: An Eclectic Bazaar."

It was October of 2002, and the Brightons had recently returned from India.

As I stepped into the former grocery store, the space was unrecognizable: Indian handicrafts and glassware were stacked across wooden tables, hand-blocked tunics hung from circular racks. Where once there were dairy cases and aisles of chips, there were leather satchels, linen lampshades, yak-wool blankets, mosaic mirrors, and silver jewelry. Karen Brighton wore a gauzy peach sari, Hank Brighton a brocade tunic. Their teenage daughters, Morgan and Riley, donned full-skirted lehenga cholis. The lights were low and moody. Bollywood music throbbed from speakers. My mom had so many free wines—chased by crunchy, spicy snacks—we went home with a lamp, a pair of slippers, and three scarves.

"I still don't know how we pulled it off," Karen Brighton tells me in her Manhattan town house, where the Brightons relocated in 2005. "I don't remember it all, to be totally honest, we were so stressed." Karen, who insists on first names, looks at Hank. "Fine." She laughs. "*I* was so stressed."

But the Brightons didn't merely pull it off; Kaleidoscope soared. After a breakout success in Eugene, they expanded quickly into Portland and Seattle in 2004. A year later, when both Brighton daughters chose New York for college, Hank and Karen followed behind and opened the flagship store that stands in Manhattan's Columbus Circle. Today, the Kaleidoscope empire contains seven brick-and-mortar locations and a thriving catalog business.

Just how much business? Hank Brighton gets this question a lot, and he isn't sharing.

"We do okay," Hank tells me, winking. A sandy-haired former surf instructor from Oahu, Hank has a playful, easy-to-like demeanor. When I compliment his summer Nehru jacket, Hank offers me one. "Come by the shop next week," he says, and when he takes down my measurements, I realize he means it.

Karen Brighton, a wiry second-generation Chinese American, wears a silk kaftan embroidered with birds of paradise. We sit in a room that looks like the Kaleidoscope catalog brought to life. There are iridescent drapes from India, butter-soft Moroccan leather club chairs, an ivory Turkish carpet with mineral-colored filaments, an antique Tibetan birdcage, a Japanese tea set. Did I mention their brownstone, tucked in a row of russet and brick, is painted a deep cornflower blue?

But life wasn't always so good for the Brightons. In 1993, financial constraints steered them from Honolulu, where they worked at the reception of the Hilton Hawaiian Village, to Eugene, where they hoped to find a more affordable life. The transition wasn't easy. Hank was unemployed for nearly a year, while Karen worked part-time in the shoe department at the now defunct Emporium. They rented a small duplex next door to a cemetery where their daughters, a year apart in elementary school, shared a room meant to be a nursery. That first year, the Brightons worried they'd made a huge mistake.

"The girls had no idea how broke we were," Karen admits. "Thank god leggings were fashionable back then, because that was all we could afford. I could get them for a dollar at the end of each season [at the Emporium], so the girls had leggings in every color but no real pants, no jeans. They just wore two pairs during the winter."

"No one wanted to hire me!" Hank leans forward on the batik-upholstered couch. "I applied all over town. A year went by and we had to do something. So when we finally sold our Oahu house, we used the money to get the grocery store. We figured, at least we'd eat."

Eugene is a small city of about 150,000 people. When Om Organics first opened, it was unlike any market in town. Customers could scoop their own grains and beans from bulk bins. Karen scratch-made prepared foods that were discounted at eight o'clock every night. It was a small, homey operation where their young daughters ran around freely. Over seven years, Om built a devoted clientele of health-focused, hippie-minded customers, many of whom followed the Brightons to their beguiling new enterprise. When Kaleidoscope opened in Eugene, Indian food was still a novelty; a stylish, high-end Indian mercantile was unprecedented.

"India changed everything," Karen says. "We took the girls for the first time and it just blew us all away. Then we got home and thought, how do we bring that feeling back with us?"

A 2005 story in *The Oregonian* found reason to believe that the Brightons met an investor on this trip, a claim the Brightons have since refuted. "It was hard work," Hank tells me. "That's all it was. People think travel is fun and games, but building a business is work. Sure, we get the occasional cocktail by the pool, but how do you think all this stuff gets to the store? I'll tell you what, it's not magic."

Soon enough, customers were asking when the Brightons were going to India next. They wanted to know the dates of new shipments. Part of Kaleidoscope's charm is that every item is a limited run. There are signature designs, like the bestselling Effortless Kaftan, that are always in stock, but the fabrics are changed constantly. The Brightons go on buying trips at least three times a year to ensure this variety, sourcing vintage and small-batch fabrics from local artisans. Kaleidoscope has since expanded beyond India: knee-length African wax-print blazers, kimono-inspired wrap dresses, and tennis skirts with Mexican embroidery are all recent hits.

"Sometimes [a piece] lasts a whole season, even for the catalog shoppers. Sometimes it's a week. Sometimes less. By now our customers know not to hesitate."

Karen isn't exaggerating. The next week, when I visited the Columbus Circle store to pick up my summer Nehru jacket, I watched a shopper torn between three versions of the Parachute Jumpsuit ($180). She left with all three.

Morgan Brighton, the older daughter at 22, is Kaleidoscope's Chief Designer and a notable new force on New York's fashion scene. Next year, she will graduate Parsons School of Design with a degree in Fashion Design and Merchandising.

These days, when Morgan finishes a new design in the Brighton's brownstone workshop, it's released limitedly in the Columbus Circle shop on a special rack called "Morgan's Closet." According to Karen, "Morgan's designs usually work."

Beyond the garment side, Morgan oversees the window displays, whose wooden and woven, voguishly pastiche aesthetic won Kaleidoscope a 2006 Visual Merchandising Award.

"Morgan is a powerhouse," Karen says with a smile. "And she's only getting better."

Younger daughter Riley Brighton, 20, is a junior at Barnard College, where she studies Anthropology. "She's smart. She's confident and independent," Karen says. "Nothing like me when I was her age."

At one point during the interview, Morgan and Riley drop by the house. Together, they are striking opposites. Morgan, as tall as Riley is petite, is fair and distinctive. Riley is brunette, bespectacled, and olive-toned. Morgan wears a vintage dress knotted above one knee, while Riley is dressed in cutoff shorts and sneakers.

"They're taking a trip." Karen looks at her daughters. "It's a graduation gift for Morgan. Next summer, they're going to Asia for two months. Alone. And I said yes but honestly, I wish she would have asked for a car."

"We didn't know that was an option," Riley says, making Hank chuckle. Morgan walks across the room and gives her mother a loving squeeze.

The family resemblance crosses so many borders—physical, behavioral, conspiratorial. While Riley may look like her mother, her eye goes to her father, while Morgan is drawn to her mother, but enters and exits with her sister. Family bonds have never been easy to explain, and the Brightons are no different. But together, they make the vision of Kaleidoscope feel genuine and true. They have built something as collaborative, as beautifully eclectic as their family.

Last Bell: New York City

When Morgan thinks back to high school, she doesn't remember James Greenly.

Riley can't exactly fault her for this. Her sister never worked on the yearbook, where James assisted on Tuesdays and Thursdays, the TA to Mr. Hastings, or Adam, as he preferred to be called. The point is, James remembers Morgan.

It was 2003. James was graduating college that spring, but even so, it was Morgan who made him nervous. Morgan who made him feel younger and clumsier than a classroom of teenagers, flirting in braces, writing bad captions for amateur photography.

On Tuesdays and Thursdays, Morgan won't remember, James wore a collared shirt and a zip-front hoodie. He put hours of thought into this combination, this attempt at looking both relevant and mature. James asked his little sister to take him shopping at the mall, and in the dressing room of Macy's, he realized for the first time how tragic he looked. The way his cargo pants fell like tubes around his legs, how his faded Frank Zappa T-shirt was slightly warped from his mom's old dryer. James forced eye contact in the mirror, shaming himself, letting the image gore him as his sister waited, as she called his name, impatient, from the entrance.

After that, James got contacts. This was before the rise of nerdy chic, before retro-vintage frames flooded the market, before glasses could be considered sexy. All of that would come later, but in 2003, in small-town Oregon, James Greenly was invisible to Morgan.

On occasion, Morgan might remember passing through the yearbook room, looking for Riley after the last bell, stopping to glance at a photograph fastened to a light box, the tiny square picas showing through the back. Sometimes, the picture was of her, and as Morgan inspected it, James would remember that he'd borrowed the negative for that shot. That he needed to return it to the files before someone noticed it was missing.

It wasn't that James was a pervert or a stalker; Morgan knows this as well as Riley. Morgan was eighteen at the time, essentially a woman, and James was a man who, like many men to come, was taken by the strange combination of her beauty. He took the pictures so he could look—*really look*—at Morgan's skin, like honey in a glass jar, held up to the light. And Morgan's eyes, the color of granite, enormous and penetrating, difficult to look at for extended amounts of time. When James was done, he disposed of the photograph. He ripped it to pieces or held a match to the corner, let it smolder in the basin of his bathroom sink. At the time, he lived with an older professor and his Russian wife, who accused him of smoking heroin in their guest bathroom.

Riley is the only one who knows this, the only person James has ever told. The admission didn't come at once. He cracked himself open bit by bit, first that afternoon on an Indian beach, then later, as they stood looking out over Bangkok, a year after the accident, a lifetime after that day at Macy's. It returned them to their most vulnerable selves; it made Riley remember things too.

That entire year of high school, James never spoke to Morgan. Once, Morgan spoke to him. She asked if he knew where Riley was. Twenty minutes before, James had sent Riley to photograph the girls' basketball practice in the main gym. They'd been joking about crouching low, shooting the freshmen like they were giants, and Riley had gone on her assignment with a quick, warm pulse that made all the pictures a little blurry. But then Morgan arrived. Morgan looked James in the eye and asked her question, and it made him so nervous that he must have forgotten. At the time, Riley imagined James was the kind of person who didn't recognize beauty, who perhaps didn't really care. When Morgan said she'd looked all over, that the TA didn't know where she was, Riley found no meaning until, six years later, she was made to revisit it. To understand the enormity of her sister's reach. How she'd always had this complicated, charismatic magic, this ability to make others arrange themselves around her oblivion, around her will.

The year after Morgan graduated high school, when Riley was a senior, James did not return to yearbook. Riley heard he'd gone to New York, to attend the journalism program at Columbia, a fact that impressed her a great deal. How spine-tingling it felt, James going to New York the year before Riley moved there too. Riley would be at Barnard. James across the street. Three thousand miles from Oregon, she pictured them crossing paths—both of them older, enhanced by time. So it was only Riley who recognized James that Sunday afternoon, sitting in her living room interviewing her parents, wearing jeans and a cobalt-blue sweater, a gray blazer, horn-rimmed glasses.

PART TWO

THE RESURFACING OF JAMES GREENLY

December 2007

I woke up to the day I'd emptied, sat up in bed, and let time shake out in front of me.

It was winter of my junior year and I'd come to love this feeling: nebulous nothing, solitude and possibility. In the bathroom down the hall, I brushed my teeth in the shower as two girls small-talked at the sink, invisible behind my plastic curtain. I tipped my head back, rinsed and spit, and as I kicked the foamy pile toward the drain, I thought of the text message from my sister. *What up.* A nothing text, and yet swollen with context on a Sunday morning at nine a.m. It meant Morgan had not gone out the night before, or if she had, it wasn't enough. She had no plans today, or if she did, she hoped for more. My sister had given up dating for nearly a year, worked obscene hours, and her appetite for platonic company was growing quietly ravenous.

In a way it made sense: Morgan had been different since the abortion, two summers before. She was quieter and more serious somehow, but she always denied it was linked. What was the point of meeting someone when she worked like she did? She didn't have time for dating, not with Kaleidoscope speeding along the rails. The winter before, preparing for the opening of the Columbus Circle store, Morgan moved out of her dorm at Parsons and into my parents' brownstone, where she'd made the basement into her laboratory. Mannequins stood sentry in her airy, sharply tailored designs, windblown kaftans and harem jumpsuits. Since then, Morgan had made a media splash, her big startling eyes and golden hair made even more mediagenic by the fact that she was genuinely talented. She had more going on than anyone else I knew, beholden to my mother's round-the-clock emergencies (shipping delays, bleeding fabrics, a dinner in forty minutes and nothing to wear), a regular happy hour with the Kaleidoscope managers, a Meatpacking tour most weekends with a crew from Parsons. Morgan was right; she didn't have time for a boyfriend, and yet she was somehow always in need of company, checking in on me the way a mom might, if our mom was the type to wonder how my night had gone, if I'd gotten home safely, what I was doing on this sunny-ass day. Each time I saw Morgan's name light up my screen, I felt a small knot of guilt, which in turn made me feel guiltier. It wasn't that I was avoiding my sister. I texted her back promptly, edited my sentences to make them funny and loving, agreed to as much as I could. But I was protecting something of my own, this small world cloistered from my family's antics and mounting spotlight, a place where I answered to no one but myself.

Three years and Morgan never learned to dissolve into the city the way I could. A set of earbuds and twenty dollars were all I needed to vanish from sunrise to sunset, longer if I went into airplane mode. At the bodega, I'd get a bacon, egg, and cheese ($2.50), then walk it ten blocks to my bench in the middle of Broadway, put in my earbuds and take greedy bites, holding the hot foil in my palms while cars whooshed by in both directions, pausing for the pedestrians who paraded before me, at perfect intervals, to Lauryn Hill. Afterward I might walk to the park. The entrance at Eighty-First was the place for dogs dressed like babies or men in suits on Razor scooters, stuff like that. With a little Hall and Oates, it made me feel like I was in a John Cusack movie. There was a train right there, transfer once for Union Square ($2), where I could digest the rest of my sandwich in the Strand stacks, picking a letter based on some private intuition and then standing in its row, looking at the spines of Cormac McCarthy and Frank McCourt and Elizabeth McCracken, Pearl Jam making the experience feel somehow, vaguely, alt-rock. I could get a paperback—heavily used—anything around ($5) to keep me company for the rest of the day. Then Vampire Weekend might come on shuffle and I'd just stop and think about how they went to Columbia, and what it must feel like to be both smart and cool in a musical way, the thought revealing a small pang of hunger. Usually, I liked to nurse it, to smell the oniony waft off the halal carts and the yeasty, cheesy slice shops. I held snacks in my mind, tasted them there as I inevitably pushed south, awash in Bon Iver, whose soft, sad falsetto made the walking, the sheer movement through the city, feel heroic and sentimental. There was a Vietnamese deli, just past the park in Chinatown with the rowdy betting and gambling scene, that did counter-service pho for ($5.50). I'd sit in the window slurping from the plastic spoon, little by little, trying to read Murakami by holding it open with my elbow, one ear listening to Fleetwood Mac. Afterward I could take a spin through Pearl's and play with the pens or go to Hong Kong Supermarket to visit the frog tank. Most times, if I picked the right cashier, I could buy a beer ($3), then I'd take the Q to Brooklyn, ride it high above the East River, and return for a sunset view across lower Manhattan ($2), sipping my beer from the privacy of my backpack, the Killers all the way home.

About a year ago, when Morgan figured out what I was doing, she insisted on coming along—just once, she said, just to see what I did by myself for so long! From the onset it felt like a negation; what she gained, I lost. Morgan wanted to play with the dogs in the park, coo with the owners, read to me from the jackets of books. She gave dollars to all the homeless and hungry and destitute (of talent)—completely fucking up the twenty-dollar day. This doesn't count, she'd say as she reached into her purse, and it frustrated me more than it should have. Morgan still couldn't understand why, now that we had it, I wouldn't take money from our parents. They paid for my tuition, what was the difference? But there was a difference. I needed my parents to put me through school, but I didn't need them infiltrating everything I bought or did or ate. I had earned the privilege to be broke: I spent my evenings babysitting the children of the Upper West Side, the overadored, undersocialized little dinguses who, at five years old, as I read to them from *This Is London*, would correct my pronunciation of the river *Thames*. Even at sixteen dollars an hour, I worked hard for that money, and I wasn't about to pass it out to every drunk guy yelling the words to "My Way." Morgan left me alone after that, conceded me the space I needed to do my lone cheap thing.

Twenty-dollar day, I texted. *Fucking freezing, we'll see how long I last. Lunch Thursday?*

Once, five days was a lifetime not to see each other. But with time, with effort, I'd made it normal.

You're demented, Morgan texted. *See you Thursday.*

28

I got dressed, slipped out down the stairwell of the dorm and into the day.

I'd arrived in New York a supernova, exploding with all the hope and vitality I'd so carefully sequestered and saved. In my new school, I was no longer Riley Brighton, that Asian girl, but Riley Brighton, anthropology major and playlist keeper, long-walk taker, vault of obscure food knowledge. Among classmates who were raised in second languages, with parents who packed their dorm fridges with banchan and roti and worked in countries I could not handily locate on a map, I had become a girl whose primary trait was no longer her Asianness. And yet it was that very Asianness that helped ease me into this new existence. Everyone was from somewhere else—a suburb of Tegucigalpa, the Jewish hills of Michigan, the Colombian part of Queens— and we were here, at this hallowed institution, precisely because we'd proven ourselves different from normal people. I'd spent my childhood in Oregon striving toward the dominant culture—the narrow hips and spaghetti straps of the white and outdoorsy. For the first time, it felt strangely advantageous to be me, good even, being half-Asian with a pollen allergy, an avid reader with lumpy social skills— it made a natural entry point to connecting with my peers, with the city, with this gateway to the larger world. I'd been stripped of my tokenism, and what was left surprised me, this desire to explore what it meant to be me.

In New York, for the first time, I was acknowledged as a woman— the doors held open, the careful smiles, the piqued interest as I passed. This attention, it was for *me*, had nothing to do with Morgan or my parents. When I first arrived, I'd put on lipstick and sunglasses and walk ten blocks out of my way, just to feel the warmth of eyes on me, just to remember it was available. Along the way, I suppose it hardened into a habit.

I waited for the train, my earbuds laying a thick Afrobeat as I bounced softly to the horns. There was a book in my bag, a Eudora Welty for class, but I wasn't in the mood. I began to think of the train as a stage, an improv set of humans reading and dozing and taking bites from bagels in paper bags. I was feeling the music, feeling the feeling; that day, I wanted to be a part of the audience. I changed at Times Square, slowed for a moment to watch three teenagers, one of them sexy, all of them in extravagant sweatpants, clapping as a fourth spun on his head. I heard the D and ran down the stairs, footwork tight, and slid between the closing doors.

My freshman year, I ate alone in a restaurant for the first time in my life. It was part of the program to harden myself, and after a while, I got good, then really good, at being alone in a room full of strangers. Going out for lunch was my first friend. I had a place in most neighborhoods where the lunch was cheap and no one bothered me, where I sat and disappeared. This place was one of them, the windows permanently fogged, the soup broth so gorgeously pungent, so fortified with shrimp carcasses, that no one I knew wanted to eat it with me. I walked in and unzipped my coat, humidity from the open kitchen gathering along the back of my neck. I smiled at the waiter, signaled to my usual table, and there he was: James Greenly. He looked up as I recognized him, surprise opening his face. Then suddenly he was standing up, saying, "Oh shit," pulling out a chair for me to sit in, all of it so far from how I'd imagined it happening. We hugged, arranged ourselves across from each other, and a dozen pleasantries ran through my head—nice things, normal things.

"What are you doing here?" I said instead, surprising myself.

"What do you mean?"

"Do you like this place?"

James looked at me, clearly amused.

"Sorry." I paused, tried to pivot. It was too hard. I decided to say it. "It's just you have very Chinese taste in soup."

"Wow." James laughed, low from his belly. "That's the nicest thing I've heard all day."

I felt my cheeks flush in the restaurant's warmth. "I'm sorry. Was that rude? I'm not saying white people make bad soup."

"It's totally fine. Soup's not really our strength."

"That's not true," I said, thinking. "Chowder's pretty good."

"Yeah. It's all right. Do you need a menu? I got this brisket thing. I've had it before, and let me tell you, fuck chowder."

"There's French onion," I said. I felt weird and I couldn't stop. "Lentil's good."

"Lentil's not really ours."

I looked up at the waiter, and when he came over, I ordered a wonton noodle soup with a side of greens, yellow mustard, a pot of tea. When he returned a few minutes later with James's bowl, I realized we'd shipwrecked, conversationally, on the Caucasian soup diaspora.

"What's going on with you?" I tried. "Are you still living up by Columbia?"

"Say you had to choose a food for the rest of your life." James looked me in the eye, entirely sincere. "A category of food. Like pizza or sandwiches or soup. What would you pick?"

"I'd pick soup." I returned his eye contact, pinpricks along my neck. His insistence on the subject, his disinterest in social pleasantries, was unraveling something in me.

"I'm asking seriously."

I nodded. "I'm answering seriously."

"I think I'd pick noodles."

I made a face—again unintentional.

"What?"

"I don't know. Seems like a boring choice."

"Says the person who just chose water-based food."

"I believe we talked about chowder."

"Great, you get milk. But you'll never use a fork again."

"See, that's where you're wrong. I can put noodles in my soup."

"Can you put a sandwich in your soup?"

"If it's a tiny one floating on top—like a mini grilled cheese?"
James waited.

"Then of course."

"Oh really!" James leaned back, incredulous, his brain working harder now. "Then I choose dinner."

"Dinner?"

"Yeah, dinner. Which includes breakfast for dinner, and dinner the way farmers say dinner for lunch."

We looked at each other, the first silence jamming the space between us, making us awkward, until the waiter brought my soup and I snorted and James released a loose mouthful of air, our collective sound startling the waiter.

"Cool," I said, nodding around me. "I feel cool."

James grinned at me, a deeply knowing expression that made me look away.

"Every year." I blinked into the fluorescent lights, tried to collect myself. "Winter strikes and I have no idea how to talk to other humans. I become this social deviant."

"Please," James spat. "I haven't left my apartment since . . . god damn. Since Thursday. Since *Thursday*." He shook his head, hard enough to jiggle his skin, then he selected his utensils from the cup between us and began to eat, head down, at a pace that astonished me. I watched him for a moment, realized only then that he had waited to start until my soup had arrived.

"But you like it here," James said. It was an appraisal that flattered the hell out of me. I looked up from my bowl, told him I did, and it occurred to me then that James and I, we were doing the same thing. Here we were in New York, molting our skins, shedding ourselves of who we were back in Oregon. Morgan's sister. Yearbook James. And we liked it here. We were happy here, growing strong and capable off the long, frigid winters, the authentic soup and snazzy banter. Something infallible reflected between us, and collectively, we let it drop. Because how did we say it? How did we congratulate each other for making it here, without admitting we'd both been losers?

"I never got to ask," James said, scooping me from my thoughts. "How did your parents like the article?"

"Ah." I flushed. "The article." James quieted, a flash of self-consciousness in his gaze.

"A friend from high school," he said, "is the features editor at *Oregon Mag.* It just made sense, you know, to get a journalism degree from Columbia in order to land an article from my buddy."

"My parents loved it," I interrupted.

"Did they really?"

"They loved you, actually."

"What does that mean?"

I smiled into my napkin. "Nothing," I said, swatting at the air because, at the time, it had felt like nothing.

"Yeah, you're going to have to tell me now."

"They . . ." I laughed. "My mom, I guess, but really both of them.

They've been trying to get Morgan to ask you out." I touched my eyes to the ceiling. "You're a nice Oregon boy. You made them look like the shahs of the Upper West Side."

"Did they say that?" James leaned forward, clearly flattered. "Honestly, the work has been so depressing lately, this is all very nice to hear. Please, go on."

I removed my glasses, shaking my head, cleaning them with the hem of my shirt. Until this moment, I'd taken little offense to my parents pairing my sister with James. She was the one living at home, in the crossfire of their meddling. "They liked you," I said. Without consent, my voice had weakened. "Enough to sell your virtues to Morgan. She hasn't been on a date in like a year; it's starting to weird us all out. I think you get the point."

"I think we're wearing the same glasses," James said, and I felt grateful for the gesture, took the opportunity to inhale, to shake away whatever anxiety crawled along the curves of my thoughts. James had a knack for this; I learned it early on, how assuredly he could diffuse the discomfort of others. We were not wearing the same glasses, not even close. Mine were larger than his, lighter in color, different in most every way save for the fact that they were both glasses and, perhaps, that they were vaguely tortoiseshell. James knew this, I could see it in his expression, the way his lips suspended in an easy half smile. I tried to draw the connection between this James, snappy and confident, and the James I'd had a crush on, Yearbook James, standing in the corner, hands in the pockets of his sweatshirt. There was little left of that skinny, timid guy, and yet the transformation didn't entirely shock me. In a place like Manhattan, there was no one to remind you that you've never worn a blazer before, that you wear hoodies, that the horn-rimmed glasses *don't look like you*. That's the entirety of the point. Come to New York, wear the blazer, put on the heels, walk the streets until you've mastered your brand of facial expression, some hardened amalgamation of wearied belonging, and more often than not, something will click. One day, New York will look good on you, which is exactly what had happened to James Greenly.

Dark stubble, nearly thick enough to be classified as a beard, lent him something ruggedly academic, journalistic facial hair, good for crossing Eastern borders and on campus, for picking up women at the Pour House. He'd put on weight, but it was virile weight, in his chest and shoulders. James wasn't a tall man—in fact, later, when he and my sister would stand side by side, I would notice how the wave of his hair, the front section that flipped a couple of inches off his head, was the only part that made him taller. But that was all right as well. In Oregon, the boys grew gigantic from the sheer amount of oxygen, but in New York, tall was a rarity, a curiosity. On a Manhattan résumé, *tall* would be listed under Special Skills.

"I'll say both pairs are a vast improvement from our high school glasses." I breached the past, almost hoping for a reaction, suddenly filled with a desire to draw that line between us.

"Riley," James said, his voice heavy with gravitas. "We never talk about those glasses." James reached for the bill as the waiter brought it, another wholly unfamiliar gesture, especially from someone who had met my parents, who had been to their home and seen their worldly tchotchkes. He pulled the leather booklet from my fingers.

"At least pretend like you think I have twenty dollars." He opened his wallet, looked inside. "Because I do. Are you headed back uptown?"

I hesitated, feeling the end and how unprepared I was to stop it. "No," I said, as if this was a plan to make him stay. "Not yet."

"Good for you." He slipped a twenty into the booklet and

gathered his things. He led the way to the door. Outside, he paused to put on his hat. "Spring James is incredible, by the way. Not weird at all, you'll see." He leaned in to hug me. "Good to see you, Riley. Take care."

I walked around the corner, wrapped my arms around my chest, and watched him cross Canal. I felt a rush that made my pulse pick up, my mind still jittery with conversation. My eye followed him, his body stiff against the wind, hands in the pockets of his pants—and it dawned on me that James had paid, this time with consequence. James had left me with all eighteen of my remaining dollars, and at the time, as I watched him disappear down the street, I couldn't tell if it was the sunlight in my eyes, clobbering my face with vitamin D, or the free meal that extended the potential of my day or this strange cape of confidence that had settled over my new existence or something else entirely—but there I was shivering, standing on a Chinatown sidewalk, smiling for really no reason at all.

BRIGHTON FAMILY VALUES

Eightieth and Riverside. It had been ours since the summer of 2005, when my parents followed Morgan and me to college and promptly, quietly bought a house. Back then, I knew enough to understand it was expensive and not quite enough to question how we could afford it. But as the story goes, Mom fell in love with the single blue building on the park-facing block: blue like Gaudí would use, blue like her favorite Moroccan city, Chefchaouen, a city she insisted on pronouncing badly, despite our objections, would always anchor with a heavy *chow*. But I fell for it too, I'll admit that even now; when I first came to look, I remember the smell of the sun warming the wood and the plaster, emitting an aroma that even now I associate with a kind of hopefulness.

The house was narrow, but it spread vertically onto three floors saturated in pale, tree-filtered light. On the very top, my parents had a floor-through suite. Morgan and I were on the second floor, separated by a Jack and Jill bathroom. We lived in the dorms; we couldn't believe they'd gotten us rooms. The ceilings soared between colonial paned windows, above thick plaster walls wrapped in crown molding that curled majestically at the corners. We ran up and down the stairs, giddy with the feeling of kids being spoiled with something they never thought to ask for. The Columbus Circle store was about to open. My parents weren't supposed to be in New York, yet there they were, and the house was something of a distraction.

On the main floor was everything else. A kitchen and a dining area, a living room with a massive three-paneled window that looked out over Riverside Park. Doors slid into walls, a fireplace clicked on and off. The basement was unfinished, stacked with their infinite Kaleidoscope boxes, waiting to become a workspace. In my mind, this was a different house, separate from the one it became; it was a house that survived just the one New York summer, before my parents got their hands on it, before they stripped the parquet floors and put in wooden planks that they stained the color of blueberry jam. Before they laid their Moroccan rugs, hung their Turkish chandeliers and iron birdcages and replaced all the doorknobs with crystal orbs and mosaic handles made by some artist they'd met whose name they could never remember. By September they'd buried their couches in tasseled pillows, spread patchwork quilts on their hand-whittled beds. It was a busy fall: no corner went without an antique trunk pushed into its angle; no window went undraped in curtains that pooled linen and lace on the blueberry wood. Golden birds flew from the ends of their curtain rods; candlesticks shaped like tree branches sprouted from the center of the dining room table; at the entrance, they hung a massive gold-framed oil painting of the number four; their arm chairs, upholstered in Guatemalan ponchos, looked like they should be performing the pan flute.

Progressively, assiduously, this is what their lives had become. In the last three years, my parents had grown ridiculous by an order of magnitude, together gave the impression that John Lennon and Yoko Ono had been dropped into a new decade, allowed to roam freely under the condition that they wear as many accessories as their bodies could carry. We're talking sunglasses dangling from woven chains, leather bracelets that fastened with tiny buckles, felt berets worn somehow backward, tasseled smoking slippers, rings that told time. Many of these things we did not sell at Kaleidoscope, and if we did, they were certainly not meant to be worn together. But this was my parents' new shtick, openly absurd and gaining a small reputation for being creative kooks, visionaries in their aesthetic field. A half dozen celebrities had been photographed in the Manhattan wild, wearing Kaleidoscope at Momofuku and Balthazar. My parents' names, always accompanied by Morgan's, were regularly printed in brief six-inch columns tucked into the folds of the Lifestyle section. These things decorated the basement now, framed little trophies that hung on the wall, including the picture James had taken of them in that very room, posing against their bolts of fabric like a couple of zany douchebags. As a result, my parents were now considered, and considered themselves, "Eclectic Lifestyle Experts" as well as budding humanitarians. Kaleidoscope proudly donated "a portion" of its profits to charities. My parents gave speeches and sat on the board of an Indian NGO, where they consulted on how to spread wealth to India. They had a Wikipedia page, an energetic publicist, a Puerto Rican woman named Rosa who cooked and cleaned and did their grocery shopping. It made me feel weird, watching Rosa unload my parents' dishwasher while they sat on a call, another member of staff briefing them on sell-through rates. Less than a decade ago, my

DOORS ON THE WORLD GALA

*A collaboration between traditional Indian artisans
and ethical American fashion*

JANUARY 5TH 2008, 7 O'CLOCK

Presented by Kaleidoscope and The House of Mewar

Welcome Reception

Dinner, Masala Mahal

Keynote Address, Hammir Bindal

Auction of Doors by Kaleidoscope,
Hank and Karen Liu Brighton

*All proceeds benefit The House of Mewar,
a charity dedicated to educating the children of artisans
in Rajasthan, India*

Black tie welcome, Indian formalwear encouraged

When he'd asked two months ago, I'd written these words for
him, but not without offering my commentary. How could an auction
of doors be the gala's primary draw? How much money did they expect to raise from *doors*? It was 2008, I'd said; there had to be another angle. But their doors, my parents had argued, slightly insulted,

were extremely popular! People were on waiting lists to receive their doors! Looking at my dad's computer screen now, I'd clearly lost this fight, and doors remained the main event. He smiled at me, satisfied like he'd just eaten a nice meal, and I swallowed the desire to warn him, once again, that this would fail.

"Good." I nodded. "It looks really good."

"Come on! I worked all day on this. What do you think of that border?"

"That border," I said. "That border is nice. Regal." My dad nodded. "Like a pro made it."

"There we go." He laced his fingers behind his head. "I'm going to send it to Hammir. I'm hoping he'll like it too."

He waited. When I realized he wanted another affirmation, I laughed at him.

"What?"

"Nothing. It's just sometimes I think you love Hammir more than any of us."

"That's not true!" My dad bristled. "I love him the same amount as everyone else." He grabbed me with his arm, squeezed me like I was a kid. "I'm kidding. I just want it to go well! I want us to sell a lot of doors."

"I know," I said. "Don't worry. You will."

The year before, after Kaleidoscope opened in Columbus Circle, my parents and Morgan threw themselves into their work. They'd since become a three-headed machine, eating Chinese delivery while standing among a mess of floor cushions or woven baskets, arguing. My sister was the chief designer, her clothing Kaleidoscope's primary draw. The recycled sari infinity scarves. The boho-luxe dresses. The swimsuit cover-up *Vogue* declared "you could wear to dinner."

Thanks to Hammir, Morgan had access to hand-dyed fabrics in heritage patterns, antique buttons, artisan silk at unspeakable discounts. We'd met Hammir on a package tour to India, his sandalwood shop of clothes the most memorable stop on an otherwise stressful trip through the golden triangle. The tour group was knocked out by Hammir's things, and by Hammir, who was a handsome, playful man with an oiled beard and arresting voice who made you feel like you could open his fridge and have whatever you wanted. All through high school, we'd flown back and forth to India trying to court this man, following my parents' intuition that he was the ticket to our success. And somehow, my parents had been right. What began as a one-sided wooing, selling him on some cockamamie idea, had turned into a wealthy Indian man's pet project, before becoming a legitimate business partnership. Hammir was a part of the family now, and I think of all of us, he was most amazed that Kaleidoscope had taken off as it had.

But everyone knew, at least now, that it was Morgan. Morgan was the reason, the aesthetic eye under which everyone organized. My mom oversaw the practical stuff, the dishes and furniture and blankets. She also watched the money, the cost of production, made sure Morgan wasn't overspending on beaded tassels. My dad, always the smiley handshake guy, handled the people, shook his head at the vendors and apologized for his hard-bargaining wife. And while I was not especially involved, I'll admit that the doors were my fault. The year before, our favorite Moroccan restaurant had gone out of business and I'd joked that we should buy their décor. If we were going to have a bright blue house, why not have a giant keyhole-shaped door? It was a moment of familial bonding, propositioning the owners for their door. We had our entrance enlarged and arched, and the new door fit perfectly, getting so many compliments from the various professionals who came in and out of our house that soon enough, we were selling them, sourcing doors from around the world. Indian doors. Turkish doors. Morgan and I made up the names—jokes that, in my parents' hands, became real. The Rajasthani Arch. Turkish Turquoise. People were using these names in earnest now, spending thousands of dollars, as one article put it, to "add some ethnicity to the house." The Kaleidoscope collection of doors had become so popular, we were about to auction them off to rich people, whose door money would go toward helping poor people.

My parents were especially invested in this. It combined two of their favorite things: helping the less fortunate and talking about how they liked to help the less fortunate. As with everything else in the last few months, Morgan was involved with Doors by default. She lived with my parents, worked with my parents. She had no boyfriend, saw very little of me. And while I knew all this, could tally it up and see for myself, it was only much later that I understood how much time she spent alone in that basement.

Silent down the stairs, I scared my sister. "I'm back!" I yelled and Morgan jumped, spat out a mouthful of pins.

"Jesus!" Morgan shoved my arm as I laughed, still slightly delirious from the exertion of finals. I fell backward onto the Persian rug, spread my arms like a starfish.

"Could it be?" Morgan stood above me. "My long-lost sister come to visit at last?"

"God," I said. "You're worse than Mom. You know I go to school, right?"

"How'd it go?"

"Crushed it."

"I assumed." Morgan walked across the room. "Which is why I

made you a little celebration piece." She stopped at a garment rack and I sat up. Right away, I knew what it was. The thoughtfulness of my sister—it still regularly took me by surprise. Months ago, we'd gone to the Young Designer's Market and I'd picked up a chiffon kimono, told her I'd like it in a less obnoxious color. She shook out the gauzy indigo material and released it over my body like a parachute. "It's for the trip."

I slipped my arms through. I rarely wore Kaleidoscope, all of it a bit too flashy for my taste. But when Morgan made me clothes, they often became my favorites—her gift for knowing what people liked to wear especially sharp on those she loved. The kimono was understated, sensible yet luxurious—admittedly an ideal piece for the trip we planned to take when Morgan graduated in the summer. The material had a soft cascading weight. "Oh shit," I said.

"Oh, come on. At least take off your sweatshirt, or I'm giving it back to her."

I looked behind Morgan, where my mannequin wore a powder-blue smock with lace garters and a straw hat at a jaunty angle. Back at Parsons, she'd ordered it from Holland in my exact proportions. The black wig came later, along with the glasses. She called the mannequin "Trendy Riley," entirely deadpan, suppressing her joy as she dressed Trendy Riley in wide-legged velvet overalls and cropped tees that read, "Bitch Please," anything, really, from the rejected design piles of her classmates. Of course she used her for making considerate things as well, but Trendy Riley was dressed differently, more ludicrously, each time I saw her.

"She looks like a slutty Mennonite."

"It's a spring look," Morgan replied, pulling me from the floor. "Mom and Dad want to know who you're bringing to the thing."

"What thing?"

"You know, the doors thing."

"Oh you mean the *gala*." I said it the way our mom did, heavy *gay*.

"Yes." Morgan pinched her voice. "The gay-la."

"Hey," I said. "We shouldn't be so hard on her. You know that people who—"

"Mispronounce a lot of words are just really well-read?"

We sat on the couch, knees toward the middle.

"She's so annoying." I tipped my head back. "She doesn't even read."

Morgan looked at me. "So who?"

"No one," I said.

"You have to bring someone."

"And why is that?"

"Just ask that sexy middle-aged desk attendant."

I had briefly contemplated not telling Morgan about Javari, the thirty-two-year-old guy who worked the front desk of my Barnard dorm. It was the kind of thing that could haunt me indefinitely: a revoked degree for sexual misconduct, an inebriated wedding toast gone horribly wrong. But then, after our first few dates, he began to write me poetry and I had to tell someone. This meant Morgan knew every perverted detail about the last two months: how he idled with a black car on the west side of Claremont, how he tasted like sucking on Jolly Ranchers and batteries, how I'd unknowingly had sex at his mother's apartment, thinking it was Javari's.

"Are you loco? Mom and Dad would poop themselves."

"And since when does that concern you?"

"Can't we just go solo? Two half-Chinese sisters in Indian clothes, enjoying a night of expensive doors?"

"Nope." She was holding something back, I could see it in her cheeks. I didn't like it.

"What are you doing?"

"Nothing."

"Morgan. Who are you bringing to the gay-la?"

"Well." She was grinning now. "It was totally random. He called last week and it actually took me a minute to remember who he was."

"Oh wonderful. You're bringing a stalker."

"He's not a stalker! It's that guy from Eugene, the one who did the interview with Mom and Dad. They both say they didn't have anything to do with it, but they're clearly lying, which I'm not ungrateful for, but—"

"*James?*" I felt my mouth open, quickly put it back.

"Yeah." Morgan stared at me. "What?"

"James asked you out?" I stood, moved from the couch. Morgan got up to follow me. I felt suddenly hot, claustrophobic.

"Wait," she said behind me. "Wait. Hold on. What's going on? Do you like this guy?"

I closed my eyes, just briefly, squeezed them shut to reset my face. I hadn't told Morgan about running into James. What could I say now, that I'd convinced myself it was practically a date? That I'd assumed if James was asking anyone out, it would be me? James had called Morgan. I swallowed it down. Morgan, who remembered nothing about him from Oregon. Who had no idea who he was. I turned around and smiled like my sister was being ridiculous.

"Riley," she said. "I'll cancel. It's not a big deal. We'll go together."

It wasn't until that December, until James, that I took a good look at my sister and saw something strange looking back. My sister, generous as the ocean, was never a pushover. You want James? Great, we'll both date him and slowly lure him into polygamy; or, James? You really like old dudes. Those were the answers I expected from Morgan, a little fight, a little respect before coming to a sensitive solution. But the girl in front of me had already surrendered, had handed over what I wanted like it was nothing. It rattled my confidence, raised my old defenses.

"No," I said. "Don't be silly. I'm surprised, that's all."

My intonation, the gust of air inflating my voice, I still wonder what she sensed. If it was possible I'd put so much distance between us that she really didn't know. Or if she knew, which is what I know is true, and she simply chose to pretend with me, to let me keep my pride, if that's what I wanted.

"Frankly," I laughed, "I've been worried about you. It's about time you got back out there."

Relief bloomed against her skin. "Exactly! Riley, I figured you'd be happy. He knew about the doors and I just figured, maybe he'd want to go." She put her hands on my shoulders, so practiced at throwing that second line when I was too proud to take the first. She looked at me as if to say, He's yours but you have to say it. You at least have to say it.

But I often ignored the second line too.

MORGAN BRIGHTON, SUPERSTAR

My first true memory, something I can conjure, to varying degrees, in each one of the senses: the year we moved to Oregon, the fall the weather changed from balmy to brisk and never switched back, Morgan began to grow breasts. That's as far as my memory will go, and even then, there she is, the two of us crammed together in a metal bathroom stall, her shirt raised above her chest, backpack on her shoulders. They're ugly, she told me, pushing the puff of flesh with her index finger, what's wrong with them, why do they look so sad? I examined my sister, always taking her so goddamn seriously. I recognized the problem straightaway. Morgan's early breasts dipped only at the sides, below her armpits, forming the slightest impression of a frowning face. The bathroom stall, which I know now was at the Honolulu airport, smelled like bubble bath, tasted like the car wash, sounded like the haphazard morning announcements at school. I remember all these things, more details than I have for the rest of that day, for my first airplane ride across the Pacific, my first glimpses of Oregon—and yet it's my sister's panicked face that snaps like a whip, sharper than anything, set against the sterile silver of the toilet stall, my earliest and soundest memory. I reached out to touch her, lifting the skin at the sides, reshaping them with my fingers. Does it hurt? I pressed gently, treating her budding puberty as if examining an infection. Morgan insisted that it didn't but still, I felt the alarm in the air. We'd packed our lives in boxes, seen the moving trucks, hugged our relatives a tearful goodbye, and none of it had resounded. But Morgan, to see her body change like this, it hit us in our frailest spot, in that nebulous, intangible space that separated her from me. It was the first time it occurred to me that we could change, that our bodies were singular and capable of blooming in strange directions at different times. We were going to Oregon, a place that might as well have been Narnia. Morgan didn't want her own room, didn't want to make new friends in a new school. That first week, when my teacher suggested I skip the first grade, Morgan begged my parents to let me skip one more, so I could be in third grade with her. She was never competitive, her scheming always in service of our togetherness. I was two years younger, barely six, and my sister was like an extra appendage, something I was required to love, and did love, by virtue of it being a part of me.

It's difficult to explain Morgan's puberty, how it changed practically everything. But perhaps it's easy: one day my sister was small, straw-haired, and scrawny, and then one summer she was three inches taller than me, the summer after six inches taller, one of us bleeding from the vagina and one of us not. Over two summers, I watched my sister expand into a creature I barely recognized—first spindly and big-footed with eyes that took up too much of her face, then womanly, her lankiness rounding into hips and ass, her nipples swelling from actual breasts. Then suddenly she was thirteen, five foot eight with bee-stung lips and hair the color of wet sand and lightning, and

I was eleven with a face that made my classmates pull their eyes at me. It forced our lives startlingly off-kilter. Since coming to Oregon, Morgan and I were the half-Asian sisters with the Chinese mom who ran the organic grocery store, the big white dad who walked the aisles opening bags of seaweed strips and offering them around. We wore secondhand clothes, had no friends but each other, ate dinner sitting on buckets in the walk-in. But Morgan's puberty dug us from our cave of obscurity. Boys were suddenly in the store, feigning interest in my mom's roast chickens. Girls from school came and brought their parents, asked Morgan what she was doing on Friday. Morgan's looks put our little slice of the world on display, Om Organics more interesting because of her. I remember watching my sister at the cash register, her long trim legs and heart-shaped butt, the smooth curve of her shoulder blades, getting ready for my turn to grow. Up until that point, there was very little terrain that separated us, very few experiences we weren't forced to share. For a time, I got such a thrill from looking at Morgan because that's where I was headed soon, and I still remember how long it took me, how much it fucked with me, to realize that height and beauty was not a stage that eventually befell us all.

Right before high school, thanks to her new body, Morgan became interested in fashion. We'd go to Goodwill as a family and Morgan would take her jeans home and chop them into shorts, shorten the straps on a sundress and braid the scraps into a choker. That summer she took our sewing machine to her wardrobe, spent entire days making things and ripping them apart, trying again. She shortened everything she could, made halter tops and circle skirts from big T-shirts and old curtains. All of this only made my sister cooler, more popular, and yet we both still had to work at Om, hauling crates of milk and scrubbing the bathroom toilet, signing our names on the cleaning chart for all our classmates to see. We both still needed to be home by ten, to share the car, to bring our friends inside so my mom could "check them out." Easier than resenting my sister's beauty was aligning myself with her, combining our weight against our parents. Morgan convinced them I was old enough to go with her to parties, that I was ready to take my driver's test when I could barely merge. In return, she kept me near her, always at the center of the party, and I drove her home as she hung her head out the window, wind on her cheeks. During the years Morgan and I might have drifted apart, we were bonded by our teenage impotence, the particular trauma of being raised within the same family. So when, my freshman year, my parents announced we were going to India—that Om was doing so well we all deserved a little vacation—it didn't matter that Morgan and I were not interested in a forty-person package tour, whose informational material featured smiling middle-aged people in drawstring hats. We both had to get on that plane.

I remember stumbling off the plane after a day and a half, our first time abroad, the fluorescent airport opening to a warm, fragrant night. The next morning, we gathered with our fellow travelers in the hotel lobby, all of them older, slightly pinker versions of the brochure models. An enormous bus idled in the circular driveway. Our guide, a jolly Indian man named "Ed," shouted into his microphone as we pushed our big plastic nose into the street, as Morgan and I fielded questions from the others about how old we were and if we liked school. That winter, you could have tied a string between Morgan and me, ten feet long, and it would not have broken. We spent two weeks in the back of a bus, crawling through traffic. We woke up in different cities, toured temples and markets and did as we were told, meeting here at this time, always waiting for Nancy to pee or stopping so Randy could buy more magnets. I was fourteen, Morgan sixteen, and we were in turns shaken by the experience, by the chaotic hysteria of the streets, the children sleeping facedown on bits of cardboard as if they were dead, and profoundly bored in a way we could not articulate. We shuffled from site to site, temple to ruin to museum, until finally we were dropped at an airy, glamorous shop of Indian clothes, and a bearded man opened the door.

Hammir's store, with its big, wood-framed windows and satin green walls and air that smelled like a rich person's underwear drawer, appeared like a fever dream after fourteen days of sticky heat. Hammir was in his early thirties at the time, strong-jawed and browed—and he carried himself like he knew he was handsome but would work for our attention in spite of it. We followed him around his store as he explained the heritage of his clothes, how the scarf with pale hexagonal dots was a royal pattern, used for two hundred years, handling it like a work of art. It would be great on you, he said to Marjorie, startling the old Canadian woman. With your eyes, he said.

At a certain point, my dad started getting involved, backing up Hammir's recommendations, making his own. Together, they began complimenting the women, making them blush, the women in turn scolding them for making them blush, which only made my dad and Hammir play off each other more, like they'd been palling around since elementary school. It was a wholly confusing dynamic—my dad and this Indian man being treated like movie stars, while our tour group stood in front of mirrors, smiling at themselves in Indian clothes. We stayed nearly three hours, Ed checking in on us again and again, reminding us we had more shops to visit. But no one cared about the other shops. Hammir's place was like a party; he put on music, turned it up when he liked a song, called out a line in a deep, arresting way, and punched the air. By the afternoon my parents and Hammir were hugging and exchanging contact information, still laughing at the door when everyone else was on the bus. They promised to stay in touch. By the time we landed back in Oregon, January frost on the ground, my mom and dad had become convinced that we'd stumbled upon a-once-in-a-lifetime opportunity.

My parents started exchanging emails with Hammir, crowded around the computer, writing careful sentences like they were nurturing a relationship with a celebrity. At first, Morgan and I thought they'd taken a weird liking to Hammir. But it soon became clear this was something more. Everything in India was cheap, they explained, by way of telling us we had to go back. In Oregon, we could sell these things for a whole lot more. Clothes weren't perishable. Selling blankets and pillows required no special equipment, little of their labor. The next summer we were on a plane again, back in Hammir's shop, and I realize now how badly this could have gone had Morgan not stepped in.

Frankly, Morgan astonished us all. There was something sobering, even for me, about watching my seventeen-year-old sister in this Indian stranger's shop, offering her opinion with absolute sincerity. The lighter tunics could be beach cover-ups, she said. The starchier ones they could lift into blouses, raise the slits to just below the waist. The Anarkali dresses, with their empire waists, could be hemmed into baby dolls. The salwar pants would make great pajamas. Hammir stood staring at my sister, arms crossed, clearly amused. He turned to my parents and laughed, openmouthed and loud. Please, he nodded, go ahead, and I watched my sister do just that. When Morgan said something would be nice if it was airier, maybe even crinkly, Hammir knew exactly what fabric to show her, what it was called, what it cost, where to get more. This will fray, Hammir advised, this won't lay flat; this silk was better for scarves and skirts, things that required some gentle weight. There was a natural, conspiratorial collaboration between them, something I recognized, I realized, from my own relationship with Morgan. Half-private, half-performative; the way children behave when being surveilled by adults. I remember looking to my mom, then to my dad, trying to pass a funny look and instead seeing how heavily they were breathing, watching them work, quietly freaking out.

Those Indian summers, Morgan and I tested the limits of our togetherness. The country was flooded with monsoon rain, Morgan and I confined to our hotel room for hours, no cell phones, no internet, just the two of us burrowing deep into the other's psyche, getting on each other's nerves. If we had to spend all this time in India, couldn't we at least do something *interesting*? I pointed out the food stalls, the auto-rickshaws, the craggy city beaches, and Morgan agreed, halfheartedly, that she wished we could do these things too. But there was work, always work, the four of us accompanying Hammir to textile factories and rattan manufacturers, making deals with hairy men who looked at my sister like they wanted to eat her. I stood in corners, waited on benches, wishing they would hurry up.

At night, we got dressed up and Hammir took us out to dinner, which was admittedly the best part of these trips. We ate superbly— fluffy lamb biryanis studded with pomegranate seeds and cream pastas twirled from silver platters—and yet I couldn't quite enjoy it. I felt out of place sitting at these dimly lit tables, eating with heavy silverware as my parents flirted with Hammir, as they consulted Morgan like an adult. Every night I went to sleep with Morgan in my ear, my beautiful sister talking about her important work, changing subjects when I went quiet, frustrating me with her easy sense of purpose and worth.

I began to ask my parents to leave me at the hotel. I took books to the lobby, stared out the window with my thoughts. I started using the hotel gym, sprinting on the treadmill until I couldn't breathe, straddling the rushing belt, panting over the display. Above the treadmill was a poster of the New York skyline, white with light, which I ran toward every day. The poster functioned as a distraction as I heaved along, and eventually, without really noticing, I began to envision myself there, slid between those lines, what it might feel like to exist in a city all my own. A city where I could start over, a place to melt myself down and recast. Day by day, as I grew stronger, the poster morphed into a challenge, my ability to live in New York in direct correlation with my progress on the treadmill, the music in my ears making it real. New York adhered to every song and every feeling, became a symbol of everything that mattered to me. Going to New York, it was the most radical thing I'd ever allowed myself to want, and with my parents doing so well, taking us on planes, living in hotels, it seemed like something I could ask for. There was a guilty image I held of myself, standing on a busy corner, hailing a cab in a long wool coat, miles away from my family. I knew Morgan planned to stay in Oregon for college, and all summer, I'd said nothing to change her mind. She caught me entirely off guard when she found me that night, fall of my junior year, passed out on my covers. Kaleidoscope had opened the year before to wild success, and I felt my need deepen and expand. On my desk, my computer glowed with evidence of my interior world, everything I hadn't told her, not quite yet.

Morgan switched off the screen, and without a word, she got into bed with me. She pulled the covers over us both and it occurs to me now that she never slept, because I awoke to her, just before dawn, looking into her eyes like staring down a well, moisture flickering at their depths. I could live in New York, she said the instant I opened my eyes. She said it like an apology, blinking slowly. Whatever school you choose, I'll go somewhere else, promise. I looked at my sister, took in the need she so easily displayed, and it startled me. It humbled me, how quickly I changed my mind. Perhaps it wasn't that I needed to be on my own. Perhaps I was pretending all along, hoping for someone to call my bluff, because when Morgan did—woke me up and willed herself into my future—it felt so distressingly good. So much better than I wanted it to.

A coward, I couldn't bring myself to look at her, so I said it to the ceiling.

I said: I don't think I can do it without you.

Morgan left for Parsons and I hyped myself up. I had one year left in Oregon, a single year of high school, and without my sister, I felt a strange, optimistic bloom of possibility. Homecoming weekend, I put on my senior sweatshirt and drove to the football game, TLC on the radio, rapping over Left Eye. I'd told people at school I'd see them there, let my parents know I'd be home late. I was still singing in my head as I climbed the bleachers and realized, with a clarity that hit me like a bird flying into a window, that I had no idea what came next. Unlike every time before, a space did not open for me to sit. No one yelled my name and called me over. I got to the end of the bleachers, turned around, walked back through the row of people I'd known for years, with whom I'd eaten birthday cake and dissected cows' hearts and sat with idly in the commons. It was Friday night and everyone was rowdy, yelling over the marching band, cheeks flushed with pregame vodka, and I felt, for the first time since we'd first come to Oregon and Morgan and I lived entirely in my parents' palm, like a creature from a lesser planet. I kept going, my legs escaping beneath me. I crossed the parents' section, crunched across the gravel until I was outside my car, and then finally, in it, taking dizzy sips of air, backing from the parking lot, my wrists shaking softly at the wheel.

I drove myself around town, in indecisive circles, along the stubby stretch of highway where it was impossible to really speed, up Chambers, down Lorane, out to where Willamette turns to big houses and forest. I sat in my car for fifteen minutes outside a 7-Eleven before going in, emerging with an armful of supplies that I drove to the parking lot across the street, turned off my lights, opened the crinkly bags and plastic sleeves, stuck a straw into my drink. It was only eight. I watched my parents inside Kaleidoscope, my dad leaning across the checkout talking to the closing manager, my mom straightening the glassware, the powdery taste of nacho cheese and chemical caramel keeping me company. I chewed, I drank, I watched for another forty minutes, when the lights went off and my parents walked across the parking lot to their car, a new gold Lexus, and drove home. Still, I stayed a bit longer. When I hit ice in my drink, I gathered my bags and wrappers and walked them to the trash outside the store. Then I took the long way home, passing by the football field so I could look at the score and tell my parents we'd won by six.

When Morgan called, even when I had nothing to do, I began to ignore her. I sent her texts to appease her efforts, full of lies: I was at the movies, I was hiking the butte with Rufi Patel. Something terrible was happening to me, and I knew if I picked up the phone during a moment of weakness, I might tell her. She might come home. I might never make it to New York. A few weeks after the fiasco at homecoming, my mom took me out to lunch and I readied myself for her lecture: how I needed to get involved with something, how I couldn't spend all my time moping around the house. It came almost as a relief. By then I was so lonely, I'd stopped making excuses for all the time I spent watching TV, waiting for one of them to ask what was wrong. I sat across from my mom, fiddling with my napkin. I watched as she poked at her phone, read the menu, and commented on how they'd raised their prices. Then she looked up at me and smiled.

It would be part-time, my mom assured me. They'd find themselves a little place, be in and out, mostly away. The numbers were crazy, she told me; Kaleidoscope was poised for growth and they'd spoken with Hammir. New York was the next step, the natural step, the city where they could really take off. I buttered my bread, ran my knife across the crystals of salt that poked through the surface, felt my heart give a little shrug. Outside Morgan's force field, these disappointments began to feel inevitable. It wasn't that I'd changed in her absence; the problem was that Morgan had left and I'd been forced to see myself. I couldn't articulate what I wanted, had little practice making myself understood, forming the kind of logical arguments that might compel my mom to pay attention to me, but to leave New York alone. I was fine—instead of her, I reasoned with myself. What did it matter? New York was huge. I was small. Two months without her and who was I to say what was right or wrong or mine or ours.

When I finally called Morgan, I apologized for my spotty correspondence, and when she said, Riley, I'm worried about you, I laughed too hard into the phone. Worried about what? That having some privacy was making me *happy*? I copped to nothing—still alluded to a respectable outside life—but I began to pick up her calls. I injected my voice with pep, and from across the country, shrouded in three thousand miles of radio frequency, it landed. By the time Morgan came home for Thanksgiving, two weeks later, everything seemed to be smoothed over. I remember she returned differently than I'd expected. She spoke of New York like she would a mediocre restaurant or a Spider-Man movie: it was good, she told us, she liked it a lot. Nothing more, and at the time, I assumed she was sparing my feelings.

She left again and it only got worse. The silent evenings wrapped around me, formed something of a shell. I decided I didn't need people the way others did. On the weekends I drove around for hours, listening to songs that made me feel like my life was about to begin. I found pleasure in my own ways: reading Nick Hornby novels, getting high, making stews. I've found that loneliness has a way of feeling significant, no matter how frivolously the hours are spent.

When Morgan came home for Christmas, I promised myself I would be fine, was ready to be completely fine, but things slipped quickly from my control. She'd been at Kaleidoscope all day with my parents, and now Morgan stood in the door of my bedroom, a look on her face I couldn't quite read.

"Hey." She stood there, polite in both her tone and distance. "Are you okay?"

"What do you mean?" I said. "I'm fine."

Morgan moved slowly inside the door, leaned against the wall, and I realized then the look was pity.

I raised an eyebrow, impatient. "What?"

"It's winter break. I don't know. You've been up here all day. Are you having any fun?"

"Am I having any *fun*?" The question startled me. The precision of her accusation, the tender packaging.

"You know what I'm saying."

I shook my head. "I really don't."

My sister nodded, frustratingly calm. "Mom and Dad said you aren't going out much."

My jaw opened, incredulous. "Am I miserable without you? Is that what you're asking? Am I ruined by your absence? Has life lost all meaning?"

"Riley, come on. That's not what I said."

"Holy shit. I'm working on my thesis, Morgan! Otherwise I wouldn't be here." I was escalating too quickly; I knew it then. But seeing my sister in my room, after all those weeks alone, asking me this question like she could see right through my soul—I couldn't take it. "Believe it or not, I'm not slitting my wrists up here. Do you have any idea how refreshing it's been? Spending time with people who aren't so goddamn full of themselves!" I looked her in the eye, smiled at her with so much condescension. "Yes, I go out. Rufi said there's a party tonight—is that fun enough for you?"

Morgan said, clearly pained, "I ran into Rufi at Kaleidoscope today."

I held my face still and tight, so still and tight I could feel it trembling. When Morgan didn't speak again, when I could feel my pulse in my face, I said, "So *what*?"

Morgan straightened off the wall, anguished. "So she said you're a *hermit*, Riley! She said no one sees you anymore except at school, and even then you're totally spaced-out. She said you never hiked the butte with her—that they asked you to come but it was the same weekend you were in New York. *Visiting me.*"

I felt my lie detonate. Then the next. Every one of them, one after the other, so many lies in the last four months. I flung my head back. From the depths of my lungs, a yell pushed wildly into the air. "Well, *fuck*, Morgan, what did you tell her?"

"What do you think I told her?" Morgan's arms flailed helplessly. "I said we got fake IDs! I don't know! I said we drank a bunch of pinot grigio!" I wanted to laugh, so badly I wanted to laugh at my sister, but it came out all wrong; the humiliation and rage, the strange slap of relief, everything I'd withheld from her, spewing, all together, hard as I tried, it would not produce the sound I hoped for. "*Riley.* Who gives a shit that you're lying to Rufi, but why the hell are you lying to me? I'm on your side. I love you. What the hell is going on?"

"I'm fucking weird without you!"

"You're weird *with* me!"

"Wow! Seriously?"

"I miss you, Riley, I miss you so much. You've been this shady nutcase since I left, and lately I don't even know what I'm allowed to say to you."

I closed my eyes, tried to breathe. "I know."

"So how do we fix this! What do I do? Riley, you can't shut me out. Not this year. I'm too far away."

"I know."

"So what?"

"So give me a minute!" I yelled at her, willing myself to take in air, to feel less combustible. "Can you do that? For once, can you give me a goddamn minute?"

Morgan paused. My face was soaked, my breathing pounding against my throat.

My sister crossed the room and without warning, her arms were wrapped around my head, the fabric of her sweatshirt shoved into my ears, my snotty face mashed into the wedge between her breasts.

"No," she said, "choose something else."

A BRIEF HISTORY OF JAVARI

Two weeks before my run-in with James, a month before the Doors Gala, I went on what I thought would be my last date with Javari.

As with everything else that year, I was wrong.

Javari and I had been seeing each other for two months, during which I saw him nearly every day as I passed through the lobby of my dorm. In the beginning, there was a thick, mutual pleasure in the veiled language we exchanged, in the looks we flashed between hellos and how are yous. I was taken by the register of his voice, which shared all the good qualities of velvet: smooth, dense, distinctive. I enjoyed bringing him snacks from the basement vending machines— the red plum juices and the little sleeves of Oreos—loved the way he had no idea what Kaleidoscope was, had never heard of such a place, so treated me like a college girl he hoped to impress and nothing more. We'd gone out to eat a handful of times. We knew more about each other than taste and touch. I'm not saying it was a whole lot more, but it was enough to justify the circumstances in my mind. Javari made me feel wanted in a way I'd never felt before, the way

I felt a real woman might, being wooed by a man with a complex world that extended far beyond the campus gates. Compared to Javari, the Columbia boys seemed like arrogant tadpoles. Javari was from Harlem, born and raised, with a father who was something of a neighborhood legend. Javari Sr. had been the subject of a recent documentary, which I watched in my dorm room after we ran into him on the street, a distinguished man in a flat-billed hat who kissed me on the cheek and smiled like he was finally meeting his son's woman.

Our first and only proper date happened early on, deep in West Harlem at a spot called the Den. We ordered cocktails in martini glasses lined with Pop Rocks and smothered chicken with macaroni and cheese. When we sat down I told Javari I wasn't hungry, my insides frozen from the frigid walk over, but as I thawed in the whiskey-colored room, settling into my worn leather chair, my appetite found me and I only realized I'd eaten all the food when Javari leaned over and said, You like to eat, don't you?

Javari smiled from his side of the mason jar candle, doe-eyed, and I understood that this was a compliment, or something akin to one. I found that I liked this about Javari; his slow, syrupy cadence, his laconic observations, entirely frank. There was nothing left to interpret with him. Indeed I did like to eat, and it seemed Javari regarded my hunger as a positive. We licked the rims of our martini glasses and guessed the flavors of the Pop Rocks. Javari was sensitive. He had a degree in poetry. The milk-coffee skin, the newsboy caps, the acrylic-knit sweaters that faded from gray to blue as your eye traveled south. Javari was a big guy, six foot two with wide, knotted shoulders, and yet the man smelled like vanilla, like vanilla and tobacco and, as the evening progressed, like baby powder, the base notes making their delicate appearance.

We said it out loud once, that he would lose his job if we were ever found out, and in my mind, Javari was falling for me. It made me feel equal parts rattled and wonderful. The first time we had sex, Javari looked me straight in the eye and expelled the air from his enormous lungs. He lowered his eyelids and opened them again, as if he didn't expect me to be there still, and he said: Riley Brighton, I'm not sure what I did to deserve this. I had him wrapped around my finger, and it bears mentioning that this was the only time, in my entire life, that I have ever felt this deep, unfathomable pull of being absolutely desired. I fed off the illicit romanticism of what was happening, this gorgeous man who was addicted to me. In the dorm's dim, drafty basement, in a jazz club's bathroom, under nightfall in the North Woods of Central Park. I thought of all the things I'd gotten that I didn't deserve either.

Our second dinner, which I thought would be our last, took place at two in the morning, at a fifties-themed diner in Times Square. We had arrived there by accident, walking aimlessly south from Barnard's campus at 116th when his shift was over. On our way downtown, Javari had told me he needed to pick something up, and as we entered the building on Broadway with a key, I had assumed the apartment was his. It wasn't until I walked to the bathroom—after he'd already lifted me against the kitchen fridge, pressed me against the alphabet magnets, rattling them until they fell to the floor—that I saw Javari's middle school portraits hanging in the hallway. Sixth-grade Javari wearing a Knicks jersey, a thin gold necklace, and a toothy grin. Seventh-grade Javari in a rainbow-striped polo, an early version of what he wore now, his hair cropped into a miniature Afro. Next to the bathroom was a bedroom for children, sparse but clean, two thin mattresses on two cot-like beds, a small set of cubbies for toys and pajamas. From the doorway I could see a picture of a mother, stern and attractive with two young boys, hung between the beds.

The apartment was Javari's mother's, the two children his little half brothers. I considered this information as I sat on the toilet, his mother's toilet, wiping her son from between my legs. For the first time I wondered what the hell I was doing; I wondered where Javari lived. I wasn't upset, exactly—I hadn't asked, he hadn't told—but what I saw in the hallway was more intimate than anything I'd been doing with Javari. I was an intruder in a family's home; my skin cells and sweat marked the family's fridge; my naked ass pressed against the place where they stored their milk and their butter, their fresh and porous groceries. Afterward, as we walked downtown, I declined the train at each eight-block interval, insisting that we walk instead. You're sure, he'd ask, and I'd nod, and we'd take another ten-minute stretch in winter silence, rubbing our hands together, remarking upon the chilly night. I didn't care to explain that I needed the air, needed the fifty blocks to walk off the feeling that clung to my insides, tender and hollow.

At the diner, we ate pancakes and drank hot bourbon ciders. When the bill came, he made a slow reach for his pocket, and when I told him I would get it, he thanked me.

"Did I spook you at my mom's place?" Javari asked as I signed my name on the receipt.

"I'm not sure," I said, and I was surprised that I had told the truth.

"I wasn't trying to. I knew no one was there, but that whole fridge thing wasn't my plan." Javari's expression was openly, somberly concerned, and I blamed myself for what was happening. I had slept with Javari that first night, after the Pop Rocks and the macaroni and cheese, and on every occasion after that. I'd wanted to; if we plotted out the events of our meeting, technically I had pursued him. Breaking my own light bulb so I could go downstairs to report it, so I could flirt with Javari in the lobby as I waited for maintenance to come and fix it—I'd been playing a girl who would enjoy being taken against his mother's fridge, who wanted the thrill of being discovered. And I realized, suddenly, that Javari was trying to impress this girl.

"It's just that Afro you had in the seventh grade," I said, closing the bill, fixing my face into something remorseful. "I'm afraid I can never take you seriously again."

A warm pause followed, one of Javari's signature silences, pensive and unknowable.

"That's not a problem," Javari replied, smiling now. "I'm pretty sure you don't take me seriously now."

When I got back to the dorms, I packed a bowl and perched myself halfway out my window, blowing smoke into the quiet, brisk night. It was four in the morning on a Tuesday; everyone was asleep. Everything would be fine. The thought settled over me as I held the smoke in, let it spread through my blood, realigning my thoughts. I would keep seeing Javari or I wouldn't. I could stay out of the dorms more, spend more time at my parents' house. People had done worse things than get involved with a guy who ate where they shat, or however the saying went. From the window ledge I dropped into my bed and pulled on the blanket, shivering. I reached for my purse to get out my phone and remembered the piece of paper Javari had given me at the end of the night, when he kissed me on the forehead as I slid into a taxi. Read it when you get home, he'd said.

I unfolded it then, the sheet of standard printer paper, the lines typed neatly in a row.

My manhood in your womb
moist like dew
draws from the honeypot
that unctuous nectar

Slow, slick, supple, stretch
Tender how
my Southern bell rings and
I surrender

Darkness, my thirsty tongue
Beneath my weight

Fusion and
shuddering frames
a feast of sweet ambrosia.

I folded up the paper immediately. I tried to smother the deep, unspeakable anxiety I felt. That Javari had gone to school for this. That he felt comfortable, confident even, gifting me these nasty, lumbering stanzas. I pictured him in front of a computer, poking at the keys, alight with focus as he typed, *my manhood in your womb*, sitting back and squinting with pleasure. I sat motionless on my bed, trying to scrape the words from my memory but instead giving them more life. Why would he give me this? The rawness of this offering, the sincerity, it mortified me, poked at something nervous and mean.

Where did he find the sureness of self to slide these words into my hand, this piece of him to read and dissect in private, to keep as evidence forever? Even more, the poem was terrible, and the audacity of this fact made me feel strangely insecure—both about myself and about what we were doing. The poem made Javari suddenly real, a man with tenderness and blind spots and mess. It filled in details about him that were previously blank, and which I could no longer fill in as I needed.

Under different circumstances, I would have gone to the gala alone. But James drew out something competitive in me. James was taking his shot. If I showed up alone, the game would be over; he would never see me as an equal. If I brought Javari, at the very least there would be an attractive, thirty-two-year-old smoke screen. James didn't know about the poetry. I assured myself of this, threatened Morgan when I agreed to her plan. Maybe, I hoped, Morgan and James would find Javari somehow cool or intimidating. We were from Oregon. A man raised in Harlem, a decade older—I told myself it just might work.

DOORS ON THE WORLD

At first, I was against the turban station, but it helped to break the ice. James and Javari were buttoned to their necks in Kaleidoscope kurtas, James in mahogany and Javari in a dusty blue, the two of them grinning like goons, sitting in wingback chairs as two Indian men worked the lengths of fabric around their heads, wrapping the circumference and smoothing the piece that trailed, wrapping and smoothing, expertly turning and forming the turbans that appeared on their heads in a matter of minutes. Around the ballroom, there was a headdress on nearly every man, elegant protrusions of colored fabric like neon buoys in the low light. Coupled with the women, who were mostly in saris or kaftans or salwar kameez, the effect was exactly what my parents had envisioned: a glittering, moneyed affair with the festive pomp of an Indian wedding.

The boys had hit it off. Once they realized what they were up against, they'd allied themselves almost immediately. My parents—my mom wearing a flashy gold bindi and my dad in his signature silver brocade—were thrilled to see James and too frenzied to properly question Javari. With his hair covered, wearing what he kept calling a "kutie," I told myself he looked nearly Indian. A tall, muscular Indian man whose beater I could see through the tunic's silk, black jeans underneath, his feet in Jordans. When he placed his hand on my back, or around my waist, I had to remember to take it off. He was attending as a friend; those were the conditions we'd agreed to. If a picture was taken and somehow printed, there was nothing wrong with he and I being friends.

"And how do you two know each other?" My mom was smiling, and I could see from its strained confusion she was torn between her excitement that I had brought a date, something I'd never done before, and her concern that Javari was a full-grown man.

"Oh, I live in the neighborhood," Javari explained, and I remember feeling that old secret rush. "We kept hanging around the same places, and one day I decided to say hello."

"Are you a graduate student?"

"I do some stuff with the university, sure. I'm a poet."

"A poet! You know James here is a journalist. Graduated from Columbia too."

"I was just learning that about him."

"Karen-ji!" a voice called, and there was Hammir, his turban crown-like with two jeweled broaches and a tasseled end. We'd seen him for dinner the night before—gone to the Italian place with prosciuttos hanging from the ceiling and stayed through three bottles of wine. Hammir kissed Morgan and me, shook the boys' hands, and stood back to tell us we all looked ravishing.

"Meet James." My mom beamed. "He wrote that nice article I sent you, for the *Oregon Magazine*."

"A pleasure to meet you, James," Hammir said, and then realized what my mom was talking about. "Ah, of course! The *Oregon Magazine*. Now, James," he scolded. "I hope you do not think I am this mystery investor! I can tell you right now, I am simply a man who loves beautiful things."

James laughed. "I'll cross you off my list immediately."

Javari said, "I like your hat."

"Thank you." Hammir nodded graciously. "It belonged to my great-grandfather. He was a very stylish man."

"Oh, look." My mom took Hammir by the hand. "The Cantors are here. Let's go say hi, I know they're going to buy a door."

The wine flowed, glasses balanced on silver trays, carried by men dressed entirely in white. At the bar the four of us took a shot of whiskey, which made everything a little softer. Morgan and I were tasked with saying hello to this person and that person, complimenting their Indian clothes, laughing gamely with all the screwing-in-the-light-bulb and petting-the-dog jokes, the tikka-tikka sounds of rich men doing bad accents. Morgan especially had to step away to bullshit with those who needed bullshitting. She wore a sage-green lehenga, three inches of skin between the waistband of the skirt and her pale pink, scalloped blouse, a delicate headpiece draped over her forehead.

"Mind if I ask how much a ticket cost?" James said, leaning over.

"A thousand a plate."

Javari whistled. "And they're still supposed to buy a door?"

He'd been looking at me funny all night, like I'd forgotten to mention a huge part of my life. But I wasn't exactly comfortable either. I never attended these things, was a bit dumbstruck myself. Morgan was the one who made the rounds with my parents, sipping champagne and declining the tiny foods they brought around on trays— like a one-bite filet mignon with cilantro aioli, a tiny lobster samosa, was nothing special. James and Javari and I, we ate everything, took a

snack and a refill every time they came around. I would have preferred to be cooler in this setting, but I couldn't manage it. I felt
trapped between pleasure that this was my family's event and embarrassment that we were all in Indian clothes, about to auction a bunch
of doors.

"I guess we'll find out," I said.

James shook his head, tipped back the rest of his wine.

We took our seats and Javari immediately put his napkin in his lap,
which continued to bother me until the lights lowered and my parents took the stage, waving big and happy.

"Welcome!" My father beamed to the sound of applause. "Welcome to the first Doors on the World Gala. Thank you. Thank you.
You all look absolutely dazzling tonight.

"As many of you know, Karen and I started this venture about six
years ago, when we decided it was a good idea to sell fine, hand-
crafted clothes from a converted grocery store." He paused for the
laughter and smiled at my mom, who said, "There was a dry cleaners
next door!" This was the way they spoke in public; he carried the
narrative, she jumped in to show she was there, that she was funny. I
looked over at James, listening attentively, and realized why my mom
had taken such a liking to his article. James had made her the star.

"We've come a long way since then. To be honest we're overwhelmed to be here today, and so proud to be able to share this evening with you all." My parents looked genuinely elated, authentically
nervous. Watching them, I couldn't help it; my heart flipped to
warmth.

"Kaleidoscope has benefited from the help of many, many people.
This room is filled with generous souls who have brought Kaleidoscope to the world, and I'm excited to say we have one of the most

important with us tonight. Hammir Bindal." My dad paused, radiated with a wholesome joy. "How can I begin to describe this man? Hammir is the definition of a gentleman. Charming. Gracious. Generous to a fault. He's a shrewd entrepreneur. He's also the most elegant man I've ever encountered."

"Same," James whispered, making Morgan and Javari laugh.

"To make matters worse, Hammir happens to be a member of the Mewar dynasty, a royal Indian family with a history of thousands of years, and he's here to tell us a bit about the role of textiles in his family and in India, as well as some exciting stuff happening in the industry today. Ladies and gentlemen, thank you for being here tonight. None of this would be possible without your generous support. Without further ado, I present to you Hammir Bindal."

Hammir strode across the stage, handsome as promised, hugging my parents and shaking his head like he'd been ambushed. The applause held steady. Music had begun to play, some kind of Bollywood track with a heavy sitar that made the handoff look like three middle-aged musicians trying to induct each other into a hall of fame.

"Oh shit," Javari said. "He's the king."

My mom leaned into the mic. "Kaleidoscope has taken a tremendous amount of talent and sacrifice and sweat. It feels so good to be celebrating that work tonight." She paused, looked out over the room like a proud pastor in front of her flock. Then she quickly added, "Dinner should be served shortly," which I knew was a scolding for the caterers, because the popadum and salads were supposed to be served with the opening remarks, and she could see from the stage that no one was eating.

"Wow." Hammir adjusted the microphone. "What a welcome. Thank you so much, Hank and Karen." As always, there was a posh, foreign rhythm to his speech.

"I must start by saying I love New York. No matter how many times I visit, there is always something new to marvel. New York is one of the great cosmopolitan cities of the world. There is little this city cannot accommodate. Just today, I was riding in the underground and I began to count the different ethnicities in my car. I counted at least one dozen, and I am sure there were many more. I am always amazed by this New York way of life, to see a woman in hijab next to a man full of tattoos, both of them reading the same magazine! What I am trying to say is that New York is a very special place. A very special place indeed. People here are allowed to be themselves, and so culture can stay alive. When Hank and Karen invited me to come to New York for this event, I began to think about what I could say about India, and about the clothes from my country that many of you are wearing tonight. So I must first ask your forgiveness, as I know this is a party and not a lecture hall, but to do this I must tell you a little history, and I hope you will indulge me."

The salads arrived, the wine refilled. Hammir was so good at this.

"For many centuries, all of India's textiles were controlled by one group, the Mughals, who were in fact a very important and powerful dynasty. The Mughals ruled the continent from the 1500s until 1857, and they became very accomplished in manufacturing during this time. In the eighteenth century the Mughals supplied one-quarter of all the world's cottons. People forget that the cotton gin, in fact, is an Indian invention, and that even centuries ago our cottons were worn by societies across the world. The Japanese. The Europeans. And cottons were only the beginning. India was also famous for silks and muslins and for weaving, for the incredible dyes that we plucked from the trees and, of course, for the work of the artisans who made these beautiful things by hand.

"The Mughal factories were quite remarkable. We called them

karkhanas. The royal Mughal families would find the best artisans from across the land and invite them to come live in the city and work in the karkhanas. Embroiderers. Potters. Calico printers. They all came to work in the factories. Every noble house had their own karkhana, where they made clothes for their household and also gifts for the emperor. In return, the artisans were provided for by the Mughals in a kind of royal patronage.

"My family, the Mewars, our ancestry dates to the first century. We lived in the state of Rajasthan long before the Mughals came to power, as we do to this day, long after they left. Throughout the years we have managed to maintain a kind of autonomy. We did not submit to the Mughals. We settled our own affairs, fought our own battles, managed our own commerce. After the British Raj took hold in India, my family made a treaty with them to let us live in peace, in our own princely state, which we now call Udaipur. The British went to war with the Mughals, and the Mughals, having been weakened by the Persians, were fully defeated in the nineteenth century, during my great-grandfather's reign.

"What happened next, I must say, is one of the darkest parts of colonial history. The British destroyed the karkhanas. They took all the raw materials; they purposefully destroyed the looms. You see, the British did not want competition. They were building their own manufacturing center in Manchester and they feared the power of Indian manufacturing. Within years, the subcontinent was a mere shadow of its past. The artisans went back to their villages with no work. This was when my family realized they must do something.

"My grandfather and his brothers tracked down the karkhana artisans. As soon as they saw that the British were destroying everything, they saved any materials they could, and they reconnected them with their owners. The artisans began to work for us. My family created a network, a discreet network of craftsmen who lived in their villages but supplied our family with their beautiful work. To this day, six hundred of them still work for the house of Mewar, and for Kaleidoscope."

Hammir twisted the top off a bottle of water, took a small sip. The ballroom was almost entirely still, the plates of fish and chicken barely touched.

"Today, as much as centuries ago, crafts need our patronage. The generational passing of skills is in decline. The Indian government views handicrafts as a sunset industry that must surrender to modern industrialization. But they are wrong. Indian weaving is one of the world's great art forms, and we must support the people who still know how, in whatever way we can.

"In recent years, it is the West who has come to understand this best. Collaborations with Western designers like Kaleidoscope have been absolutely critical for the survival of my country's traditional handicrafts. When Hank and Karen came into my shop some six years ago, we had a cup of chai and chatted about what they hoped to do, and to be honest, it sounded crazy! They wanted to buy my clothes and sell them in a place called Oregon!

"But then I met their daughters, both of them so beautiful and with such interesting ideas. I thought, at least these girls know what they're doing!" The room had a good laugh at my parents' expense. Hammir had always known who was at the helm, had always treated Morgan like the talent she was. And while I was a rare participant, he never left me out. "But in all seriousness, I knew there was something special about this family, about their ambition, and I wanted to be involved.

"Since then, it has only become better to watch them grow, and to see my country's ancient art become New York City fashion. So I'd like to raise a glass." Hammir looked around until a waitress scuttled on stage with a flute of champagne and the room laughed again. Hammir lifted his glass into the light. "To Hank and Karen. To Morgan and Riley. To preserving a legacy, and to the beauty that has come from its evolution. Cheers, my friends."

The tables erupted in applause, a feeling of triumph soaking the room. Attorneys and bankers and journalists in turbans, their wives in saris—they were making history, wearing history. Even I was a bit overcome, Hammir's impassioned history lesson lending the emotional muscle needed to crack open the evening. It was the perfect time to auction off some doors. Behind Hammir, white-clad waitstaff pushed the doors on small dollies into the center of the stage and my parents returned to the Bollywood track.

"All right, folks," my father said. "I won't try to follow that up. I'll just remind you that we're building a school for the children of these artisans. Let's make sure they get an education."

I watched, strangely rapt, as my parents sold all fourteen doors in twenty minutes, the most expensive of which went for twenty-seven thousand dollars. Everyone was eating with great enthusiasm, remarking upon how wonderfully spiced the chickpeas were, how the naan was so light and chewy, chatting loudly, looser and happier in the third hour of wine. At a certain point, Morgan and I were pulled away to take pictures with our parents and Hammir on the stage, then in front of the doors and in the grand archway of the foyer. I was happy, you can see it in the picture—flushed skin and glossy eyes, radiating an easy, obvious joy—that still hangs in my parents' office.

It's hard to say exactly how it happened. At some point, while we were running around with the photographer, Javari said something to James. James told Morgan. Morgan brought the admission to me.

It could have waited until morning, yes; under different circumstances, it might have waited forever. But at the Doors on the World Gala by the Royal House of Mewar, when a thirty-two-year-old man in a borrowed tunic began talking about women who were not his date, righteousness came without delay.

Outside, caught up in the chain of indignation, I called Javari a piece of shit.

Riley, I heard my sister's voice. *Let me in.*

I stood in the bathroom, walls pulsing at my sides. It was fancy, a wallpapered little room with a sink and carpeting and a chair. I leaned against the vanity, properly smashed, thinking about what a fucking lunatic I was. I looked at my phone: *Sorry R I didn't mean to upset you.* And why had he? Javari and I weren't a couple. Not even close. We'd been messing around with the understanding that this was a temporary thrill, an inappropriate relationship that could crumble at any minute. At face value, I understood this—in fact had brought him here to display my nonchalance and mystery—and yet I'd allowed my feelings to distort. To believe that this man belonged to me, wanted only me, and so I'd yelled at him on the street, told him to go fuck himself. I'd handled the situation so dementedly, so drunkenly, I'd been in the bathroom for half an hour trying to explain it to myself. It was almost impressive, the trifecta of my humiliation. Morgan now pitied me, James wanted to avenge my honor, and Javari thought I was obsessed with him.

Riley, come on. My sister knocked again. *Open up.*

I lifted my face from my palms and looked at myself, crying in a sari. It was everything I'd fought against, coming to New York to be my own person—and seeing myself like this, wearing too much makeup, swept up in my family's pageantry, it rattled me completely.

I turned on the faucet, splashed water on my face, tried to scrub the eyeliner and mascara, my red-stained lips. *Riley.* My sister knocked. *Please.* I looked at myself once more, smiled as big as I could, teeth appearing on the sad, smudged landscape, then I shook myself sober and opened the door to let in my sister.

HOMECOMING

For three years, James had been renting a room from a twenty-two-year-old small-time drug dealer in a full-service building in East Harlem. He found the room through a J-school acquaintance, who vouched for Mark being a decent guy, adding that he was *pretty sure* he only sold weed. As a single guy who slept on a Craigslist mattress, who sustained himself on bodega sandwiches, James could deal with the occasional sticky situation. Once a month, no more than twice, someone would pound on the door when Mark wasn't home. How they got past the doormen, James wasn't sure, but after the first year he'd learned to stop answering. He'd broken the rule once since then, the summer before, when he'd heard a woman crying on the other side. It was Mark's mother, a heavyset Dominican woman wringing her hands, hot off the rumor that her youngest son had gotten caught up with the Bloods.

Angel the doorman told James not to worry, he'd known Mark since he was a boy, and more than that, he knew the neighborhood. Mark was fronting, he said. Mark was a stuntman. But when Mark's girlfriend delivered their son late last year, Little Mark Junior, they bought a red stroller. Mark began to wear red sweatpants, red hoodies, red hats. Early in December, Mark had knocked on James's bedroom door and led him to their shared bathroom, pulled open the shower curtain, and pointed to a streak of blue shower gel wiped menacingly against the beige tile. "This your blue goo, man?" Mark had stared at James, hard in the face. "No, man," James had replied, shaking his head earnestly. "That's not my goo."

In the weeks after the gala, as James and Morgan's relationship steadily ramped up, they found that Mark's apartment, with its resin-sticky countertops and bloodred upholstery, was not an ideal place for their canoodling. Luckily Morgan lived in a four-story brownstone, and James, having already won my parents with his article, was welcomed into my parents' home with the warmth and zeal of retirees.

Over the book I pretended to read, I watched the four of them around the kitchen table, peeling the wrappers from the miniature cupcakes James and Morgan had brought to share. My sister was twenty-two, James four years older, with enough facial hair to prove his maturity to my father and enough harmless, boyish charm that the sight of him extended across our couch, limbs relaxed and hair askew, did not give off the impression of sex with a daughter. It was March, nearly two months since the gala, and in typical Morgan style, they were always together or else making plans to meet up. They hung out with my parents, bringing them snacks, offering advice on this and that, telling stories like actual friends, which I found both sad and mesmerizing.

The tiny cupcakes, I knew, were Morgan's idea. But the difference was that James had said yes where I would have said no. In my mind, cupcakes were apology food, sad food, a small defensive cake that screamed: Perk up! Morgan and I would have disagreed on this, arguing until I refused to enter the infuriating, sterile bakery made to look, for no reason at all, like a scientific laboratory that sold microscopic cupcakes. And while James had ultimately agreed, he made fun of them openly, called them Lab-Baked Turds, which made it, in my reckoning, somehow better. Without meaning to, I began to keep track of them, their strange and confounding dynamic. The two of them were so ill matched—he nerdy and eager to please, she glossy and effortlessly cool—and yet there was some degree of logic. They were both good at sitting around a table, talkative, generous in spirit, patient with others. I watched them carve out a rhythm I enjoyed, even if I didn't completely understand, and it was the first time, since coming to New York, that I was drawn back to my parents' house, back to my sister, if only to see how this went.

The situation with Javari had bothered me deeply, more than I could admit even to myself. The whole thing made me feel young and stupid, easily blown off course. If James hadn't provided a distraction, inserted himself into our lives at the very minute Javari had split, I knew the damage might have been much worse. It helped me, that James had been outraged first, that he'd flared up in my defense, especially because he would never know how outsize my reaction was. And so I held on. I followed them to my parents' house, telling myself it was totally fine, it was my house too. A few times a week, I started sleeping in my room, going to class and coming back, eating dinner with my family.

My sister and James, they'd become inseparable since the gala, nearly athletic in their hanging out. Grocery shopping, dry cleaning, picking out sheets at Bed Bath & Beyond—nothing was too mundane for them to do together. Morgan was in her last semester at

Parsons and was barely on campus. From what I understood, James had a patchwork schedule of shifts at the Columbia library, tutoring sessions with rich high schoolers, and when he could get it, freelance writing. I wanted to know what they talked about, how they fit into each other's worlds. But James rarely talked about his life; he left for his jobs, came back, took them on and off like a raincoat. Once, my dad said he should really consider working at a newspaper or a magazine and James laughed so hard it took us all by surprise.

"Sorry," he replied, composing himself. "It's just . . . I'm not a tutor by choice." He nodded. "I've tried."

Most days, James and Morgan would show up to the house around five or six, keys jingling, batting back and forth their various topics: the rip-off that was boxes of cereal, if breeding dogs to have short legs was cruel. Morgan would take out the ceramic bowls and fill them with the yogurt pretzels or the cheese crackers or the dry-roasted edamame they had brought and yell upstairs to where, without having ever discussed it, I had acquired the habit of quietly waiting for them. By March, a routine had begun to take shape around us. Conflicted as I felt by their relationship, I found I still wanted to be there, with them, and they won me over by acting like they wanted me too. I seemed perpetually invited to stick my nose into what they were doing, to plop on the couch and make fun of what they were watching, to put my fingers into what they were eating—and so I did.

It was surprisingly liberating, returning to the old comforts of my sister, letting her guide as she had in high school. There was refuge in the shift that was happening in my mind: I was invisible again, and I could stay in my parents' house, with Morgan and James, for as long as I needed. In a way it felt like the natural Brighton order had finally found us, had caught a flight east after a three-year delay.

"Come on," Morgan said from the door of our bathroom. It was noon on a Saturday, freshly spring. "We're smoking this joint and going to the natural history museum." I followed her into her room and perched against the windowsill, where James was running a flame along the joint's seam. He lit it, took two long pulls, then passed it to me.

"You going to try and pay a dollar again?" I held the smoke in my lungs and the words came out pinched.

"Pay what you wish, Riley. If you want to pay twenty-three bucks, that's your wish."

"*One dollar*, though?"

"Hey, I didn't make the rules. I pay a dollar, they let me in."

I looked at Morgan. "You go places with this cheap bastard?"

"Look who's talking."

James made a sound like I'd been called to the principal's office.

"How can you even put us in the same category?" I took another drag and passed it to Morgan. "I look for deals. This guy's a miser."

"A *miser*?" James said the word back, made it ridiculous.

"Shut up," I said.

"Look." Morgan coughed into her elbow. "He can buy his one-dollar ticket, and we can stand in another line."

But at the museum, when Morgan and I saw the line of kids and families and tourists, all of them blisteringly sober, we were forced to change our strategy. James was a remarkably functional high person, able to sit around a table with my parents with the same ease he could look the ticket woman in the eye and ask for three one-dollar tickets. He had a good time shaming us when we asked, laughed with his mouth tipped in the air, called us little carpetbaggers. Then he went to stand in line while Morgan and I giggled beneath the Tyrannosaurus rex, which we decided looked like a party dinosaur, a groupie type with that open mouth and eager gait.

Inside, the dark was soothing, almost viscous. We went straight to the Hall of Ocean Life, that big-bellied basin awash in blue. I stood in front of a manatee suspended in its diorama, a sad concave arch to its body, and wondered how long it would take to feel better. In theory, I wanted to reclaim my life at school, but sliding backward like this, it made me question what I had to return to. Going to the dorms meant seeing Javari. It meant confronting a reality I suddenly feared was lonely and small. I looked over at them, a few dioramas down, and felt a big depressing gratitude. They were doing this for me, filling my Saturdays with little projects and excursions. Each weekend I told myself I would decline, get dressed and go out and snap the fuck out of it, and each weekend we'd be in the kitchen making banana bread or walking to PetSmart to pick out a fish tank. I couldn't stop. It startled me how simple it was to be with them, and as time passed I began to picture us old together, they happily married and I in the spare room, and through the fog in my heart, I thought to myself: *It could be worse.*

Upstairs, in the halls filled with artifacts from indigenous people of the world, there were too many jokes for me and James, too many thousand-year-old pillows and native costumes that looked like they belonged to my parents. We paused before a diorama of a rural Hindu wedding scene: a husband and wife with the priest and the matchmaker, the woman draped in fabric, buried in jewelry, a veil on her head topped with a towering floral headpiece.

James said, "Your mom would like that."

I said, "They have been talking about renewing their vows."

James leaned in to read the plaque.

"Do you think your parents are from the same caste?"

I thought for a minute. "Dad's a Brahman. Definitely. But Mom's actually more of a laborer."

"You think your mom's a Shudra? What the fuck, Riley."

"Sorry, did you have her pegged as more of a scholar?"

"I mean, I don't think she's sweeping stairs for a living. I don't think of her as a peasant."

"God," Morgan groaned. "You two are the epitome of bad museum company."

James looked at me, lips in a line. Morgan had said epi-*tomb*. We waited for the other to make a move, unsure if we should, when I turned to my left and felt my bowels drop. Across the way, the back of a man in a leather jacket, a paperboy cap, six feet something with a wide, square stance. He was looking at a Chinese opera scene, a woman beside him in stiletto boots. I backed slowly into a wall, and when the man turned around, I let out a low, crazy sound.

"What?" Morgan was beside me. "What are you— Oh god. No. No, it's not him."

We left the indigenous people. They followed me through the Asian mammals, into the African mammals, where I looked up at the elephants, at the two floors of hippos and buffalos and lions frozen for eternity in the same position, trying to think of something witty to say that would put them at ease and make me look like a sane and balanced human person, when I understood that I needed to leave, to be alone, to shake the blanket of smog strangling my thoughts.

"Stay," I told them. "It will make it worse if you leave too."

"It wasn't him, Riley." Morgan stood in front of a giraffe, and the two of them together made me want to scream. "And if it was, he would have come over and apologized. I'm sure he feels terrible. I'm sure he just doesn't know what to do."

"Morgan," I said, closing my eyes. "Please stop. You're making it worse."

By April, James was sleeping in Morgan's bedroom, drinking coffee with my parents before they left for work. He showed up at Kaleidoscope and helped move boxes, held mannequins still so Morgan could dress them. My parents accused us of staging a coup, but they so clearly delighted in what was happening. Their new house echoed with voices, shook with laughter. Their countertops and floors were marked with crumbs, scratches, and stains—all signs of children, of life. My parents flew to India, came back and asked where all the coffee had gone, pulled out secret stores of toilet paper and laundry soap with the joy of people in their nineties. Cries from the pantry, from the couch when they opened their DVR, from the bathroom when they realized that instead of doing laundry, we'd used all their towels—each lecture from my mother and chuckle from my father had an unmistakable underpinning of amusement. Their complaints were halfhearted; we learned to open a bottle of Oregon pinot if they returned at night, to buy smoked salmon and bagels if they arrived in the morning. We paid for these things with our own money, and it gave us the impression that we were even.

New York, for the first time, it felt like home.

By May, James had his hands in everything. He edited my final papers, gave me little pep talks when I showed signs of distress about my future—was, in fact, the only person who took this seriously. I worried that forgoing a summer internship to go backpacking with Morgan would make my career indecision worse. The trip would help me, James said. It would expose me to weird things, unlock parts of my thinking that wouldn't happen staying here, stuck in an office. No one knew what they wanted to do, not really; Morgan was an anomaly. Look at him, a graduate degree and still no real job. No, don't look at him. He was a bad example. The point was, there was plenty of time. It was remarkable, how James made an effort with us all, sharpened the kitchen knives and reconfigured the routers and explained to my dad the concept of cloud-based storage. Morgan graduated from Parsons and James sat with us, wore a suit and held a velvet box with earrings that were so perfect for her, it made my pulse beat lopsided and hot. As Morgan and I prepared for our trip, James was there, attacking all the tasks she and I had passed back and forth, effectively avoiding. Questions about visas, USB chargers, partition—they were now directed at James, inching us closer to our grand adventure.

How long had Morgan and I dreamed of this trip? All those weeks together in hotel rooms, we talked of traveling on our own. We would go to India, we decided, but only to see the places our parents had refused to take us, the beaches and the holy cities and the deserts that spanned the walls of Kaleidoscope. We would go to Thailand, howl at the moon. We would run through rice fields in Bali, take boats into the sunset. We'd talked about these things until we made ourselves crazy, imagining ourselves older, scheming until we fell asleep. But it had been some time since we'd been those girls in Mumbai, steeped in that interdependent, sisterly talk. So when Morgan asked for the trip as her college graduation gift, I hadn't expected it, felt both flattered and alarmed. I was confronted with the reality of a summer traveling together, just the two of us, and I found it made me slightly nervous, trying to imagine it, unsure what it would feel like.

With departure two weeks away, we'd transformed our rooms

into a headquarters for the trip. James had convinced us to cede half of what we wanted to bring. He'd backpacked through Europe the summer after college, two months all alone. A couple of shirts, a pair of pants, some shorts, a swimsuit, a handful of underwear. We knew how to shop, didn't we? We'd been to Asia, seen the markets and bazaars, the air-conditioned malls; we'd find what we needed, he said, and we rolled our eyes, parroted his advice to each other in increasingly offensive imitations (Morgan, come on, doesn't floss seem excessive? A book, Riley? Don't they have books in Asia?). But we did what he said. We did almost everything he said. The truth is we were anxious about leaving James behind. Morgan and I had been at a distance for so long, and we worried, I think, it was James's presence that made us work again. If we asked him, we knew he would come, but we never asked. The trip was for us, a way to bring us back together.

"I've been thinking," I said to my sister as we sat on the floor of my bedroom one rare, James-less afternoon. It was a week before my birthday and I had been thinking, had been working out a way to make it disappear. June ninth. Every summer my birthday struck first and Morgan's followed, ten days behind. Seven hundred and twenty days separated her birth from mine, and yet, within the scope of vast possibilities, the universe had chosen us both as Geminis, had marked us as twins. We realized this fact in middle school, came up with the idea when we were twelve and fourteen. Matching outfits, tandem bicycles, dinners with food served only in pairs—over the years the tradition had hardened, became as serious as Thanksgiving or Christmas, but it was just for us, a way to renew our sisterly vows. For nearly a decade my parents had stuck candles in a cake and opened the door, let us run off to whatever we'd devised for each other. The summer before Morgan left for college, she presented me with a certificate for a binary star and we climbed to the top of Spencer Butte. I have ninety-five pictures tucked away in a file, endless, stubborn frames of pitch-black night: a nebulous, plausible twinkle in the distance. Not once did we bring up our impending separation.

"Hear me out," I said.

I'd laid out the argument before bringing it to Morgan, knowing that she would put up a fight. We were about to embark across the world, two months just the two of us, was that not celebration enough? We should save our money, be reasonable, focus on the trip. Besides, had we not exhausted the options for buying bullshit in twos? Did we not creep out James enough as it was? All her other boyfriends I never gave a shit about, but did James need to witness yet another inane family tradition?

Morgan listened. She heard me. She nodded at the appropriate times, interjected mostly in defense of us, how we didn't have to change our behavior for James, how twenty-one was a big deal, how she could do it differently, that she wanted nothing for her birthday in return.

"It's not about James and it's not about us." I finally came out with it. "It's about me. I'm in a weird place, Morgan. I think you know that, and I don't have the strength for a birthday. I can't this year. Please"—I held her eyes on mine—"tell me you understand what I'm saying. You tell me to communicate, you tell me to talk to you. I'm trying. I'm talking."

I watched her process what I was saying. She took her time. Never before had I given voice to that sentiment. I couldn't handle another grand Morgan gesture, for fear of my debt growing even larger, for fear of it making me defensive and weird when all I wanted was to be the good sister, the one with parts to spare, the one doing the giving. It stemmed from my knowledge that our impending trip was, in so many unspoken ways, a gift from my sister to my teenage self—the girl who needed to dream herself elsewhere and older and better. And here we were, making it come true. It touched me deeply, and yet I didn't trust myself to behave accordingly, not yet. Before we spent all summer on the road, just the two of us, I needed some time to work out my knots.

"Okay." Morgan nodded, clearing her throat when the word came out scratched. "I hear you. I understand, I really do."

She smiled at me, faintly, and in my memory I hugged her. Every time, I add that in; I scoot myself across my bedroom floor, across the mess of clothes and cables and plastic containers of delivery lunch and I wrap my arms around my sister. It doesn't change a thing, I know for certain it changes nothing, and yet it's important. Of course there's a hug, the last time I can remember just the two of us alone, together, my memory demands it: there absolutely must be a hug.

I embrace my sister; she pulls me close; our bodies are warm, pulsing and alive.

THE CRASH OF 2008

Before I knew what was inside, I was endeared by your shitty envelope.

Eight in the morning and you were gone, your bed made, your phone switched off, James's too. It all felt like a trap at first: the bloated envelope taped to our bathroom mirror with my name scrawled across the front. At first I simply glared at it, groggy in my underwear, angry with you for yoking me to this ploy when all I wanted was to pee, to go back to sleep, to ignore my birthday as I'd plainly requested. And I nearly did, Morgan. I turned around, took three steps toward my still-warm bed before you caught me.

The envelope was a piece of shit; this was your bait, and it worked beautifully. The business rectangle that had been used before, the lettering like you'd woken in the middle of the night and spelled my name with your left hand; it looked more like a ransom note than a birthday present, and the image of you selecting this terrible envelope, the thought of you rummaging through our parents' junk to find something as ugly as this, it softened me just enough to peel the packet from the mirror, to open the flap and shake out what you'd stuffed inside.

A leaf of college rule, folded in thirds, the left edge frayed from where you ripped it from a spiral notebook. As I stood in our bathroom unfolding the paper, picture me smiling: know that I was. From you, Morgan, this stab at dispassion was respect in itself, proof that you had indeed listened. The nonchalant handwriting I imagine you practiced, at least a few times, probably on nicer paper than the final product; the free city map you made an effort to procure, to ensure it was free; the two twenty-dollar bills running loose in the mix, the defense for including two instead of one—all of it, it was nothing short of perfect, and by the time I understood how they worked in conjunction I had already turned myself away from the mirror.

Better than anyone else, you understand how I hate seeing my reflection when I'm moved unexpectedly by surprise, by emotion.

I picked up the two twenties and I smelled them. I don't know why, but even now I can recall their metallic tang, like a handful of dirt, a ring of old keys, sharp in my nostrils. They smelled like Oregon, somehow, and even now I wonder how you did it. How you managed to gift me even this memory, this vestige of childhood already doing its work: pulling me closer to what you understood, even then, that I had lost.

You got everything right. It's essential that you know this, will be the first thing I say when I see you next. All the places you circled on that free city map were like molecules of my strongest DNA, coded in red for sustenance and blue for entertainment and green for relaxation, strung together to display a rendering of myself I'd nearly discarded. I stared at that map for a long time, matching circles to the places they represented, or trying, at least. There were eleven points, and only eight of them, from an aerial view, did I know by heart. I twitched for a computer, to lay bare the unknown three, but I knew it would be a breach of contract. You hadn't labeled them and I wouldn't either. For an instant I considered going back to sleep; it had been six months since I'd spent a day like this, and the thought of it exhausted me. But the map felt like a challenge, you knew it would, and I changed my mind: I turned off my phone. I brushed my teeth, wrapped myself in your kimono, and when I realized I didn't own a watch, I took the alarm clock. Then I followed your instructions on how to disappear.

I took the train to Chinatown first. Did you know I would start there? The beauty parlor opened early, at nine thirty, and so I went to get my hair washed, my head massaged. It was the same woman, the one who cackled when you said your honey hair was natural, that you were half-Chinese like me. I'll admit the experience is different without the scene that trails your special face. Alone, I melted into that porcelain basin. I closed my eyes and let her thick, brawny fingers knead deep into my scalp, pull in circles at my temples. The weight of the water, the eucalyptus lather, the competent hands—how could you not like this? I felt my eyebrows crease, the woman's thumb glide over them. I decided I would make you try again.

Afterward, facing the mirror, the woman blow-dried my hair with the roller brush that scared you off. This time too, she insisted on teasing the top and curling under the ends to frame my face, but when she pulled out the hairspray I blocked her. The pleasure has almost nothing to do with the end result; it's about the low-pressure hour of fingers and conditioner, of warm, soft blown air, of nothing to do but eye the styles on the wall: the men with feathery mullets, the women shaking out their orange bobs. For six dollars, this is my kingdom. I tipped two more, and when I came out onto the street at the south side of Canal I heard your voice, counting my change, telling me that I had thirty dollars, 1980s hair, and an empty, footloose birthday in the city I loved.

Following the sun, I walked east. My alarm clock told me it was ten forty-five. At a certain point I unfolded your map and found the circle nearest me, holding my finger to the location as I made my way slowly toward it, feeling equal parts tourist and detective. I didn't recognize the spot, couldn't remember what stood at that intersection until I physically came upon it. How was it possible that you had remembered when I barely did? Did you walk the blocks yourself, prodding your memory, or are you really that good? There are so many questions I have saved up to ask you. I suppose this one can wait.

The café had no tables, only a counter that ran along the windows. I went in, ordered what I'd brought you to eat that morning, three years before, when I first came to visit you in New York. And while you had navigated us down on the train, located the street, pointed me in the right direction, I made you cover your eyes as we approached. I had you sit at that counter, eyes shut as I whispered my order to the woman. There was one thing we missed from that terrible layover in Singapore, when Mom got poisoned and we missed our connection—and while we couldn't find it in Oregon, we got it there. Holy shit, you'd said. We'd ordered three more, but that day I had just one, sat by myself with my toasted sandwich spread thick with kaya coconut jam, thinking of you, thinking of all the stupid shit we'd done for each other, all the inevitable things to come.

The walk to Union Square was about thirty blocks, a mile and half, a straight shot north. I liked this walk, had done it with you a dozen times, but never before on a Monday morning. Elizabeth was nearly empty, Chinatown almost clean. Men with cigarettes suspended from the sides of their mouths moved their crates of cabbage and wet boxes of fish; some of them napped in their trucks, bare feet on the dash, hands above their heads, armpits reflected in the side-view mirror. A woman spraying down the sidewalk in front of her shop moved her hose to let me pass and I smelled the herbs stacked in the cartons behind her, licked the jam from the slats of my teeth and laughed too loud, all alone, thinking of our failed attempt that summer, the summer you lost your virginity to Kyle Webber, the same summer I had my braces removed: a sexy summer for us both. There were no pandan leaves in Eugene, and so we'd used cilantro instead. On the internet we read that the two could be used as substitutes, but the internet had lied. Our kaya jam was disgusting, do you remember? Dad said it tasted like soap and sweet mayonnaise. But we ate it still, stubborn as hell. We convinced each other it wasn't so bad. We'd spent most of the weekend shopping for it, making it, trying to convince other people to eat it. I can still taste it spread on that sourdough from Barry's; your idea, not mine. Did we have weed of our own that summer? As I crossed East Houston, turned onto the Bowery, I hoped we were a little high.

The villages were your territory, the areas around your school and dorm. You were always more of an uptown girl, but I'd taken the north for myself, and so you'd embraced the little Italian joints in Alphabet City, found a nail spot where they knew your name, an old Polish man who fixed your shoes. It's hard to be in the village without thinking of you, and at first, when I returned to New York, that's exactly why I lived off Cooper Square. I stayed two years, did you know that? Until all the places you loved shut down.

My plan was to find the second unknown, just east of Third coming up on the right, but I decided first to pass through Union Square.

I had to remind myself this was part of the day, to swing by places and see what was happening. On the days I hated everything, the many piss-and-shit-filled days, this was one thing I still cherished about this city: even when there was nothing, no farmers' market or heritage-day parade or circle of breakdancing Puerto Ricans, there was *something*. If you put yourself in the way of New York, she always gave you something to look at, something to change your state of mind. A woman driving a remote control car with a Chihuahua sitting behind the wheel. A white dude furiously nunchucking his way up some stairs. Two toddlers being pulled by a leash. I bought a dollar coffee at the deli and went into the Barnes and Noble, rode the escalators to the reading floor and found a spot against the window. I took your map from my purse and shook it out, adjusted it to the right direction.

Whenever I orient myself in real life, in real time, I picture the shape of the United States; did you know this about me? The whole thing is ridiculous, one of my saddest, most patriotic traits. I determine a single direction, north or east, south or west, it doesn't matter, I just need one. For most anyone else it's easy from here, but I've fucked it up so many times, hit West End on my way to Central Park, that I made myself a little tool. I conjure America, its whale-shaped body, and use its coasts to find my way. North, I'll think, toward Canada, and if the next turn is west, I'll head to California; if east, I'll walk toward the Atlantic. Don't ask how it's helpful or why it works, but it does explain why, as I looked out over the soccer balls and Hula-Hoops of Union Square, the bodies pounding on drums and guitars, smoking cigarettes, accosting strangers for haircuts and donations, I thought of Mexico. I thought of that first trip Mom and Dad took to Puerto Vallarta, without us. You were in middle school; you'd left me behind in elementary, but that week, staying with the neighbors, you came to the fifth grade as a special guest. You must remember. You'd talked to the teachers yourself, ran it by the old neighbor couple—*just for the week!*—and somehow, they'd each agreed. Only in Eugene. Only in a town of a hundred thousand hippies would this be considered a reasonable deal to strike with a twelve-year-old in the absence of parents. But in retrospect, perhaps it was. We were overjoyed. Nothing went wrong. We followed the rules; the next week you went back.

So south I went, down the escalators and into the wild, searching for the unknown circle just a few more blocks toward Mexico, surveying every storefront for what you might be trying to show me, when there it was.

Shit, Morgan. You play the game almost better than I do. That was my first thought, hand on my heart: I hadn't given you nearly enough credit. The basement taproom was my kind of place, mostly wood, mostly empty. I watched the bartender restock his olives and limes as I hesitated outside. The sandwich board said FREE BIRTHDAY DRINK.

My hand reached into my purse and fumbled for the alarm clock. The neon light glowed 1:17.

I understood that I would not go inside.

How could I allow my first legal drink to be alone on a Monday at 1:17? It mattered to me; in the bottom of my throat, in the way my hand still clutched the alarm clock. It mattered to me, and at first that's all I could concede, that I wanted to share that drink with you. I told myself it was natural to want the hoopla, the announcement you'd make to the bartender, the excitement you'd bring, the celebration. I'd changed my mind. Perhaps this was your plan all along, to make me miss your little spectacles. This was the second thought I'd allowed to land, a fraudulent little theory that reeked of what I wouldn't say.

There's no doubt in my mind you assumed I would go in, relax into a booth with a free birthday beer, and there I was, incapable. For five months I'd slipped back into your protection, and that day, I understood how little of my bravery remained. I could not bring myself to the one ability I took pride in more than anything else: simply being alone in a way that you could not, comfortably, unselfconsciously. You liked to say that I had the thick skin but Morgan, you had the flesh. It was your tissue, your muscle and fat, holding me taut, keeping me tough.

I opened the map again; across the way, a familiar circle came to my rescue.

I knew it to be food by its color, and to be sushi by its location. Specifically it was our dollar-sushi spot, everything on the menu deeply, comically discounted from regular prices permanently struck through. We were obsessed with this place: you for the kitsch, the dangling paper lanterns and glossy pictures of octopus balls and yellowtail collars strung between the wooden tables, and me for the menu's twelve-page bravado, the way the servers yelled above the booming hip-hop, the patent disregard for how discounts worked. The restaurant exploded, did you see? A gas leak killed two men, leveled the building and three others adjacent, smoke and flames rising like the apocalypse, all the way to Midtown. When I heard, I walked out into the street and around the block, around again, made circles until it was dark.

But that Monday in June my legs moved from sheer adrenaline, propelling me around the corner and down Second Avenue, past the smoke shops and the Jewish bakeries, the water pipes and towers of shriveled rugelach. I was high from your game, from what I perceived then as a personal challenge, and my pace turned in rapid succession from stroll to stride to trot, until I was nearly jogging, kimono fluttering as my hand held down my bouncing purse. A hole was growing, a greedy pit that bloomed like an emergency. I was starving, Morgan, please know at least this: despite everything I did not know, I was blurry with the desire to fill myself up.

A dollar for five gyoza; a dollar for a fried, trembling block of agedashi tofu; a dollar for blistered shisito peppers. I ate four pieces of salmon nigiri, three pieces of tuna, two eel, a mackerel, a tamago. I ate in a way that pinned me down, took all my focus, a vacuum of determined pleasure. I've learned it takes a certain level of energy, a high level, to do anything with genuine abandon. Dancing, drinking, fucking—eating is no exception, pairs naturally with oblivion. This was a tenet of my New York existence, but that day the pleasure would not come, and so I continued to summon it: a spicy tuna roll, a plate of kimchi, anticipating what I would order next before the desire even hit. I ate until the food lost its distinguishing features, until it was salty mash and pulp, the dull flavor of binging. I ate as if a camera was on me and you were on the other side; this, perhaps, is the most true. I wanted to show you I would be all right; I see the irony in this now.

By the time I paid the bill, twenty-three dollars with tax and tip, I knew I'd fucked up the budget. I felt disgusting and yet I conflated this excess with satisfaction. I thought you might be pleased. It was nearly three.

I made my way to Tompkins Square Park, where a teenager accepted my dollar and handed me a cigarette, lit against his. I crossed slowly through, passed the girls in their bikinis, their ready-made sandwiches and iced coffees laid out across their dorm-room towels. I remembered my sunglasses, fished them from my bag and put them on. I tried to get into the mood. Up ahead, along the benches, a pair of Caribbean nannies sat in the shade with their strollers, fanning themselves as they watched two boys shoot around on the basketball court. I paused for a minute, watched the taller boy attempt a layup and miss completely, and I moved along, pretended like I hadn't seen. I remembered my headphones, plugged them into my phone and turned it on, switched it immediately to airplane mode. On the jungle gym, a bit farther along, it was all adults on the monkey bars doing pull-ups and arm dips and upside-down sit-ups. I stopped, took a drag, put my music on. The cigarette allowed me to think, to disguise my wandering as something purposeful. I liked that about New York: you never had to buy a pack, never had to commit to smoking. An implicit pact said a dollar could buy me ten minutes of thinking, and by the time the cigarette had finished, I'd found my beat, and with it came that quivering sliver of perspective. I held on, exited the park.

Walking in New York, it comes with practice, has a specific tempo unique to itself. There are no hard-and-fast rules, no walk to the left or pass to the right, not like the Tokyos of the world. This drove you crazy, but I always admired the hustle of the sidewalks. Like driving up and down the avenues, the lanes don't even matter; it's just avoidance, anticipation, a zigzag that speeds and slows with the flow of human traffic. When I walk in New York, my brain stays watchful, keeps itself always a little warm so when the reflexes gradually became comfortable, when I realized I could match my rhythm to a beat that made me feel alive, it morphed into a kind of addiction for me and then, slowly, into a type of therapy. I used to do it two, three times a week to keep my balance. I don't think I ever put this into words for you, how I spent most of those days alone. It was the walking, the music, the fleeting contact with humans set against a dramatic, synthetic pulse that gave me the impression that I was a part of the thing I wanted most, that I was in the middle of it, vibing off the city without ever extending myself personally. I must have walked the length of Manhattan a hundred times, eyes glazed, filling myself with wonder, with swagger. I needed this time; it built me up. Somehow you understood this years before I could put it into words myself.

Not much has changed, Morgan. I still wander the streets when I feel myself jumping out of my skin, but now I'll get on a treadmill if it's too late, or I'll blast my music and clean the oven, vacuum my carpet like I'm fighting a war. I still think about things I want to accomplish; I still wonder what I'm doing with my life.

But that day, something clicked. For the first time that day, that week, perhaps since James picked you and everything shifted, I thought to myself: *I am a lucky motherfucker.* I reminded myself: *I am exactly where I hoped I would be.* Full, exhausted, alone, twenty-one years old and making my way west, across the island that I had coveted so badly and, in that moment, that felt like mine. Somewhere in between I found myself on a bench, head dipped backward, arms spread along the wooden seat back. I must have been smiling. I shut my eyes, allowed myself to zoom slowly out, picturing my splayed form getting smaller and smaller. I watched the black lines dance across my eyelids, conducted by the sun.

At seven o'clock, you wrote in your note, you and James would happen to be eating dinner at the Frying Pan, a lightship turned seafood restaurant docked in Pier 66; join or don't, it was up to me, but of course you'd chosen a place that screamed celebration. I opened the map one last time. Along the way was a third unknown, just west, coded simply for entertainment.

You took a chance with this one, but I'm grateful you did. It was exactly as you'd described it to me, as Mom had marveled, and as I passed through the doors I heard the term you two had coined: Fancy Goodwill. Only in New York, where the FIT students donated their excess couture, where West Village mothers dropped off their things, tags still attached, could there exist a Fancy Goodwill. It smelled nothing like the soured, stagnant musk of the racks we'd learned on in Eugene. The Fancy Goodwill had mannequins with handbags, with raffia sun hats and leather slides. I wove through the racks, scoffing at price tags, wondering what I might find for my remaining three dollars, when I saw it. Opposite me, hanging on a display wall: a red backpack, nylon and canvas with a thin leather trim, large enough for a laptop, small enough to be a purse. I crossed the store to touch it. It was the kind of backpack that would break our girlhood treaty. It was the kind of backpack we had battled over, the one frivolous item we both coveted deeply, and yet we understood that two inseparable sisters wearing two red backpacks would negate any kind of cool the backpack might provide. I tried it on, turned myself in front of the mirror, remembered that hostile day at the mall, when Mom said she'd buy us each what we wanted and we'd both chosen that red fucking backpack. It was one of the rare instances I can recall of Mom intercepting our conflict. We went home with nothing, pissed off with each other. We made the pact a week later, when we became so lonely we had to do something, when the backpack had bloomed into a symbol of something much worse. We would not go to battle over an object, a thing, a city, a man. Neither of us, we promised, would ever own a red backpack. But I never stopped wanting it and neither did you.

I wore it up to the cashier, reckless, exhilarated. I bought it for you.

The West Side Highway is one of the sunniest places in all of Manhattan, and that day felt radioactive. Slabs of sunlight, heavy, whitewashed beams fell from across the Hudson River, blinding me as I crossed west, toward California. The pier opened before me, flanked by wooden planks that formed Xs, steel braces at their centers: a maritime acropolis funneling me toward the bright red ship docked at the end. A thin, towering mast rose from the center, yellow in the lowering light, a lantern like a jewel at the very top. At the gangway, I fussed with myself, smoothed out things that needed no smoothing: my tank top, my hair. I made my ascent, and at the top, I paused once more.

James from across the deck, at a table along the railing, sunglasses on, handsome as hell. I'd grown so accustomed to seeing him around the house, fluffy-haired in a sleeping shirt, that the sight of him startled me. He sat in a chair, one leg raised, not crossed, but an ankle rested on a knee, hands in his lap, gaze out over the Hudson. Sitting there, alone like that, James matched you, Morgan: in that moment, paused at the entrance, it all made sense. Light has a way of altering its subject, making a god out of something perfectly ordinary, but even then, I knew the effect was his, was, of course, yours. The look on his face, Morgan. He was at peace in a way I have not seen since.

James would like the backpack, I knew he would. He would get it, and the anticipation made me flush with excitement. I hid it behind my back, expecting you to appear at any moment. If you tried to gift me something, I'd gift you something first. The ungiftable, the illicit, I would stump you with what I held in my hands. But you hadn't yet arrived.

Where is she, I whispered by way of greeting, sitting down across from James, sliding my package below my chair. *You made it,* he smiled. *Happy birthday.*

He'd call you, James said, but you were playing the day by the rulebook: phone off, fully unreachable. The two of you had spent the morning in the park, hiding from me. You'd packed a go bag: a canvas tote with chocolate croissants for breakfast, cold cuts and pasta salad for lunch, a change of clothes, a pack of baby wipes, two protein bars in case of enemy capture. After lunch, the two of you separated, James to the library, you to run your secret errands, with plans to meet back up at seven.

I marveled at the strategy, all of it just to make me feel alone.

When the waiter came by, it was seven fifteen. We waited for you. We joked that you'd gotten lost, that without the internet, how could you know what time it was? I pulled out my alarm clock, set it on the table between us. At 7:25 we tried to call you. I connected my phone back to the network, found nothing waiting, but still, your phone was off. When the waiter came by a second time, James insisted we get started with drinks. We sensed you right around the corner, swiping your card in the back of a cab, hitting that button for a 25 percent tip, the driver turning around to get a good look at you. We imagined you with a mess of balloons, an armful of cake, running along the pier, up the gangway, late.

I reached for the list of cocktails and James mirrored me, pulling the menu from my grasp. No menus, he said, no signature cocktails. He used air quotes for this last statement, told me we would be adhering to an authentic twenty-first-birthday experience.

James laid out his instructions. I was supposed to pick a drink I recognized but that I'd never had: no Manhattans, no cosmopolitans—nothing classy. It's important, he said, that the drink be out of place, inauthentic to the region but iconic to somewhere else, something that perhaps I'd heard of in a movie. An appletini, a piña colada, a tequila sunrise. A drink that lent itself easily to statements like, I could drink five more of these, or, I can barely taste the alcohol. I deliberated for a minute, landed on mint juleps, and when the cocktails arrived we cheered twice, found both statements to be true.

At what point did we become wrong? Tell me, at what point did we fail you? At eight o'clock? At eight fifteen? Should we have paid our bill, gone looking for you? Earlier even, should we have felt you gone? For all the talk of being your Gemini, your second half by celestial means, the person who would always know, *tell me*: How will I ever forgive myself?

Instead, we stayed. We ordered a second round of mint syrup and bourbon, assured the waiter that we'd have dinner just as soon as our third person arrived. We joked that the go bag had run dry, that low on protein, you would be ravenous. We'd order the hummus, the burger, the ribs for your deteriorating nutrition. We talked about you; despite our deeper oblivion, Morgan, we held you close. Loose from liquor, slackened by sunshine, we got smart, we grew funny, but we kept your name on our tongues, passed it between us like a balloon, like the game we'd played as girls, reaching well before it touched the ground.

We didn't check the time again until my phone rang, startling us both, Dad on the screen. I laughed into the phone: Have you seen Morgan? *Come home*, replied a voice that sounded only vaguely of Dad's. *Just come home*, it said again, and the way it shook, it was about you.

A twenty-story crane had fallen in Midtown, Fifty-First and Second, and there you were, just as James and I had imagined you, but four miles away, five hours earlier: a pastry box in hand, three perfect éclairs in white paper wrappers. Rushing.

They identified you first, within the first couple of hours, because someone had been watching you. From a fourth-floor window across the way, a middle-aged man with a wife and a kid told the police what you were wearing, the color of your hair, the white and blue box you held in your hands. They remembered you at the bakery, too, remembered you well. They pulled the credit card receipt, the police told us that Monday night, as we sat in the living room, Mom and Dad, James and me. I know we were all there, but I couldn't tell you what we said, couldn't say for sure who screamed from the upstairs bathroom, who broke the hallway lamp, which one of us collapsed on the kitchen floor, body folded into a ball, heaving on the rug beneath the sink.

I read your autopsy. For months, I was the only one, and James was right, I shouldn't have. But after that I saw you regularly, waking from visions of what I'd read, choking in the middle of the night and grappling in the bed you'd never use again, your room exactly the way you'd left it, the old sheets, the same laundry, and in the worst way, the most gruesome possible way, it helped me. I needed to see it to understand, to sear into my consciousness that what had happened was real, that there had been an accident, because for months, Morgan, the concept would not take.

You were everywhere. Where you are, I don't know if you saw, but they clung to you, printed picture after fucking picture to feed the story that was selling papers, taking up airtime, turning you into some kind of devastating spectacle. I don't know if I handled it right. I mean that honestly, I really don't know, because after you left I lost all perspective. I looked out over my life and saw nothing of my own, because who was I now, how did I sound, what the fuck did I know, Morgan, without the chorus of us?

PART THREE

February 2009, New York City

They sit on the tarmac forty minutes before the voice comes on the loudspeaker above, apologizing for the delay. It takes a moment for the voice to round on its point, for the listeners to take out their earbuds and shake from their various hypnagogic states. It is February in New York and the general population is sucked dry by steam boilers, chapped from commutes in blizzard winds, and tired, mostly, caught in the ides of New York's worst month. It has been half a year since summer, nearly eight months since a crane fell in Midtown East, killing four, and while many on the plane remember this news, only two are thinking of it now.

The captain's voice is blithe. It has the small-town lilt of a Greg or a Jim, with no trace of alarm, so when he says the crew is below the plane, locating and extracting a piece of luggage that belongs to a passenger who checked into the flight but who, oddly, did not board, there is no detectable threat. It's an eight-hour red-eye from JFK; those not already sleeping are working, pulled deep into the tired glow of their screens. News of a passenger who has seemingly disappeared between the ticket counter and the gate, whose suitcase still sat on the plane, is met with a flicker of displeasure that straps promptly back into eye masks and spreadsheets.

In just a few minutes, the voice assures us, they will be in the air and on their way.

It's a full flight, 374 passengers in all. As the pilot speaks, across the aisle in the twenty-eighth row, Riley and James strain to make out the announcement, a quiet pulse slamming in their ears and their throats. They say nothing to each other, eyes stolidly ahead, and arrive separately at the same conclusion: the contents of that suitcase are likely catastrophic. The plane will not take off at all. The plane will explode with fire. The plane is a figment of their ravaged imaginations, a slip of consciousness they know well from months of chasing sleep with pills that bleed the line between true and false. For months they had been smothered by the same relentless sensation, a feeling they have described to each other at great length, in aching detail, with a clarity that extends to nothing else.

A shortness of breath, a restless insanity in their bodies, the once vitalizing city streets. All of it was closing in on them, the buildings blocking out the sky, the traffic like a defective siren, the freezing cold snatching at their wits. They felt trapped in the elevator of their minds, panicked and furious, pressing every button, lungs full of helium jammed in their throats. They needed to get out. They came to this conclusion over and over, until they worked up the nerve to do something about it.

Ten minutes later a second announcement is made.
The bag has been removed. The crew is aboard.
Clear skies ahead. A nice tailwind from the south.
Thirty-one degrees, folks, a beautiful night for flying.

RILEY

Seven Months Earlier

The silent war of slights commenced at the funeral, when Riley excused herself quietly to the bathroom. She turned left out of the carpeted, wood-paneled room that held her sister and two hundred others, walked down the hall, past the bathroom, and out into the blistering day.

It was the start of summer. Late June. The city was beginning to drain of its locals and repopulate with families in sneakers and backpacks, long European sleeves in the afternoon heat, Chinese tours in a huddle of umbrellas. The funeral was held downtown, where Riley's mother had opened the day to the public. Karen Brighton had insisted that anyone who wished to mourn her daughter be permitted, and so the little chapel room was too young, too fashionable, too curious in their grief. Two hundred of them pressed against one another in black dresses with mandarin collars, the men in leather despite the heat. They watched Riley, Riley and James both, and when either of them stood or moved, their attention fluttered.

Riley was meant to speak at the service. Despite her misgivings she intended to go along with her mother's plan, to play a song her sister liked, to share a memory. But instead she left. Not twenty minutes in, Riley was fleeing down Sixth Avenue in her blue kimono, skin tacky with defiance, head filled with words she refused to waste on a room of strangers. At a newspaper stand, stopping to breathe, to buy a bottle of something cold, she reached for a tabloid—the daily circular with thick-lettered headlines blown across the pictures— and the next moment, as far as she will remember, she was sitting on the stoop of a town house, someone else's town house, paper open to page four, a three-by-five-inch black-and-white frame of her sister smiling up at her.

It was a precarious lifeline, these miniature portraits of her sister tucked into the pages of the week's news. Riley knew all their locations, which paper on which date, which page, which picture. She'd developed a habit of buying them, repeatedly, whenever she needed a fix. Already, she owned three of these tabloids, three of these pictures of her sister on the Great Lawn the summer before, legs crossed in a wax-print dress.

Riley put in her headphones. She took a breath that felt like the gulp of a whale, a gush of nutrients and debris, the krill of the city charging her lungs with the oxygen she needed, indivisible. She looked at her phone; the song was queued up for the service. She lowered her sunglasses, hardened her gaze out over the morning traffic, and beneath the slow scrape of the snare drum, the sting of the guitar and the tender howl of Eddie Vedder, a voice that will forever transport her to the hardest, most painful year of her life, she extracted her voice; she told her sister about her funeral.

The flowers, white lilies and gladiolas, she would have liked: the

Eternal Affection Arrangement, Riley added, pausing to let her react to this name.

Kyle Webber had been there, Rebecca with her Maltese in a Zabar's shopping bag, Jimmy the super from her old dorm, wiping at his eyes, still in uniform. Dozens of classmates Riley didn't know, everyone who worked at Columbus Circle.

Hammir had been there all week.

And Rufi had flown in. She was staying at the Hyatt with Kyle. Not together, she clarified. Just as friends.

The parlor didn't allow food, but there was a bar across the street—they'd been there before, Lucky's, did she remember? Mom and Dad had opened a tab, which was cool of them, for everyone to get a beer when it was over.

Was it already over? No, Riley shook her head. She'd left early. She was worried she might say something wrong. She felt in perpetual danger of getting in her parents' way. All week they'd stayed up well past midnight, sorting pictures, making lists. Hours later they were back at the table, phones pressed to their ears, wading through a mess of brochures. *Were they okay?* It was just like Morgan to ask this, to worry about their parents on the day of her funeral. They'd be okay, Riley assured her. They would all be fine. She insisted on this point because everything that had happened so far felt oddly, satisfyingly chimerical. They were living on a stage, a reality ensconced in a veneer of impermanence that would eventually be packed up and stored away.

The funeral was happening, but it was hardly a proper funeral, full of young people in lipstick and Rag & Bone—but Morgan's room, the Brighton house, the Upper West Side—the things that mattered, they were all exactly as they'd been before. Soon enough, the newspapers would forget, the mess of the crane would be cleaned up, and while she didn't allow herself to overthink it, Riley had a nagging suspicion that with time, Morgan would alight from wherever she'd gone and the fog would clear, her life would return to her. While everyone else lost their heads, Riley would stay in touch. She would send her sister news while she was away.

For nearly an hour, as the funeral pushed forward, as James was pressed to fill Riley's absence, made to announce himself, haphazardly, as the grieving boyfriend, when the whole room was wiping mucus and tears into their sleeves and her phone had collected fifteen missed calls, three from her mother, twelve from James, Riley sat on that Chelsea stoop with the newspaper spread across her lap, chatting away, a bottle of water in her hand, having a conversation that appeared, to anyone who passed, to be perfectly ordinary, a girl on the phone, her sister on the line.

It took until August for the pictures to mess with Riley, when the days were scooped out and hollow and the collecting kept her warm and moving in the void. Over the weeks it had evolved into this: walking the city end to end, seam to seam, checking for pieces of her in mini-marts and grocery stores, hair salons, public libraries, a slap of terrible dopamine each time she saw her, each time she bought her, threading herself around the city before heading home and hauling herself up the silent stairs, getting into bed with a pair of scissors and trimming with great care, producing perfect squares of her sister like talismans, like physical remains.

When her mother called that first afternoon, after waking up to find her missing, Riley told her that she had gone walking. The call came later than Riley imagined, when the sun sat low against the avenues, bathing the buildings in pastels. Karen repeated the word, surprised by it, as if she'd said something impossible. But walking really did sound like walking, and not like a bar or a hospital or a ditch. Riley had prepared to deliver it evenly, and when she hung up the phone, she found herself unbalanced. She was stung by the victory. Come home, she'd imagined her mother saying, to which she was planning to refuse.

Two a day for six weeks, Riley walked nearly three hundred miles and collected:

(27) Morgans on the Great Lawn, cranberry headscarf, wax-print dress;

(23) Morgans atop Spencer Butte, running shorts, arms raised triumphantly in the air;

(19) Headshot Morgans in a low bun, cotton-candy lips, gray eyes like an Abyssinian cat;

(11) Teenage Morgans at her sewing machine, dress at her needle, pins in her mouth.

It was a way to keep busy, a way to see Morgan every day. It gave her a jolt each time, a punishment she thought she deserved, a private penance, a sucker punch she'd begun to imagine came from her sister. All day she was alone, the feeling chasing her twenty blocks south and six avenues east. She ripped the skin off every day. As she walked out the door in the mornings, she made plans to get coffee, to visit a museum, as she simultaneously dismissed these vacuous interruptions. It was summer break. For a while it felt like her life was simply on hold, temporarily suspended between problem and solution—and the best plan of attack was to stay there, exist in that space, until something changed. But soon the walking and collecting began to feel like a day job. The task, the sense of purpose, it was all there, pouring cement around her life. What Riley couldn't admit was how much she feared reaching the other side, empty-handed. She looked at the newspapers and felt clobbered each time, astounded that she was reading it again—crane collapse, four dead—and yet it was exactly this that made her feel most alive. She depended on that clobbering, because without it, she never heard from Morgan. She became a wayfarer of the Upper East Side, of Hell's Kitchen, of Little Italy, atoning and receiving, pausing before the images displayed in the newspaper boxes, block by block, shielded by cases of metal and plastic like little shrines, embalming her sister.

In August, Riley stood in a Murray Hill bodega staring at the newspaper racks.

From behind her counter, the cashier asked if she was looking for something, and Riley looked up, startled, as if the electricity had gone out. It was the third shop she'd tried that morning. Yes, Riley said, did they have any copies from the week before? The cashier flicked her head. Maybe in the back, if the guys didn't throw them out. She shuffled her way to the employee door, and when she reached the back, the cashier paused. Riley remembers this in slow motion, in grotesque detail, the first villain of an unspeakable summer. The skin on her face was puffy and dimpled, like overproofed dough, as she looked at Riley over the soft mound of her shoulder. She squinted her eyes and in a damp, brassy voice that did not match her words or the dimensions of the store or the thoughtful way she held Riley's gaze, motherly, wanting to help, the cashier yelled with unfettered vigor: You want the one with the girl killed by that crane, right, honey?

Back home, in Morgan's room, Riley located her sister's old tennis shoes and held them in her fists, squeezed her palms into the mesh until they marked her flesh like a layer of webbing. She rifled through Morgan's makeup and found the soft pink lipstick, testing the colors against her wrist, holding them systematically to the photograph. In the back of her closet, in a plastic garment bag, she found the dress she'd made on that old Singer sewing machine.

She couldn't explain why, but this was her plan, to piece together the girl who got killed by that crane, to make her more real than a stranger's voice, yelling in a gingham muumuu, taking up all the space in her head.

"Back from your walk?" Karen asked, appearing in the door of Morgan's room. "What are you looking for?"

"Hair dryer," Riley said, because by August they were already lying.

They did it for each other and they did it for themselves. If they wanted to be left alone—which they did, more and more as they sank deeper into their private worlds—they understood it was a reciprocal courtesy. Any deviation from a gentle affirmative was an invitation for concern, for conversation, for deeper probing into how they were faring against the tide. They didn't need a second opinion; they were all doing horribly, sedated and delusional, reclusive and unwilling to acknowledge the potential hazards of their gelatin composure. The less they used their words, the three of them groping syllable by syllable, the more they mistrusted them. The lying let them exist together at the surface, eyes bobbing as they treaded water, a pact to never look down. Did Riley want lunch? No, she'd already eaten. Did Dad sleep well? Much better than last night. How are you, Mom? Fine, thanks. How are you? I'm good. That's great.

As summer gave way to fall, Hank and Karen withdrew with practiced routine, slinking like burglars in their own home, creeping at odd hours to avoid interception and, now that Riley was no longer walking, the burden of remarking upon the day or the hour or the armful of supplies they were smuggling upstairs. They worried about Riley; if you asked them, they would insist they worried about her all the time. She was taking a leave of absence from school, which worried them. She spent all that time in Morgan's room, which worried them more. But devoid of the intention to extend themselves further—to convince their daughter that life had to resume, to help her make a plan to do it together—every sight of her, every passive word exchanged, every question left unasked, reminded Hank and Karen only of their failure. And so they sought reassurance in the harrowing images broadcasted to their bedroom wall, where they fed off an unending loop of needless, wrongful trauma. Good people held hostage by Colombian rebels. Eleven mountaineers killed in an ice avalanche. One hundred fifty-four dead in a horrific Spanair crash. Their days unfolded to the urgent, electronic melody of breaking news and the echo of sound bites, wind and sand crackling through the microphone. They descended into a soothing darkness. At the top of each cycle, Hank and Karen would be an hour drunker, an hour more medicated, and they would watch the stories reported again, rapt as if it were the first time, a prick of unspeakable pleasure because they knew the words by heart, and this time they were prepared.

When Riley did see her parents, late in the bottomless afternoons, they appeared suspended in a woolly state of distress. The buttering

of toast, the opening of mail, the answering of a yes-no question—
they approached each task as if edging off a high dive, eyes closed,
changing their minds at the last minute. Once, that day in September the market plunged and distress seeped in from every channel,
Karen finally turning off the TV, Hank tried to joke about the dire
state of the entire world, how at least they had good company. Riley
watched her father attempt this thing that once came so naturally to
him, a little quip to make them feel lighter, but it went wrong at the
end, his eyes flickering with his breath, his laughter a ragged sawing
of air. That week she heard them on the phone, assuring each person
not to worry, it was time they returned. Fine, she heard her mom say,
oddly convincing, they were fine. They would be back to take care of
things soon.

Riley didn't push. She became the pool below, the liquid dis-
placed if they needed to fall. She allowed them the opportunity to
withdraw as parents, to avert their gaze, and so they did.

Because who was she, really, at a time like this, to tell them to
keep better track of her?

Three months after the accident—late September, just after
midnight—Riley woke to a noise she hadn't heard in weeks, a twin-
kling sound that threw her into another world. The sound triggered
a reflex, nebulous in form but precise in feeling, a promise that shook
her instantly alive. She leapt for the illuminated phone, and when she
saw his name, glowing in the dark, she nearly choked, the trappings
of reality shifting back into place.

"James," she said, and a beat fell before she heard her name back.
"What happened?"

"Nothing," James said. "Nothing happened. I'm sorry I'm calling
so late." He hesitated again and Riley sat up, turned on a lamp, as if

it might help her to see him better. She forced his attention through the phone.

"*James.*"

"Can I come in?"

"What do you mean?"

"I'm outside."

James on the front stoop, skinny and unshaven, his backpack visibly stuffed.

"I don't know what I'm doing," he said, and Riley felt a small throb of relief, seeing him there, as skittish and vulnerable as she herself felt.

"I thought you were Morgan," she said. "I thought Morgan was calling."

They stared at each other, cloaked by the perpetual dusk of Manhattan at night, the soft glow of the streetlamps, the peroxide dark. Riley nodded him across the divide, and inside, without being asked, she led him to the basement and began to make up a bed on the couch. James hovered beside her, making his apologies, wading through the words he had prepared, all the reasons why he had chosen here and her and now.

But Riley wasn't listening. James's words were like water, rising around her, making it harder to hear. Riley hadn't been in the basement since June, a reckoning that came to her with startling force, and the sound of James speaking made her want to cry, expanded the bubble growing in her chest and inside her skull. She hadn't prepared for any of this; she'd thought he was Morgan, and now that he wasn't, the adrenaline was turning to nerves. She needed to get to the surface.

Riley put a hand on James's shoulder; it took all of her resources to interrupt him. She forced her eyes to meet his, to take him in beneath the light, and for the first time she saw the blood vessel that had broken in the corner of his eye. She saw the wild mess of hair that spread in a tangle across his face, hollow in places she hadn't remembered. She was hit by an eviscerating urge to say something honest, to summon words from the hole that was opening inside her, but the courage she needed never arrived, or perhaps the words didn't exist at all.

How did she ask him to stay, to please stay, and also not to push? To look at her but not too closely, to be patient with her fucked-up instincts? How did she say thank you for showing up, knowing she hadn't done the same for him? Morgan was gone and all Riley could feel was a smoldering apathy. The loneliness was gutting her, scooping her out like the seeds from a gourd, and she hadn't known until just then, when she felt something drop in the void.

Riley leaned in and clamped her arms around James's middle, squeezing him like a stuffed animal, face shoved in the folds of his quilted jacket, still cold from outside. She counted to three, inhaling him as deeply and quietly as she could.

Then she disappeared up the stairs.

JAMES

James understood, from the minute he arrived, that he was not entitled to the house's asylum. Since the funeral, he fought every day to keep his distance. He knew things had gone wrong that day. He'd searched for Riley everywhere, in the bathroom and the garden of the funeral home, the utility closet, the walk-in refrigerator, the bike racks. He'd called her a dozen times as he strode the avenue outside, looking down alleyways and cupping his hands over his eyes, squinting into the windows of half-lit bars.

He never found her. Riley didn't return his calls and so he never knew what happened. He went home that afternoon and in a moment of frailty he called his mother, a mistake. After ten minutes, when he'd successfully convinced her he was fine, he learned all the ways that she was not. The washing machine was broken and had flooded the basement; she'd waited three hours and the plumber hadn't shown; everything had to be moved to the stairs. James held the phone from his ear, away from his shallow breathing, calling his responses into the mouthpiece as his mother drew lines between their tragedies. James hung up and threw a fist into his closet door, splicing the wood. He dropped to his bed and pulled his face into the collar of his shirt and held it there, a headless man, heaving. He'd considered punching many things in his life, but he'd never actually done it. He couldn't believe how badly it hurt, how the pain burst absolutely everywhere at once, but later than he'd imagined.

In the nights that followed, as he tried to sleep, instead of Morgan he saw the inverse of her: a crowd of bodies pressed against the chapel wall, forming a border around the chairs, a sea of foreheads, a mass of shoes. His conscience pulsed around this anxious feeling, parallel to grief but absent of anything productive. He cleared his thoughts and saw two hundred people crying, all at once, the heat of their attention melting his skin, boiling the liquid in his heart. He knew he'd spoken up there, to that crowd, but he had no idea what he'd said. The sequence of memory ended in nothing. It drained him of Morgan, replaced her with a queasy knot, and every night for the last three months, this blank spot kept him staring at the ceiling, watching the light from the cracks of his blinds change from flaxen to hazy sodium orange to shards of pale lemon, inching slowly across the room, impaling him by morning.

After the accident, James had stopped showing up for his shifts at the library, then his tutoring sessions, which led to him being graciously let go by both. At first it was a strange relief, releasing himself from these commitments, cutting himself suddenly free. Since James had graduated from Columbia two years before—had spent all those months being vigorously interviewed and then turned down, or else ghosted, for every staff job for which he applied—he'd settled into a temporary solution as he danced around his next move. Staying close to Columbia, tutoring the kids of people with connections to the jobs he wanted, James figured something would happen for him. Instead, he became a kind of lacky for the places and people who would not let him in. His ambition, that red-hot thing that had carried him to the city, warped, turned feeble and defensive. At least he was paying his own bills, unlike most of his classmates; at least he wasn't being humiliated every day, waiting for rejections to land in his inbox. But soon James found it was a new kind of dejection, perhaps much worse, not caring at all about your work, especially in a place like New York, where professional ambition was almost as respectable as actual money. By the time he ran into Riley last December, James hadn't quite given up, but he was in the process of doing so, was coming to terms with simply being one of the many hungry small-town kids who had come to the city to get overeducated, saddled with debt, and trampled. But then Riley had walked into that Chinatown restaurant, had reminded James of who he used to be, of how far he'd actually come, and it sent a strange bolt of lightning through his life. He'd called Morgan, not because he expected her to say yes, but because he had to do *something* to keep the blood pumping. What came after had blown past anything he'd prepared for. Being with Morgan, sleeping with Morgan, getting close to the Brightons, it had been the first shock of genuine pleasure in so long. It had reopened New York for him, which was now as closed and dark as it had ever felt.

The solution—James arrived at the same conclusion all summer, as he lay in bed wondering when his roommate would get fed up, ask him to leave—was in the house. He needed to reenter the realm of her, to be reminded, viscerally, of the things his memory had made impassible. Back in the house, he would find that person he was able to be, knock some feeling back into him. The idea sunk a hook deep into his psyche, and soon it became James's soundest thought. Before he slept, just a couple of hours each night, he conjured the house he knew in color and texture and sound. There was Riley on the couch, eavesdropping behind a book. There was Hank and, beside him, Karen, standing in a doorway, peering over jewel-toned glasses, soliciting advice on the piece of fabric or the electronic device they held in their hands. James was there too. He placed his figurine in the living room, sitting at the kitchen counter. He cycled through the rooms like difficult asanas, sweating through the poses, inhaling and exhaling, gathering strength.

That first morning, waking to this version of reality, James groomed and dressed in the basement bathroom, warmed by the early light and the familiar smell of citrus and rosemary and fresh pencil shavings. He ascended the stairs, wound tight with purpose, and sat in the kitchen as the minutes passed, dismantling him as they turned to hours.

At ten o'clock, no one had come downstairs. He heard a toilet flush and strained his ears. By eleven, the coffee he made was two hours' untouched, and self-conscious about wasting their sparse supplies, James drank cup after cup, hot and black, until he could wash and replace the pot. The kitchen counter was a barren landscape. A kettle on the back burner, raised on the iron grates. A paper-towel holder with no paper towels. A bottle of olive oil, mostly empty, in a greasy ring of its own perspiration, and in the corner, the only sign of food—a glass jar with a single sticky layer of apricots.

By noon James could feel his stomach in his brain. He was about to let himself out when Riley surfaced, padding down the stairs and into the kitchen. She reached for the jar of apricots and peeled a gummy orb from the mass.

"They're really old," she said, offering him the jar. James reached in and felt one, its skin like a fresh scab.

"Get your coat," he said, intense with caffeine and unspent

purpose. Riley found her coat and followed him out the door, sliding her socked feet into a pair of rubber sandals, no purse, leaving the front door unlocked because she had no keys.

Up and down the grocery aisles, they groped their way around the store. They stared into the dairy case for what felt like hours, James putting question marks at the ends of words. Yogurt? Cream cheese? Eggs? The refrigeration blew against their faces, granting them a temporary patience. They filled their basket at the cold displays, but in the middle aisles, where the fluorescent lights fell on them like arid sun, they couldn't make decisions. Everything looked like a trick. The colors didn't match the flavors. The shelves grew endlessly, dizzyingly vertical. Back at the house, James told Riley he had it handled. He felt her itching, and their outing had given him a lift of confidence. She vanished upstairs and James stretched out his hands, clearing out the produce drawer, rinsing the pint of tomatoes, slicing the cucumber, arranging the eggs in the door.

When at last the sun dissolved over the park, James was wiping down the kitchen counter. He looked up and called a startled hello to Karen Brighton in a flannel nightgown.

"Oh," she replied, "James."

She seemed affronted by his presence but not surprised. She broke stride just for a second, before walking to the fridge as James watched, like a predator afraid of startling his prey, as she opened the door and stared into his afternoon's work.

"There's ham," he said, wishing he hadn't, but feeling suddenly small and worthless. "There's mozzarella too. Riley said you like mozzarella."

Karen drew her mouth horizontal, closing the fridge.

"She might be right," she said. "I used to like a lot of things."

She reached for the jar of apricots and left.

. . .

Riley convinced him, when James told her it was time to head back uptown, that he should stay. She seemed unsettled by the thought of him leaving. She stared at his chest, unwilling to meet his eyes.

"You can't," she said. "You can't just *leave.*"

"I don't live here, Riley. It's making everyone uncomfortable."

"It's making *them* uncomfortable." She said it like a reflex. "So ten minutes a day they come downstairs and act like jerks. Who cares?"

"I care. It's their house. I should care."

"They're not losing sleep over us," Riley said, grouping them suddenly together.

The day before, Riley had gone into her parents' room and found them both in their usual condition, comatose, flushed limbs tangled in greasy sheets, the whole scene preserved by the air-conditioning blasting from above. CNN flashed muted images of the trading floor and graphs that looked like lightning bolts. Next to her mother's lamp was a pile of papers and a bottle of sleeping pills, next to her father's a bottle of vodka with no top. Riley collected the plates and bowls and lumps of clothes from around the room. She glanced at the papers, financial statements she shuffled into a pile, without the interest or capacity to read them. She switched off the television and opened the windows.

"They don't even notice." Riley blinked at James. "Trust me, we're not their main concern. I'm asking you to stay, okay? It's my house too."

So he stayed.

In the mornings, James and Riley walked to the park, or to the bagel shop, or to the bodega for hot sandwiches bundled in tin foil, griddled by a woman who called them *mijos.* On the way back they stopped for groceries because James still insisted on curating the fridge, dipping into his meager savings to replace the things that had disappeared overnight. He read the shelves each morning like tea leaves: gone were the small wax circles of cheese, the plastic tubs of roasted vegetables and chicken salad. They liked all the items James couldn't afford, but still he bought them, the fridge his soundest portal of consolation. Other than that he left no trace of himself. The blankets he slept with were folded and replaced in the chest, his toothbrush returned to the plastic bag in his backpack, his backpack slid beneath the couch.

The afternoons were the longest stretch of the day, when Riley excused herself upstairs and James returned to his couch. He spent the first week in a kind of trance, making his way through the books on the shelves, indiscriminately, one after the other as if they were all one continuous volume. The death of Nelson Mandela segued, within minutes, into a couple renovating a home in Provence, which morphed into a series of anecdotes based on business advice from Andrew Carnegie, who was still speaking in his booming, jugular voice when three hours later, James was learning the difference between a flan and a crème caramel. It helped him drown out the memories of the space, the pictures on the wall, which he did not expect to be so brutal. He needed to create new experiences on the couch he slept on, like reading books, instead of kissing Morgan, her gray eyes darting to the ceiling as if she could see through the floor, confirming no one else was home. He was stalling, James knew this, was delaying his life until the bitter end. He tried not to think too hard about it, focused on the fact that he had made it there, at the very least, into the house.

There was no TV in the basement, but after James attempted to leave, Riley brought one down, a tail of cords clacking behind her.

They set up the monitor on a small teak trunk, plugged in the cable box, and annihilated their hours, evening after evening, adding a joint or a six-pack of beer or a dozen dumplings, passing the remote back and forth.

The intersection of their interests was mostly nature shows. The mighty Serengeti. An hour on puffins. It made them talk about the meaning of life, or really, the inverse of it: the futility of what they wanted, what they once thought was important to their self-worth, set against the huge chaos of the natural world, was almost embarrassing. They liked the soothing repetition of shows in factories: a thousand pounds of bread dough slapping against a steel drum, a parade of blue jeans hanging upside down. They imagined spending eight hours a day packing frozen waffles, twelve to a box, and felt envious of such clear purpose. Some days it took until seven p.m. to realize how little they'd spoken, when one of them answered a question on *Jeopardy!* and the sound of a voice, real in the room, made the walls of the space appear suddenly around them.

A week later, in October, Hank and Karen came out of their room.

Karen made her entrance first, just her voice, calling Riley's name from the floor above. Riley and James were in the basement, about to leave when they heard the sound. Karen called again and Riley followed her name up the stairs as James stood motionless on the landing, making out very little.

"Let's go," Riley said when she reappeared.

"What happened?"

"Nothing."

"It couldn't have been nothing."

"She just wanted to know what we're doing today."

"What did you tell her?"

"Relax, James. Everything's fine."

But when they returned with their groceries, Hank was on the couch off the kitchen, leaning against the left armrest, a bottle of gin on the side table. Across the room, Karen had set up at the dining room table. Her hair blew from the breeze through the open windows as she shuffled a deck of cards. There was a phantom smell of smoke, a cigarette whisked recently away, nearly gone but not quite. The room was freezing.

James felt immediately as if he'd intruded on something deeply private. He felt this way that afternoon and every time after, when he entered a room and found them there. It was the first time he had seen them lingering out in the open, and he was unsure if they would stand or if he should approach, and so he shuffled his way toward them, shaking Hank's hand and patting Karen twice on the shoulder, the warmth they once showed him completely gone.

"Can I get you guys anything?" James asked. "We got some guacamole."

Karen continued to deal her game of solitaire.

"Go ahead." She nodded. "You know how to make yourself at home."

Hank was drunk, sunken into the couch, the gin adding strange, agitated decibels to his voice as he called them over to watch something on TV, growing slowly frustrated as he couldn't find it.

"Riley," Karen said. "Come sit with me." Riley walked over and sat. "I see you've been doing some rearranging."

"What do you mean?"

"It looks like you've been sleeping in her bed."

Riley paused. "Not every night."

Karen matched a card. "That's what I thought. And I don't think it's appropriate."

James sat awkwardly with Hank, watching him rewind and pause as he muttered curses.

"All right."

"And her closet. I think it'd be best if you left it alone." Karen hadn't stopped matching her cards, peeling them three by three from the deck. "There's only so much we have of her."

"I'm not doing that much."

"I know. I just think you'll regret it. I'm speaking from experience. Remember your mom has a few more years of life experience than you. Trust me. With some things, it's better to leave them alone."

James felt her words like pinpricks, spreading across the back of his neck. He looked at Hank, his face slack and red, his eyes like peeled grapes.

"I don't think she would mind."

"I'm asking you to respect her things. I'm telling you that I mind. Do I need to explain myself more?"

Riley said no.

"I know you're not ready to go back to school, but you can't spend all day messing with her things."

"I'm not."

"Just listen," Karen said. "Your dad and I have a lot on our plate. Especially with Morgan gone, there's a lot for us to figure out. And I'm not putting that on you. I really don't think I'm asking you for so much."

Riley nodded.

Karen put down the cards. "If you want me to be the bad guy, fine. I'm used to it. But I'm not doing anything wrong. I'm trying to hold the pieces together." When Riley didn't respond, Karen sighed. "Come on. Give your mom a hug."

Riley leaned in and the two of them opened their arms like the claws in a stuffed animal machine, closing them mechanically, ineffectively, around each other. Watching them, James ached for his Harlem apartment—to light a blunt with Mark and scrub himself of whatever was happening in this house. But how could he, knowing Riley had to stay? Most unnerving was the shift in her, in the power between her and her mother, alone. He'd been envious of Riley, of her easy superiority, in the absolute affection she commanded in Morgan. Even the memory of this shamed him now, upset him into allegiance.

James did not go home, but he no longer came up from the basement, waited for Riley to collect him each morning. When he slept, which was very little, his dreams were filled with punishment: he sat in a courtroom in a suit and tie, ate a bowl of nails with a spoon like cereal. He thought about what Karen had said, imagined Riley upstairs with Morgan's things and felt closer to her. It clarified his own behavior, which often baffled him. It was the throb of intimacy, the comfort of standing in the narrow, shifting shadow of something lost. It was Riley, he realized. For James, it was Riley. She was the closest thing he had to Morgan, the memory that recalled her best. And just as he knew Riley hadn't given up her habit, was pissing off her parents to get her fix, he felt somehow entitled to do the same.

October in the air, they began to spend more time outside, slipping from the house to run their errands, then sitting on a bench in Riverside Park. They sat overlooking the water, groceries at their feet, when one morning Riley said something had come in the mail, then handed James an envelope. He read the address in the corner, and his mouth became very dry.

"Where did you get this?"

"It came in the mail."

"Is it . . . ?" he said, and Riley nodded. He tried to hand it back, but she wouldn't take it.

"I've been thinking. Maybe we could open it together."

"What?" He dropped the envelope into her lap.

"I've given it a lot of thought. I really have. It could help us understand."

He looked at her, stunned. "No."

"What do you mean no?"

"I mean no. I'm not opening that. And neither should you."

"James, please." Her voice cracked, frightening them both.

"No."

"Why not?"

"Why not? Why *would* we?"

"Because . . ." Riley faltered. "Because how are we supposed to know? How can we be sure it was definitely her? We can't be sure unless we look."

"Riley," James said, aghast. "It was her."

"You don't know that!"

He pressed his lips together, opened his mouth but said nothing.

"Just think about it!"

James reached over and took the envelope.

"Open it," Riley begged and James stared at her, worry in his eyes. It flustered her, soaked her in insecurity. "Then give it back!"

James stood, unsure what else to do, clutching the envelope in his right hand.

"I'll put it somewhere. I won't throw it away. We'll talk about it again in a few weeks."

Riley stood from the bench, reaching for the envelope, but he pulled away.

"James, what the hell!"

"Riley! This is a shit idea. How did you even get this?"

Riley took a rickety breath, filled her cheeks with air. The woman from the records department had called the week before—had caught Riley by surprise. She'd received the written request, the woman had said, her voice concerned. It was Riley's right. She could send it now. But it would be graphic. Was Riley sure?

"It's my right to have it!" Riley yelled, rattled anew.

"I'm . . ." James blinked at her. "I'm not letting you open this."

Riley's face widened, furious. "You're not *letting* me? Oh! Because you're the adult here? Sleeping on my parents' couch! Hiding in their fucking basement! Buying them shit they don't even want to make up for the fact that they hate you!" She laughed, big and scary, out of control, and her words cut right in the place she hoped they would.

"Riley." James froze. In his bones, he knew Hank and Karen didn't want him there, but to hear it from Riley, he felt unmoored, pathetic. James focused, used all his might to shake it off, to not fight desperation with desperation. "Do the details even matter? Do they? We *know* what happened. Why do you want to know how many bones she broke? What she looked like open on a table?"

"Fuck you."

"Fuck *me*? You're trying to get me to look at that!"

"Give it back." She glared at him, shaking with rage. He extended the envelope and she ripped it from his grasp. "Don't follow me," she yelled. "Go home."

James watched her tear through the park, two dogs barking as she passed, and disappear into the street. He waited there. The sun lowered behind a bank of clouds. The children were corralled into strollers and pushed away. James sat there, shivering in the hoodie he'd worn every day since he arrived at the Brightons', in the middle of the night, a lifetime ago. He smelled their detergent, aloe and floral, inhaled deeper and deeper until he made himself faint.

When two hours passed and Riley didn't return, James finally stood. He stretched out his arms and stared into the enormous sky, terrifying and humbling now that he was alone. He picked up the grocery bag of pita chips and salami and carried it to Harlem to give to Mark, as an apology for disappearing for nearly a month, and for being behind again on the rent.

RILEY

Morgan at her sewing machine. Morgan atop a mountain. Morgan looking into the camera, an arched eyebrow, her left ear mangled as if shredded by a cheese grater.

The body is presented in a black body bag. The body is that of a normally developed, well-nourished Asian and Caucasian female measuring 69 inches in length, weighing 132 pounds. The scalp is partially covered by straight, light brown hair. The eyes are open and the irises are gray. The exterior genitalia are those of a normal adult woman.

Morgan on the Great Lawn, abrasions like a venomous rash, smears of blood and pulp up and down her abdomen, matted with grass, wrapped partially in a hand-dyed, wax-print dress.

On the right side, fractures of the ribs 1 through 7 and on the left, ribs 2 through 9. The pericardial sac is lacerated and the heart protrudes into the left thoracic cavity. Cardiac contusion has caused massive hemorrhaging.

Morgan on the crest of Spencer Butte, arms raised above a body sawed straight down the middle and pried neatly apart, spandex leggings, Nike Zooms she got for Christmas.

The heart weighs 308 grams and has a normal external configuration. The brain weighs 1,356 grams and is within normal limits. The kidneys weigh: left, 117 grams; right, 119 grams with hemorrhage in the perirenal soft tissue. Lungs are 870 grams combined with multiple lacerations of right middle lobe. The 140-gram spleen has partial pulpification. The bladder is contracted. The ovaries are unremarkable.

Four hands, four blue latex gloves with bloody fingers, reaching into a gaping cavity, some of it yellow and clotted like chicken skin, some pink and gray like freshly turned sausage; a lattice of tendon; clumps and pockets of viscous jelly shivering in the pits.

Hard and relentless, full of motion and sound, for a week Riley was assaulted by falling objects and shards of rib bone; she saw Technicolor flesh, heard the wallop of bodies against concrete, the high-pitched whistle of a punctured lung, the hum of a sewing machine tearing through traffic—a violent, cacophonous litany of sounds strung subliminally together by her imagination. Each morning she fell out of these nightmares with a mouthful of blood and gravel, her calescent limbs slicked in a layer of ice, the sensation unbearable. At the sink she gargled with her mixture of Listerine and salt, stepped into the shower with the clothes she slept in, and let the warm downpour ease her back into a reality that was only different— not better, she arrived at this conclusion each day—than the one she'd escaped.

With James gone, it was Karen who began to answer her daughter's new sounds: the yelps and thrashing after midnight, the hour-long showers at dawn. Riley's mother had recently begun seeing a therapist on the Upper East Side. It had been Hank's idea, who in return promised to clean up his drinking. Now she paused each day in her daughter's bedroom door, trying to talk to her, if only to prove the therapist wrong.

"You're up early," Karen said. It was the only pleasantry that came to her, standing there again, the fifth day in a row. Riley nodded. "I heard the shower. Everything okay?"

"Fine." Riley paused, wrapped in her sister's shirt, waiting for what came next. Since the therapy began, her mother had withheld her judgment, stood in the door practically holding her breath. When she said nothing, Riley took her turn. "You look nice," she said. "Are you going somewhere?" Her mother had begun doing a little work, sitting half-dressed at the table, the authority in her voice steadily creeping back in. Watching her, it made Riley feel somehow deficient, her own inaction standing out in relief.

Karen looked down. She wore jeans and a gray sweater, old clothes from an old life, and the compliment took her by surprise. It sent a rush of blood to her face. For a moment, she considered asking her daughter to come with her.

"The therapy," she said instead.

"How's that going?"

"Okay." Karen looked over Riley's shoulder, out the window. "I'm not always crazy about what she says. But I'm supposed to try for ten sessions."

"That makes sense."

"I'll say it again, Riley. As soon as you're ready, you should talk to someone. I think we all need to get back on our feet."

"I know."

"Hold on one sec." Karen left and returned with a bottle of pills. Instead of handing it to Riley, she placed it on her dresser, as if this might make the gesture more appropriate. "I know you're not sleeping. Since James went home, I hear you up half the night. It worries me." She directed her words between her daughter and the bottle, her eyes dragging in the space between them. "Just one," she said, "right before bed."

Riley peered up at her mother, trying to get a good look without drawing any unnecessary attention. There she stood just inside the threshold, cagey and wooden, showing vague yet evidently willful interest in being her mother again. Riley thought of her crossing town twice a week, sitting on the bus, enlisting the help of a total stranger—more than she was willing to do. She was trying, Riley realized. Her mother was trying, in her own stunted way, to extend herself, to be there.

"There's still Indian in the fridge. And I got some groceries. Are you okay?"

"Fine," Riley said. "Go to your appointment. I'm fine."

Downstairs, Riley stood in front of the open refrigerator, dumbstruck.

She looked around her, a moment that would strike again and again, the impulsive throb to share with her sister before remembering, suddenly, that she was dead.

Inside the fridge was an alien display. A package of bright red hot dogs bundled like dynamite. A four-pack of chocolate pudding. A blue tube of biscuit dough. Six squat plastic cups of "tropical fruit" with foil tops. There was no milk. There were no eggs or yogurt. She slid open the freezer door below her. A neat wall of chicken potpies appeared, green and square. She bent and picked up what appeared to be a breakfast sandwich in a translucent sack, frozen disks of egg and sausage scraping between the English muffin.

The refrigerator began to beep.

Had her mother really picked these things? Riley tried to imagine her at the store, filling her cart with six chicken potpies, deliberately pulling each box from the deep freezer until none were left. The image startled her with its intimacy. Riley shut the refrigerator doors and leaned against them. She felt the ocean in her stomach; a week of nightmares dripped from her nerves.

She did not recognize her own fridge. She felt alarmed by the state of her mother. She felt sorry for her drunk father. She was haunted by her sister's autopsy. She'd driven James away.

Riley went upstairs and put on a T-shirt from the dwindling pile that smelled of Morgan—the pile she'd promised she would not touch. Then she climbed into her sister's bed and took the first pink pill.

Sleeping, Riley came to understand, was better than everything else she had tried so far. The pills knocked out the nightmares, sent her into a pit of oblivion. Riley was sleeping twelve, fourteen hours a day, an arm's length from everything, swaddled in a distant cocoon. The pills worked instantly; that came as the biggest surprise. Before she could wonder if it was working, she felt the velvety pull of gravity, the cradle of sheets, as if she'd had a long and fulfilling day, climbed a mountain or studied for hours. It was the ultimate simulation. Sleep came no matter what. It made her more pleasant during her waking hours, jelly at the joints, sailing at her own elevation. She stopped reading into her parents' moods. It was more straightforward than she imagined. She simply discarded the desire to think, to interpret. Everything was how it presented itself, and the deafness, the freedom it brought was the best medicine yet.

. . .

Most nights, the Brightons called for delivery. They ordered enough for two meals, so that they could eat it again the next day for lunch. Riley woke in the afternoon, microwaved herself a scoop of rigatoni, and sat by the big living room window, temporarily calmed and fortified by sleep. Around six, she convened with her parents over the menus, and when the doorbell rang, they set up tray tables and watched network TV, no longer the news but sitcoms, game shows. During the commercials, they practiced conversation, a minute and a half at a time, twelve minutes for every hour. The green curry was spicy. The weather was nice. The dishwasher was acting funny.

Her parents were returning to work. Messengers rang their doorbell nearly every day, dropping off garment bags and boxes that Karen took upstairs. Once, Riley stood on the stairs, listening to her mother scold her father about how he needed to pull himself together or else they'd have nothing left. How she couldn't do it alone. Had he seen the sales? Almost December and no one was shopping; November's numbers worse than October's. How did he expect to pay for *this*? Karen opened her arms and Riley looked around, the house so much larger and grander than it had seemed before, when no one questioned anything. Morgan's absence was the shape of their collective anxiety, the gaping hole that made everything left feel a bit absurd. What would become of Kaleidoscope, of them, of this life that made no sense without her?

When Riley asked, Karen refilled her bottle of pills, but she wanted something in return. She asked her daughter to see a therapist she had found nearby, on West End, who specialized in situations like hers—youth trauma, she said it was called. Karen had made an appointment for Riley the following week. Before Riley could respond, Karen added that, on the same night, she and Hank would be across the park with her therapist. She knew this would matter to her daughter. Just once, she'd said, just see if you like it, and confronted with the desire to please her parents, to meet them in the middle, Riley had agreed.

But on Tuesday evening, leaving the house with every intention of keeping the appointment, Riley found she couldn't do it. She had taken a cigarette from her mother's secret laundry room pack and smoked it on the corner, outside the doctor's office, giving herself the opportunity to change her mind. But when she stomped out the butt, her legs walked to Fairway. She would make dinner for her parents, she decided, the first home-cooked dinner in months. She would make lasagna. With spinach and San Marzanos and the fresh ricotta from the cheese case.

She shopped in a delicious state of satisfaction, plugged into her headphones, swinging her empty plastic basket. She was functioning in the outside world, picking out groceries that had to be chopped and assembled and heated for long periods of time, unlike the things she had bought with James. The box of pasta sheets felt somehow glamorous, perfectly symmetrical and modernly designed. The mounds of garlic were buxom gemstones, undulating, heavy in the hand. She had to feel better, to be better, for her parents and for Morgan. She had to release the sack of stones she dragged back and forth, between then and now. Tonight, Riley would shake herself into competence, to make something warm and comforting for her parents. She would do something to return a speck of normalcy to their lives, and she felt a zing of hope, for the first time in so long, to be walking up Broadway, a girl with a plan.

. . .

If Riley had gone to her appointment, she wouldn't have returned for another thirty minutes. Inside the house, as soon as she opened the door, she heard them yelling.

Karen was repeating the same sentence, over and over. *How dare you.* She exploded the words, launched them wet and volatile.

"I'm sorry! I'm not taking sides, I just thought she made a fair point. Morgan is gone. Riley is still here. We can't neglect her."

"How dare you. I *never* neglected her!"

"You're missing the point, Karen. It's normal to feel this way, to put all your energy into missing Morgan."

"Oh! It's normal, Hank?"

"Nothing is *normal*! I'm just saying—"

"Is it *normal* for Riley to walk out on her own sister's funeral? Is it? It is *normal* for Riley to take *no* responsibility? Knowing that she brought her here? Is it normal for her to mess with everything Morgan owned? Including her boyfriend! Everything that's left of her! Is it, Hank? She's oblivious!" Karen was slamming drawers, opening and closing the fridge, her voice shrill and disorderly, shattering with things unsaid.

"You need to try to calm down."

A laugh. A terrible laugh Riley knew well, one that signaled her mother had no reply and yet, she would not back down. It was a laugh that meant logic would do no good and reason would bounce violently back. Karen Brighton, rational queen in professional matters, could not apply the same principals to emotion. She'd never learned how.

"Why don't you take a bath?" Hank offered. "I'll start one for you and get some dinner."

"You think you know how I feel. I'm not comfortable in my own home! I have to swallow my emotions! I have to keep Kaleidoscope from falling apart! Who else do you think is going to do that? You? The village drunk? Or our daughter who sleeps all day?"

Trapped downstairs, standing at the bottom of the steps, groceries in hand, Riley realized that she was crying. Hot, thin tears spilled down her face, caught on the line of her jaw and dripped from her chin. The plastic grocery bags shook in her hands. Her breathing was slow but the tears were relentless, like an allergic reaction, pushing out all the liquid from her body. She considered leaving, but where would she go? It was dark outside, thirty degrees. She didn't have any friends, hadn't answered a text message in months. She opened her mouth. A small sound pushed out, a damp whistle of air, and she was walloped by the sensation of being alone in the world, not in the way she had wished for as a teenager but in the way that drains the heart of its blood, makes it feel parched and thin and weak. She had no idea how to be a person without her sister, and Riley understood, for the first time since the accident, that Morgan was not coming back. The realization cut her breathing short. Her sister, her greatest ally, the person who loved her most in this world, whose tenacious devotion blunted everyone else's bad behavior, had left her alone in this family, a place she'd belonged because she'd belonged to Morgan, and Morgan to them.

Unable to listen any longer, Riley walked up the stairs and stood at the landing. She let them see her. Her father looked immediately horrified.

"We . . . we . . ." Karen stammered. "Riley, how was your appointment? What time is it?" She looked to her wrist for a watch that wasn't there.

Riley dropped the grocery bags and continued up the stairs.

. . .

Later, there was a knock on her door. Riley walked over to listen, but it was only her father. Alone, Hank didn't know what to say through a door. He worried his words, so carefully scrutinized in the echoing house, might dig him deeper into difficulty. He was tired; his wife was drowning. When Riley didn't answer, when he could think of nothing suitable to express through a door, he pushed a yellow flash card underneath.

I love you, he wrote. *I'm so sorry. It's all going to take some time.*

In the morning Riley awoke to her mother sitting on her bed, dressed in a velvet dress and tights.

It was cold outside, she remembered, already December.

"Come on," Karen said, putting on a smile, business mixed with sunshine, "I need to talk to you." Riley blinked at the dressed-up figure. "I'm sorry about what you heard last night. I don't know what you heard, actually, but your father and I had a hard session. If I offended you, that's my fault."

Riley nodded, squinting, coming around to being awake, to receiving her apology.

"I didn't mean to upset you. That's never my intention, you must know that. Sometimes it just feels so dark, even for me. I'm strong, Riley, but even your mom has bad days."

Riley bristled.

"How much did you hear?" Karen paused, received no answer. "It doesn't matter. But I don't think you heard it right. I was just saying, trying to say, that it's hard for everyone. Your sister was the glue, you know that. Every minute, Riley, I can't believe she's gone."

Riley felt everything inside her tighten. Morgan was the glue. It was true. But then what did that make her? She willed her mother to say something more, to say something, anything, to make her feel less like a problem to be dealt with. A drain on her parents.

"We'll get through this." Karen squeezed her daughter's arm, and when Riley didn't respond she added, "I'm going into the store today."

"Today?" Riley felt her skin tingle, like someone had let in a draft.

"Today's the day." Karen looked at her, eyes hopeful, blowing out a sigh like she needed her daughter's reassurance. It was done, Riley realized a beat too late. The subject had changed. Her mother had made her peace.

The night before, Riley had locked her bedroom door but unlocked it after her parents went to sleep. When Karen gave apologies it was in the morning. She was optimistic in the mornings, clearheaded, willing to face previous mistakes, and Riley, lying up all night, found that she was willing to accept. But what Karen had offered had not been an apology. What her mother had done was absolute bullshit.

Riley felt the heat pressing against her sinuses, the catch in her throat. What made her feelings so easy to overlook? Weren't mothers supposed to love the same, or at the very least pretend to? But when her mother looked at her, all Riley could see was the absence of Morgan. Riley saw all the things that she was not, all the times she had been difficult when Morgan had been easy, the times Riley had run while Morgan had stayed, all the times she had been Riley instead of Morgan. And it devastated her. Riley felt singed through the middle by how skillfully her mother swept past her pain. Karen's velvet dress, her shiny fucking tights—she'd put more effort into dressing herself than reckoning with her daughter.

"You're going to feel better." Karen leaned over her daughter and gave her a squeeze that smelled of jasmine shampoo and the light sulfur of freshly blow-dried hair. "Order the soup from the Thai place. Put it on the card. We might not have it for much longer if I don't go to work."

Riley blinked, astounded. Do you blame me? The question was still there, sitting in the chamber but ridiculous now. Not once, Riley realized, had her mother said she didn't mean what she'd said. Work. Her mother was nervous about work.

Karen left and Riley began to shake, first softly and then completely overcome.

Her mother wanted her house back, she wanted Riley to be somewhere else, to be someone else, to grieve more productively, to grieve better. Riley rose from her bed, dressing herself in raging, fevered movements, falling into her jeans, zipping a hoodie to the neck. She would prove herself different from her mother; she brushed her teeth and tasted blood. She could make herself vulnerable. She could make herself better. Riley grabbed her sister's backpack. At the very least, she could give a goddamn apology.

JAMES

It was late afternoon when he walked into his building, the winter sun reflecting low off the lobby's glass windows. James's doorman, Angel, stood in uniform behind the polished wood desk, grinning slightly harder than usual.

"Fucking private school girl." James reached for Angel's outstretched hand. "Probably not even sixteen."

Angel didn't reply, just kept smiling.

"What?" James asked, looking around. "What's going on?"

Ten feet away, Riley sat on his lobby couch, fitted into the worn leather cushions, eyeing him like a circus performer. He felt a sudden tear in the space between them.

"Riley and I been chopping it up." Angel slid into his act, distributing what intelligence he could within the public forum of his lobby. He was brilliant at this, could pick up the phone and dial up to a tenant, listen to an angry voice like it was a dial tone, hang up, and tell the visitor nobody was home. "Told her I didn't know where you'd gone, but she said she didn't mind waiting. You know me, can't turn down the company of a beautiful woman." He looked earnestly at Riley. "Funny too."

Angel knew exactly who Riley was, had consoled James after the accident. Since James moved into the building three years ago, Angel was arguably his most trusted confidant.

"Came in right after you left," he said and whistled, which meant Riley had been there for at least two hours: they had talked. "Can't have her waiting out there. No fun out there."

James stared at Riley now, surprised to see her dressed and out. Then he saw himself through her eyes.

"Do you want to come up?"

"I do." Riley stood in her winter jacket, a smile threatening her face, and followed him into the elevator.

As the gold doors closed James inhaled, deeply and silently through his nose.

"If I ask," Riley looked at him, "are you going to tell me the truth?"

"Ask what?"

"I guess that's my answer."

The elevator doors opened and she followed him down the carpeted hall, past a peeling gold-framed mirror, and stopped at the door marked 5F. James heard his roommate moving inside and understood, in every scenario, he'd have to answer to someone.

"Do you want to go somewhere? I could eat something."

"No, thanks, I'm good."

"Look." James lowered his voice. "If you want to come in, you have to relax. Let me talk to my roommate and then you can ask your questions after. I'm not promising anything. I'm not saying you'll get what you came for, but if you act suspicious, Mark's going to want you out."

"What I *came for?*"

"Riley, can you do that or not?"

"Of course I can."

"He'll probably hit on you."

Riley raised an eyebrow.

"He'll probably hit on *you*. Does he know you're dressed like this?"

The front door opened directly into the living room, where Mark lay on the leather sectional, watching football on full volume. The coffee table where he propped his socked feet had three cans of energy drinks, a crumpled white paper sack, and a giant glass ashtray overflowing with the brown, crushed ends of blunts. The air smelled like tobacco and semen.

"There's my pretty boy," Mark said, sitting up. "Went all right?"

"Great. Full ask."

"Zah!" Mark stood and offered James his hand. He looked at Riley. "Who's this? You fucking with Mr. Model?" He flashed a sloppy, clowning grin. Mark had the heaviest-lidded eyes, no eyelashes, a baby face with a shaved head, red T-shirt, red basketball shorts, red socks.

"Oh no," Riley sounded truly appalled. "Oh no." She turned to James, trying to recover from the strength of her reaction. "I mean, Jesus. Look at him. How could I compete with that?"

Mark erupted in laughter, fell back into the couch and beat his thighs.

"This is Riley." James nodded at her. "She thinks she's funny. We'll be in my room. We can settle things in a minute?"

"Course, man." Mark shook his head, winked at Riley with one bloodshot eye.

. . .

"Damn." Riley covered her mouth with her hand. "I had no idea you were this cool."

"Fuck off." James dropped his wallet and keys on his dresser and took off his wool blazer. He unbuttoned the collar of his shirt, which was expertly pressed, a professional job. He was wearing slim gray slacks, a leather belt, cognac oxfords—more style, more money than she'd ever seen on his body. His hair was slightly slicked back, long enough now to flop over his forehead when he leaned forward to take off his shoes.

"What do you want?" James sat on a folding chair, crossed his arms. His bedroom was tiny, mostly bare. Riley sat on his bed and looked at her knees, concentrating.

"I . . ." she said slowly. "I came, to apologize. To you."

"Go ahead."

"Look, I feel really badly about what happened. I shouldn't have talked to you like that. I shouldn't have stormed off in the park. It wasn't you. You didn't do anything wrong." Riley paused. "I just lost it. For a while, actually. I felt really, really shitty about things and I needed to take it out on someone." Riley looked him in the eye. "I'm sorry I was such an asshole."

"It's okay." Through the wall, they heard Mark yelling at the referee, calling him a fucking faggot. "I appreciate you making the trip."

"What's going on with you? Why are you dressed like the prince of Monaco?"

"It's a long story."

"I've been sitting in your lobby for three hours. Time's not really the issue."

James took a deep inhale, knit his fingers over his head.

"I'm leaving town."

"To take the throne?"

James looked up at the ceiling, impatient.

"I'm sorry," Riley said. "I'm sorry. Where are you going?"

"Just away. On a trip. A long trip." He paused. "Fuck it, you won't leave until I tell you."

"I will not."

James stood and stuck his foot under the bed. He hooked it around something hard and slid out a wide, flat box, the size of a sheet cake but with a thick lid, matte and black. He picked it up and set it beside Riley on the bed.

"Mark has a friend. He gets them from China." He lifted the lid. "And I sell them in my royal clothes."

Riley picked up one of the bags. The leather was supple, textured but not too shiny. She ran her fingers along the stitching: tight, uniform. The chain strap was heavy, the interlocking CCs centered. It surprised her, after years with her mother and sister, how much she knew about the real thing. What gave the strongest impression of replica was the sheer amount of them; she counted ten, side by side like chocolate-glazed, caviar-leather pastries.

"What do you get for one of these?"

"Depends. Usually about eighteen hundred. Today I got two grand."

"Fuck."

"Yeah."

They sat in silence, an air of consecration settling between them, and after the terrible night with her parents, the excruciating morning, she felt herself breathe in James's company. Her chest and mind loosened like she was standing on a mountain, sucking in oxygen.

"So where are you going?"

"Not sure yet. Just trying to get rid of them as fast as I can, then I'll figure out what's next. Doesn't really matter. Someplace cheap. Far away."

James looked at Riley, but her attention was on the handbag, rotating the clasp, studying the flap, feeling the interior.

A minute passed, then a few more.

"How have you been?" James asked. "I didn't think you wanted me to call."

"I want to say something." Riley hesitated. "But I need you to hear me out. Please, don't say anything until the end, and then if you want to say no, I promise not to tell you to fuck yourself."

She looked at James.

"Let me come with you."

"What? No."

"I'm serious, James. I'm good at this stuff. I'll plan everything."

"I don't need you to plan everything."

"I'm talking about the stuff you don't want to plan. The stuff you'll forget. Sun block. Mosquito repellant." She paused, everything contracting. "Directions. I'm good with maps." He fought the urge to interrupt her. "I'm good at reading situations. I don't wear dumb hats. Not even on boats. I'm bad at communicating with people I know, but I'm good on the road, I'm good with languages. And I sleep a lot. You'll have all your evenings to yourself. I'll leave you alone during the day too, if you want. I won't be a liability. I won't tell anyone, we'll just disappear. Please."

"*Riley.*"

"Please, James."

"This isn't a vacation, Riley. I'm *leaving*. Do you get that?"

"You think I want to go on *vacation* with you?"

"You know what I meant."

"I want to rip myself from my skin, James. Do you get that? I want to sleep in her clothes and drink her shampoo and climb into her drawers and I can't, because then she'll really be gone. I'll have used her all up, and then what happens? I'm fucking everything up. I need to go someplace no one knows about *all of this*." She shakes him with the whites of her eyes. "Let me come."

"But I would know."

"You don't count."

"What are these rules? Does money count? How do you expect to pay for this?"

"I'll help you sell the Chanels."

He nodded at the carpet. "There it is."

"I know I could sell them all. More, even, if you could get them. I'm a decent liar. Clearly not as practiced as you but I have some ideas. You were right about the autopsy, okay? It fucked me up," Riley stuttered, "and I should have listened to you. But this is a good idea. Let's get the money and get the hell out of here." She held his gaze, solemn, pleading. On the other side of the wall a whistle blew, a marching band started up to the sound of Mark coughing.

"I walked in on my parents talking about me. With or without you, I'm getting out of here too—"

"Fine," James interrupted her. He lifted his eyes to the ceiling and back. "Okay," he said. "Sure."

"*What?*"

He shook his head, ran both hands through his hair, pulling at the roots.

"Sure," he said again, as if the word was now some kind of dumb punch line. He took a long, audible inhale and for the first time since Riley arrived, she sensed he was holding back a smile.

. . .

His first year out of Columbia, James sold six Chanels, just enough to cover the loans he couldn't pay through legitimate work. It had been Mark's idea, but James had made the technique his own, taking compelling photographs of the bags, softly lit and posed in the seductive way his photojournalist friends had advised. He wrote convincing, tightly worded listings on Craigslist—on generous days, he let himself believe he was using his education, working in his field. He liked to play a man recently scorned, going through a divorce, selling off the belongings of his cheating wife, but sometimes a banker with a gambling problem, or an estranged son who had recently lost his mother. It made people think they were profiting from the spoils of misfortune, the best way, James found, to make them think they were getting an unbelievable deal. When he couldn't find work as a writer, as he cobbled together his odd jobs, he kept it going to make his student loan payments, a bag every few months, hardly a habit. The tutoring paid his rent, the library his minimal expenses, the Chanels for an education he had begun to regret.

Then James met Morgan and he stopped. He'd saved up a decent chunk of money by then and decided to just make his way through it, worry about it later. Spending all that time among rich people, James became less cavalier about playing one. He worried he would accidentally sell a bag to a Kaleidoscope person, or someone who might recognize him from the gala. Complicating matters further was the convoluted pleasure of being around these people. Rich people were impressed by him, wanted their kids to go to Columbia too, to have nice manners and date a Morgan type. In these circles, James was fascinating. He was a boy from Oregon who lived in Harlem, looked nice in a suit, and laughed warmly and appropriately. He felt oddly charming, socially dexterous. With the Brightons as his portal— Morgan whisking him in and out of introductions with her supple flattery—James had lost his will to scam the wealthy, who no longer seemed like the enemy.

But by August, James was using credit cards again. He'd showed up on the Brightons' stoop not because he expected to feel good and special again, but because he'd convinced himself they'd all find comfort in one another. He was wholly unprepared for such coldness from Karen and Hank, such frustration at the sight of him—which shook both memory and instinct. Without Morgan, the narrative shifted; James felt like an outsider, a mooch. It revealed his inner- most fear, which was returning to Eugene, to his mom's lonely house, nothing to show for his time away. Was James not biding his time, doing exactly what Karen and Hank accused him of doing? He'd gone back to Harlem riddled with insecurity, behind on his rent, and received a long and winding lecture from Mark, who was six years younger and cut his coke with his son's baby formula but nonetheless was worried about what James was doing with his life. Get back on the bags, Mark had coached him, fatherly, as if telling him he still had a shot at the playoffs if he turned it around in the second half. James was obliterated by that point. He felt the expanse of the uni- verse, throbbing like the 3D show at the planetarium, *Journey to the Stars*. There was still hope for him, plenty of it; the world was large; he was not at the center; he would take control of what he could.

When he woke the next morning, the impression was still there, like a watermark on his life, a ferocious feeling of renewed posses- sion. Ironically, it was the Brightons who had given him the next push. James had taken a walk downtown, through the park, and found himself in front of Kaleidoscope's soaring windows, looking up at the 70 percent off signs. After that, he saw them everywhere, massive discounts at all the luxury retailers, Saks and Bloomingdale's and Neiman Marcus. James had gone home and begun his research. It had been a bad year, a catastrophic sales season, and the expensive stores were drowning in stock. To get it off their hands and recoup some losses, they were luring the wealthy from their hidey-holes with unprecedented pre-Christmas discounts. And it appeared to be working. James told Mark to put in the order. He'd take a dozen, he said, and Mark shoved him in the chest, told him to get the fuck out. But why couldn't James sell twenty grand in fake Chanel? New York was teeming with people with too much money, looking for deals. He'd lived among them for nearly five months.

But it was all exhausting to sustain. Each day was a mental and physical effort to believe he was making forward progress, fighting the system, selling counterfeit bags for some higher purpose. James waded through the internet, sending his résumé into the ether, waiting for someone to email him about a job or a bag. He was losing steam, had no idea what came next. It was only when Riley showed up that James felt genuinely, truly, in possession of something valuable. And when Riley asked if she could come, could tag along on his hypothetical escape plan, James understood that he could actually go.

Nearly a year had passed since they first ran into each other. Was it really so crazy? She was Morgan's sister, stubborn and smart-assed, oddly comfortable. He got the impression that had they met under different circumstances, they might still be friends, if either of them was the type to make and keep a friend. It was clear her parents saw it differently. The memory of what he'd seen and heard in those weeks still unsettled him, made him question his relationship with Riley. James was a pleaser; he wanted to be liked, wanted to make a good impression, and the fact that Karen and Hank now shunned him was, justified or not, a tender wound. But Riley's confidence in herself, in her reaction to her parents' disregard of them—it was compelling to behold. Hank and Karen were never home, never wondered where she'd been, could not see past their own predicaments. When James asked Riley what she planned on telling them about their leaving, she replied, "The truth." She looked at him in her no-nonsense way. Did they deserve the courtesy of a lie?

Each morning, they met at James's apartment and pieced together their plan. They unearthed a conjoined intensity, focus fueling focus, powering them through a maniacal tunnel of single-mindedness. How scary it was to have nothing to do but this. Their days now revolved around a single goal, which was to make as much money as they could, in as little time as possible, and to get the fuck out of New York.

CHANEL CAVIAR BLACK LEATHER CLASSIC FLAPBAG

This bag was a gift from my mother-in-law, purchased at the Paris Chanel Cambon in 2006. She didn't know I already had the classic black, so now I have two, and I'd like to get the Mademoiselle. It's in perfect condition (see pictures), with serial number, authenticity card, and original duster. Asking $2200.

They posted the ad ten days before Christmas, Riley's idea, to capitalize on the despairing wave of last-minute husbands and boyfriends. Men were their ideal buyers; they had no idea what they were doing. They liked that the bag was black. They liked that it came with the duster, because they hoped to pass it off as new.

CHANEL QUILTED HANDBAG, LEATHER, GOLD CHAIN, JUMBO SIZE

Bought this bag for my ex-girlfriend for Christmas and need to get rid of it before I move to Chicago. I have tons of pictures which I can send on request, or you can come see it for yourself. Bag comes with everything. $2K—not negotiable, am losing enough money on this already.

They knew this ad was a crapshoot. The seller sounded like a douchebag. They shot the pictures on James's navy bedspread, a masculine touch, authentic. Nine people emailed but only four showed up to touch it. James met them outside an office building by Bryant Park, smoking a cigarette, a man in advertising who couldn't wait to get to Chicago. The fourth buyer was a middle-aged man in tweed—a Chanel authenticator, he told James when he shook his hand. The bag was a fake, he said, showing him where the top edge of the pocket was too curved, and James lost it on Sixth Avenue, railing on the bastard who sold it to him, cursing his ex-girlfriend, disavowing the city forever. He stamped out his cigarette and apologized, excused himself into the towering glass building, where he hid in the lobby bathroom and called Riley, laughing and jittery, breathing hard into the phone.

GENUINE CHANEL CLASSIC SHOULDER BAG, PERFECT CONDITION

My wife and I are moving upstate and are selling many of our things to fund our down payment. Among them is a shoulder bag my wife got for her birthday and has worn no more than half a dozen times. She is a writer. The bag was a gift from her godmother and was never her style. She'd like $1800 or the best offer. Please look at the pictures and let me know if you need further information. Thank you.

"What does it matter that the wife is a writer?"

"I don't know. Writers don't move upstate and wear Chanel. She doesn't value it."

"You don't think it's a bit much? Kind of dorky?"

"Read the ad, Riley, they're dorks."

It turned out to be their best tactic. A hundred-pound woman with a platinum bob arrived, then a Russian woman with a yappy Maltese, then a former cast member on *Big Brother*, then a woman with a daughter about to be bat mitzvahed. James and Riley sat in the window of a café near Central Park, in their glasses and sweaters, drinking cappuccinos, and sold the last four bags one after the other, playing the friendly academic couple with remarkable dexterity. They were going up to Hamilton, Riley told them. James was teaching at Colgate in the spring. Philosophy, James said. Political science. Creative writing. They gazed across the table at each other, their eye contact, their game of improv, making them both a little crazy. Could they take sixteen hundred? James pressed his lips together. He would, but there was someone else interested at full price. The women understood. They handed over their envelopes of cash, wished them luck.

It was the end of January and like some furious act of magic, all ten bags were gone. Three ads in six weeks; they had sprinted along a precarious wire and fallen on the right side of wrong, with twenty-two thousand dollars in cash that made them feel invincible. They deposited the money into James's special bank account, set up through a friend of Mark's who worked at a branch on 125th and Lexington. The bank account collected no interest, and so, according to Mark, it would fly under the radar of the IRS. James felt ridiculous explaining this to Riley, exposing how deep the roots had grown. They could add her name to his account, he said, or he could give her half the money to handle how she wished—whatever she wanted. Riley went to the bank and produced her documents, signed her name, received her debit card to their joint account. After the elaborate teamwork of moving twenty thousand dollars of East Harlem contraband, they felt tied to each other in a way they imagined long-term couples might. Exposed. Mutually indebted. Filled with admiration and plated in steel.

When Riley went home to sleep at night—she was offered the couch but she never stayed—James threw himself into the tedium of planning, trying to thwart the voices that spoke up when she left. Of course he understood the morality of the situation. She was Morgan's sister; his ex-girlfriend's sister, his ex-girlfriend who had died just last year. But what could James do? He didn't like the answer, felt bound to a different emotion that conflicted him deeper and compelled him more. James feared this turbulent escape might be the best thing he'd ever done, the greatest thing he'd ever do, and more than anything now, he wanted to do it.

The Saturday Riley told her parents, five days before their scheduled departure, she showed up at James's apartment hauling the backpack they'd researched and bought together.

"We need to sell three more," Riley said when she walked through the door. "Twenty-two isn't enough. We'll run out. Hey, Mark." James followed her into his room. "I have three thousand dollars of my own saved. What do you have?"

"Maybe two. After I pay Mark through February. Maybe a little more?"

"That will put us over thirty. That's great. That's what we'll do."

"Riley, sit down."

"I have an idea. We'll put up flyers at NYU and FIT. We'll skip Parsons, just in case we're recognized."

"Let me think about it. I'll talk to Mark. I'm not positive we can get more in time."

"We can. I asked him. He said we can."

"Riley." James pressed his lips together. "What happened?"

"It's fine." Riley smiled but her eyes betrayed her, filling in with a shiny film.

"It's clearly not fine."

"It's nothing that I didn't expect." She wiped her left eye, then her right, holding determinedly to her smile. "I'm shitting on Morgan's memory. We both are." She attempted a laugh. "We'll regret it. We have no sense of respect. The trip was meant for me and Morgan and as long as we're planning to go, I'm cut off. Financially, they mean. But I assume they mean emotionally too."

James nodded, slowly, then again. "Okay," he said. "Anything else?"

"Not really." She wiped a palm across her face. "They think we can't do it without them. They're idiots. They think we're planning on using their money."

"Did you . . . ?" James hesitated.

"Of course not."

Riley remembered the look on her mother's face, like of course Riley was fucking things up yet again, making Karen's life harder, and how it had bothered Riley so much less than she'd anticipated. Her parents had no idea what was going on with her, all their focus on saving the business, saving themselves, and so to yield to their judgment on her life felt idiotic.

"Oh," Riley said, a new carefulness in her voice alarming James. "My mom. She doesn't want you in the house."

James raised an eyebrow, amused by this. "No fucking kidding."

Riley laughed, using her sleeves to dab her eyes, hiccups creeping up and cutting her breathing in half, the laughing dropping her backward into the wall. Mark appeared in the open door. He held a bowl of cereal in his hands, pointing with his spoon. "Fuck happened to her?"

They sold three more. The city was preposterous. They held this information against it, that there were thirteen people in two months—in the middle of a fucking recession—with enough disposable cash to buy these shiny crap holders for an amount of money that could feed a family for several months. The last three bags were different. It was no longer a game, or the game was now personal. James followed Riley around the city that night, posting flyers absolutely anywhere rich people might congregate: the 92nd Street Y, the Upper East Side YMCA, Spence and Chapin and Nightingale and Brearley. They had just five days left before their departure, but it didn't deter her; if anything it made her bolder, because soon they'd be gone. Riley had withdrawn from school. She couldn't go back to her parents' house. She didn't appear to sleep at night. James encouraged her to reach out to her mother, to try to talk to her before they left, but Riley wasn't interested. Her parents made her insides harden. Her dad texted her like nothing was wrong, *hey* and *how are you* and *hope you're doing okay*, which enraged her almost as much as her mother's silence. She didn't reply, refused to act like everything was fine. Instead Riley focused on the bags, and she was right. Five days was enough.

. . .

James watched Riley in her wool coat, her knit hat and black heeled boots. She nodded blithely, showing the buyer where there was a scuff or a stain, all of which she'd applied just hours before. She commanded a confidence that felt incendiary, in her posture, in the way she used her smile, warmth and fire in the middle of winter. He waited halfway down the block, holding a shopping bag with the last purse. He watched the woman, a Park Avenue type, say thank you, twice, and point to Riley's boots, to which Riley lifted a heel and offered some story about where she'd bought them. Berlin, maybe. Secondhand in Barcelona. James smiled as he watched her work, trying out her range, nearly enjoying herself, and a feeling snapped suddenly into place. James was seeing Riley as he imagined Morgan did. Part protective, part in awe. He wanted her to get what she was after. Perhaps more than anyone else he'd ever known, James held no reservations about her happiness. Morgan had felt the same way. He held the feeling for a minute, her eyes laid over his.

A slim stack of hundred-dollar bills, removed from a pocket or an envelope or a purse. This part he knew was all their own, this sordid hit of pleasure. They had this in common, he and Riley, a self-consciously vindictive core, a desire to make uneven things even. They both worked hard and cared deeply and felt entitled, especially now, to reach their hands in and make adjustments. So they exacted their revenge. They took aim at the city they felt had taken so much from them.

. . .

February 14, 2009. It's Valentine's Day, an unavoidable happenstance they choose to ignore because the tickets were cheap and the plane was right: a Boeing 777, James's favorite. Since he was fifteen—back row in a turboprop, holding in his vomit as they descended through a fog so dense it felt like he was drowning in a bowl of milk—James flies only wide-bodied jets.

Riley discovered this piece of information early on, as she watched him sink half a week piecing together the perfect route—three legs, a layover in Europe, no flight longer than eight hours—and later, at the airport, hunched over his phone, refreshing the turbulence map over and over, checking the sky, providing unsolicited commentary on the clouds. The 777, he explained, was the only plane in existence with fly-by-wire technology: an electronic interface that read the air, a computer that fine-tuned the control surfaces, smoothing out the sky. There is something about turbulence that recalls violent death for James, makes him imagine a bone-shattering plunge, his organs shunted into his lungs. It's an inherited phobia, he told her without a trace of irony, a gift from his mother.

Riley does not have a favorite plane, but she does see the appeal in this one. The chairs are wide and curved nicely to her body. Each seat has a TV screen and a footrest that folds out from the seat in front, like first class on a train. The attendants, dressed in crimson suits and pillbox hats, passed out hot towels with silver tongs. A celestial composition of organs and synth guitar greeted them as they stored their carry-ons and took their seats. She has flown a 777 before, most every time she's crossed an ocean, but without her family it feels brand-new.

Flight attendants, prepare for takeoff. The cabin lights go off, which makes JFK appear even more consequential, the concrete vanished, leaving just the fluorescent glow of windows and flood lamps. After the captain makes his announcement, Riley barely feels the plane push off. It's only when they are already in motion, when she looks to her left and sees the streaks of colors sailing past, that she realizes they have started their journey. It's so gentle, the way they accumulate speed, and Riley imagines herself on the wing, rumble in her bones, filling herself with the thunderous purr of takeoff.

Thirty-two thousand dollars. Enough to keep them away for the rest of the year. Hostels, street food, buses, trains, feet. This is their plan, for as long as they can manage, until the money runs out. Through the forces of reciprocal necessity, they sit on this plane in the middle of February with no blueprint for how to return. Together they will take a trip not intended for them. An opportunity, an aberration, scooped up through their unspeakable loss, the presence of one enabling the other. From across the aisle, James reaches for Riley's hand, a sweaty palm clamped around hers, warm and nervous and pulsing with gratitude.

They fly into the night sky, high up in the air, finally breathing.

PART FOUR

February 2009–November 2009

DAY ONE

They climb out of the plane into a white-hot day—warm, thick air crawling into their sleeves and expanding deliciously against their skin. The heat is the first thing that confirms their distance. It's February and here they are peeling the jackets from their bodies, crossing a tarmac that smells like mangoes, the world completely upside down. They feel delirious in a zany but competent way, finally there. They stand in the immigration line, remove their glasses for the officer, follow the signs to baggage claim. When the carousel buzzes and begins to drop luggage, one by one from its big silver mouth, James squeezes through the bodies to pluck his backpack from the belt. The luggage falls like a game of Tetris, rectangles sliding into gaps, then stacking up. The bags appear and disappear, travelers strapping on their packs and Indian families amassing their rolling bags and cardboard boxes until James and Riley are alone, slumped against a metal pillar, watching the last two bags make slow, confounding loops.

In the baggage office, they fill out paperwork as the uniformed clerk tells them not to worry: the bags get lost, they miss connections, but they always turn up. Once a bag went all the way to Moscow, but it came back. It was just an example! She laughs at Riley. Her back-pack was not going to Moscow; that was very rare. Riley's backpack would be delivered to the address on the paperwork, the woman explains, lifting the form to her eyeglasses.

She clears her throat. "Vagator."

"Yes," James says. "That's where we're staying."

"I will send the bag to Vagator," she says slowly.

Riley leans across the counter. "Is there a problem?"

"Oh no," the woman says. "No problem at all."

A few years in New York have given James and Riley a natural, confrontational patience, a small bell that rings when someone is be-ing even slightly suspicious. They stand there, two jet-lagged detec-tives, when the woman raises a skinny eyebrow and says, almost gossipy, "The question is, how will you get there?"

Outside the terminal is chaos. A man stands on a bench, yelling with his hands cupped to his mouth. "The taxi drivers are on strike!" he yells, skinny and formal in his ironed clothes. "No one can leave the city limits!" Disbelief spreads quickly backward, people looking over their shoulders, exchanging the exasperated eye contact of those who have been mutually inconvenienced. Still, the drivers charge forward. "Ma'am!" "Sir!" "Chief!" "My friend!" There are hands on shoulders, hands reaching for bags, four men walking backward as they make their pitch, a surround sound of drivers say-ing not to worry, they will get to their destination the following day, just come with them. A man offers Riley and James a hotel room in the center of town, then a restaurant with mega-air-conditioning and then, after complimenting them for being so savvy, wagging his finger like he's on to them, a nicer hotel, a guesthouse, a very special place that they will love.

The exhaustion and the slap of blistering sun make the scene feel hallucinatory. Some of the touts have had quick success, hoisting suitcases and duffel bags and bulging cardboard boxes above their heads, leading a parade of passengers off and away, but James and Riley have hardened themselves for this moment, for this country, and an hour later they are the last two foreigners standing outside an empty airport, still pushing for a solution. The men marvel at the obstinacy of this American couple. The taxi strike is a serious matter; if the drivers are spotted on the highway, the locals will gather and throw rocks until the vehicle breaks or someone is injured. The locals must do this, the drivers explain with utmost sincerity, to ensure a proper strike.

Riley is close to giving in, begins scanning for the man with the very special guesthouse that they will love. She can feel the long flight, the leap in time, the glazing over of her mind and her limbs, and the heat, the balmy, sticky heat trapped between the clothes she's been wearing since she and James rode the train out to Queens nearly thirty hours before, the same clothes she'd worn as she gave herself a pep talk in the airplane bathroom, the pair of leggings, the navy kimono, the shirt of Morgan's she's now committed to wearing—her luggage lost—for the foreseeable future. As she grows tired of refusing these men, already she feels the desperation she hoped to leave at home. She puts a hand on James's shoulder. "Okay," she says. "Let's quit."

But James's resolve has taken root. Give me five more minutes, he tells her, and off he goes, toward a different group of men who gave up early without much fight. Riley sits on the bench where the man stood yelling, letting five, then fifteen minutes pass. And right before James turns around, calls her over with an excitement that makes her more exhausted, Riley feels her body melting, her patience shot. She drags her feet across the parking lot.

"Mr. Manoj," James says, nodding at a middle-aged man with a push-broom mustache, "is going to lend us his car, and we're going to drive it to our hostel in Vagator."

Riley looks to the man, then to the six others, before pulling James aside. "What are you doing? You sound insane."

"I got him down to a thousand rupees," James says, and he doesn't know if it's the lack of sleep or some alien courage keeping his face straight. "Fifteen bucks a day, three days up front, and we can take the car."

"Does that make any sense to you?"

"I don't know. He's a nice guy. He wants to help us. I think we should do it."

"We've been in India for *an hour* and you want to take a random man's car."

"Look at that guy. Seriously, Riley, look at him. He's a Hindu. I asked him why he's helping us, that's what he said."

"He said he's a Hindu so we can have his car for forty-five dollars."

"Borrow it. We have to bring it back in a few days, when the strike is over. And the other guys, they really like him. Mr. Panesh said we can trust him."

"Who the hell is Mr. Panesh?"

"*Riley*," James shushes her, looks at her like she's being impossible, and Riley is confronted with a reverse reality. Here she is, back in India, resisting the very thing she'd asked for again and again: to throw out the plan, to do something interesting.

"All right." She shakes her head. "Okay, let's do it."

. . .

All seven men lead them across the parking lot to where a lime-green sedan sits parked in the shade. Inside, fastened to the dashboard, is a statue of Ganesh and a mostly wilted garland of marigolds. They open the door to a hot, musty interior and Mr. Manoj tells James and Riley to wait just one minute while he removes his belongings and wipes the main surfaces with a series of tissues he pulls from the glove compartment. In the trunk he shows them two vinyl umbrellas and a rolled-up straw mat "for their personal use," and gathers his tennis shoes, a plastic shopping bag, and a half-empty gallon jug of water. When James opens his wallet, Mr. Manoj accepts the cash as if James is making a generous donation.

"I will write my phone number on this paper," Mr. Manoj says, doing it. "And you will call me with any questions." He opens the door for Riley, looks almost proud. "The most important part is to enjoy."

They get in the car and the men gather around them, forming a kind of human atrium, staring into the windows as James starts the ignition and realizes, for the first time, that he will be operating a left-handed stick shift. He tries not to let the realization spread to his face, smiles tight as he murmurs the admission to Riley. "Wow," she says, waving and smiling at the men as they pull from the parking spot. "Wow," she says again, louder as they roll away. James shifts into second and accelerates with a small, maniacal whoop that jolts Riley alert. She blinks hard into the sun, feels herself, her mind reappearing, refocusing in this surreal iteration of time and place.

Right out of the parking lot, straight through the exit—to the left, keep to the left! Where the blinker should be is the windshield wiper, blades swooping across the glass as they slow for turns. They shoot out onto a two-lane highway, see women walking along the dirt shoulder, saris rippling in the wind, and suddenly they are laughing, hooting with joy, swaddled in this private space and hurtling through an unknown landscape, free to lose their shit for the first time in so long.

It would be the least professional scam ever attempted; that's what they say on the first straightaway, the first words they speak without the imperative, eyes damp with hysteria. They have the car. Mr. Manoj has forty-five dollars. No matter how many ways they parse the situation, it seems to them they have the upper hand. They tally the facts: Mr. Manoj is a Hindu. He owns a friendly Ganesh in orange pants. Mr. Panesh said to trust him. They never told him their full names. They never said where they were staying. As they push north through the Goan capital—sand strewn across the asphalt roads, a bridge across a stone-colored bay, whitewashed churches and powder-blue buildings rising against an endless sky and motorbikes, their owners' shirts billowing huge in the breeze—they feel good about their odds, unsettled of course, but still validated on the basis of logic. Riley reaches for the stereo, presses the power, and a woman's voice explodes through the speakers, a high wail of a voice over an ecstatic, bouncing backbone of drums and tambourines, a piercing sitar. It's a CD, the volume set teenage-high. "Mr. *Manoj!*" James exclaims, slamming his palm on the steering wheel, and the two of them throw their hands in the air, bounce like they haven't slept in two days.

Leaving the capital, the road narrows, and they turn down the music in order to focus. They ride a winding strip of laneless concrete with no shoulder or sidewalks, no barrier between vehicle and human and animal traffic. They pass through villages, weaving through a maze of roadside stalls with steaming, crackling vats of oil and triangular mounds of limes and coconuts and packed buses with no glass in the windows and whistles blowing and scooters beeping as they emerge from blind corners and invisible alleyways. They dodge a hunchbacked woman, a pack of goats. They are serious again, back to imperatives. Watch out! Stay to the left! Careful! They squeeze slowly through a crowd loitering in the street, and when no one moves, Riley reaches out her window and pulls in her mirror.

There are cows, huge and defiant in the traffic. There are dogs and flower peddlers and low-hanging vines. After this, the coastal road appears like a blessing, vacant by comparison. The ocean opens to their left, between the palms and the bushes and the burnt-caramel sand, and beyond that, a jagged cutout of the low-lying water. It is a feeling as much as it is a landscape. It makes their hearts feel bloody, their lungs enormous. Five more miles, they are trampled by sights, by the oil and spices warm and swollen in the air, by the vibrancy of the fabrics swinging on the lines, the poverty of the houses that own the fabrics, the makeshift gas stations selling red-tinted fuel in plastic water bottles. By the time they reach Vagator they are mentally numb and physically exhausted and bursting with a furious vitality. James slows to a stop, their bodies humming. Then he pulls the key from the ignition and when the music cuts, it stills the rest of the world.

At the end of the lane, they find the two-story Portuguese house. There is a likeness to the pictures on the internet: the whitewashed building has an old-world, colonial charm. But dark streaks spill down the sides; moss crawls in the opposite direction. In front of the house is an outcropping of grass, and on the grass is a gathering of young people sitting cross-legged and side-sprawled in a circle, barefoot and unwashed with deep golden tans.

"Hey, mates," one of them says. He's Indian by appearance and English by accent, his white T-shirt and left cheek smeared with a neon-blue dust he does not address as he introduces himself as Harsh, then opens up the circle for full introductions. Four of them are English, a pair of them are French, the tall one with wire-rimmed glasses and cut-up feet, who hasn't worn shoes in four months, is Remus from Germany, and then there are two Israeli girls in crocheted clothing, two Australian brothers in gym shorts and Tevas, and a couple from the north of India, from Gujarat, who introduce themselves as engineering students. They all look up.

"Oh," Riley says. "Right. I'm Riley."

"James." He waves.

"We're American. From Oregon."

"We're cousins," James says, surprising Riley by how quickly he's fed this story into the ether. James looks at the people on the grass, waits for someone to ask a question, ready with answers they'd prepared on the plane ride over, scratching their revisionist family tree into the waxy surface of an air-sickness bag. Somewhere between Greece and Turkey, they decided they would become someone else. That they would remain James and Riley, at least by name to avoid falling into that unending trap, but this James and Riley would not be them. It was the first moment of lucidity, high in the air, sipping the free wine that blocked the oxygen to their brains. They would assume the identities of another family, a real family they would pull from Eugene. A believable cover—James poked Riley in the arm— was all about specifics, and so they sifted through the real families of Eugene, looking for a fully formed disguise, when they landed on the Swansons. James and Riley Swanson of the Eugene Bakery Swansons—an aspirational family, with a mess of attractive cousins they'd both gone to school with. Riley's father, a third-generation baker, would be younger brother to James's father, the family business accountant. James felt he could play the role of a filial young accountant with some success. Riley was reasonably comfortable with the mechanics of bread.

"What one is Oregon?" An Israeli girl looks at them, lighting a cigarette, and before either can answer, Remus of Germany turns and says, "On the top of California."

The sound the group makes to convey their understanding is throaty and pronounced, lifts with vibrato, the least American, most comforting noise Riley has heard in half a year.

"Porte-lande," one of the Frenchmen adds, extending a thumbs-up, and the line of questioning is over.

"I never thought I'd say this," James says, dropping his backpack in their room, a tiny space with two twin beds that smells like mothballs and bleach. "But that kimono is giving us real legitimacy right now. I feel like a nark out there."

"I told you, do the tiny ponytail."

"Of course, the tiny ponytail. Have you ever seen an accountant with a tiny ponytail?"

"So you'll be the first! It'll keep the hair from your eyes while you make the calculations." She bangs on an invisible keyboard. "You know, balance the books."

James nods. "That's really helpful, thanks. I need to take a shower. Then I'd be down to get something to eat if you're not too beat?"

Riley hesitates, scratches at a stain on her bedsheet, her exhaustion turned suddenly big and itchy. She feels like drinking. She feels like throwing herself into that circle of strangers and being Riley Swanson of the Eugene Bakery Swansons. The Swansons of Oregon, the one on the top of California.

"I'm good," she says. "You go shower. I'll probably just head back out there."

James pauses, looks up from where he's rummaging in his back-pack. "You're serious," he says, clearly impressed.

"Come on." Riley smiles, mischievous, and James is hit with a strange, light-bodied rush, a blink of something he cannot name smothered beneath a mountain of clutter. "Don't you want to play with the hippies?"

"I do." He swallows. "I'll . . ." he says. "I'll meet you out there."

The communal bathroom is a long, rectangular room covered floor to ceiling in once-white tiles, bordered in grout that has been scrubbed into various shades of brown. On the near end, closest to the door, a toilet rises from the floor, a loose roll of toilet paper balanced on the tank, warped in the middle by wet hands. On the wall opposite the toilet there are two knobs, a showerhead, and a red plastic pail, with no curtain from the ceiling or lip on the floor to signal where the toilet portion ends and the shower begins. *The room is a shower-toilet*, James thinks to himself, a visceral reminder that this wet room, this temporary home, the yard outside and the world beyond, exists in a universe entirely apart from anything he knows.

Undressed, clothes hanging from a hook, James opens the faucets, and as the water surges above his head, he spots the faint outline of muddy handprints, perfectly parallel, just above the set of knobs. The image stays with him, adheres to the back of his eyelids as he lathers his hair with the hard piece of soap left molded to the rusty tray. It's been six years since he stayed in a hostel. He wonders at his previous self, if there were markings like this in the shared showers of Europe that had been lost on him. He'd been fresh out of college then, had experienced sex all of five times. He'd never been with a woman in a shower, never seen one naked and vertical in a lit-up space, certainly never muddy, nothing like this. In the hostels of Spain and Italy, he remembers the puking, lots of puking tying up the toilet stalls from midnight to the early morning, a still-drunk friend cracking open the door to tell the knocker, if he was a man, to go piss in the courtyard. He remembers the couples stumbling into the dorm, whispering behind the towels they hung to hide their bottom bunks—yes, he knew there had been sex, but that was different. These handprints—he opens his eyes—they are the ostentatious, brutal remains of flashy, unapologetic fucking. They are ecstatic as exclamation points, furious as a slap of thunder. James shuts his eyes again, rinsing himself beneath the stream of water and when he feels himself becoming hard, he doesn't stop to think. He is thirty hours unslept, ten hours jet-lagged, mentally battered from the effort of operating a left-handed stick shift and drained from the confidence he pulled from that moment of hysteria, that he peddled as real, tangible competence. He takes himself in his hand, the smell of bleach and lemon and mildew lifting from the tiled walls, gulps a mouthful of balmy air, and for the first time since the accident, he doesn't stop himself. His mind melts to lava, enraged with toxins. In twenty seconds he is smeared against the cold tile wall, heaving silently, violently, his heart thrashing against his skin.

Alone in the lobby, Riley stands before the fridge of beers, which is policed by a pad of paper and a pen on a string, taped to the pad. It's an honor system, something that challenges her basest instincts. How easy it would be to take a beer, not write her name, to take two and write one. She flips the pages, reading the names that have stood where she is now, recorded their beers. She removes two bottles and gulps one right there, almost feral, cold and heat dripping through her veins. Then she wipes her mouth and adds her name, with two tally marks, among the people who can be trusted.

Outside the air smells like Memorial Day weekend, like the entire world is cooking outdoors, smoke blowing through the tang of human sweat and the thick, damp musk of dirt exploding with life. Riley finds an opening in the group and lowers herself, cross-legged, in the fading light. The circle is bigger now; the hostel has come out at night. When she tells the girl beside her that it's her first day, the girl reacts as if Riley has said she's an astronaut or a lion tamer, telling more and more people—Riley arrived today, Riley started today— until the whole group knows and Riley is the center of conversation. What was the plan? How long did they have? What happened to James? It takes Riley some time, even as it's happening, to adjust to the way she talks and everyone listens, asks more questions, listens again. Back home, if Riley told someone she was going to India, the answer was "amazing" or "I went to India; it was amazing" and the conversation was more or less done. Occasionally, someone might ask "when"? But here, the talk unfurls in strange directions, wistful in an uncomplicated way. Most of the group has been traveling for months, the last of their sand slipping through the hourglass, and the fact that Riley is at day one, everything ahead, makes them openly excited for her and woeful for themselves.

"I started in Phuket," one of the English guys says. "Bit of a mess, really, Phuket." The group goes rowdy for this statement; it's clear that Phuket is considered garbage, and that most everyone has been. They toss the question back and forth, telling each other where they started, where they've been. They have ridden camels in Morocco and climbed volcanos in Indonesia and yet the stories they like most involve sleepless nights on ferries and endless trains, amusing scams, harrowing bridges and border crossings and shit gone completely off the rails. The intelligence they share is scooped up, applied pragmatically to those headed in the same direction. In New York—and Riley knows, she must stop comparing her surroundings to Manhattan—people were stingy with sincerity. Effusive behavior conceded astonishment, which slid so easily into inferiority. But among these people, what made one of them superior? They are all sleeping in an eight-dollar bunk bed, sharing a moldy toilet, living off what they can strap to their back. Almost all of their stories end in fuckups—in a lost bag and a taxi strike and a borrowed car with a friendly Ganesh—and what strikes Riley most, what kindles a small fire in her sternum, is that none of them wants it to end. In her omission, Riley plays a person who's never been to this country before. It happens so quickly, so effortlessly: Riley is struck by the freedom she imagined would come in New York—the ability to offer her own narrative, to be whoever she says she is.

"Who is Jan Van Wolfswinkle?" James appears, walking from the lobby in shorts and a T-shirt, hair damp from the shower. The group looks to Jan, the long-legged Dutch guy in capris, who raises a timid hand. "That is a seriously cool name. This beer is for you, man." James cheers Wolfswinkle, then everyone cheers Wolfswinkle. James lowers himself next to Riley, bumps her on the shoulder. He appears refreshed, palpably lighter, his shoulders relaxed down his back, and the sight of him fills Riley with a big silvery slice of possibility. She tilts her head back and feels her sister in the atmosphere, big and soothing, a strange new feeling, a warm tailwind on her back. And while Riley can't say exactly why, how much it has to do with James or with her sister or simply the delirium of being dropped into this mysterious colony on the coast of India—a place that painted the walls of her young imagination—this circle feels like an absolution. Like the universe has opened up a temporary portal and she's stumbled inside to find something so unexpected, so necessary and good, it grants her an incandescent amnesia, an oblivion from herself. Riley closes her eyes and lets the impression deepen.

This night, this group, this uncharted feeling, she will learn by heart and carry with her for the rest of her life.

A minibus arrives at midnight, when the group is buzzed and loose and chummy. It is Remus's last night. Tomorrow he goes back to Germany, back to snow, back to shoes, and the group latches on to a singular, contagious desire to memorialize his final hours. Inside the bus they pile on top of one another, half an ass on half a thigh, a shoulder across a lap, skin everywhere, heads knocking against the frayed, duct-taped ceiling as they bump along in the dark.

At the end of a small, unlit road, the door opens and they're released into what feels like a jungle. They look up through the leaves: at the top of a hill, there is a single beam of light spearing the sky. Riley and James find each other's eyes, place a weight around this moment. They walk along an uneven path, through a maze of giant vegetation, then the jungle opens and they're climbing, one by one, into the back of an open-roofed jeep, propped up on huge treaded wheels, idling on the other side of the thicket. Inside, Riley reaches up to hold the scaffolding of roll bar as the jeep tips them backward and powers to the top of the hill. The breeze changes, goes grassy and cool with elevation, and while they do not recognize this feeling yet, there it is, numb on their faces. A new recklessness, a drop of poison in their blood.

Fire dancers. A thatch-roofed bar. Squiggles of light suspended in trees. At the top of the hill, inside the fortress, everything is bathed in neon, draped in white, shaking with bodies. The crowd is half Indian, half foreign, in Hawaiian shirts and crop tops and spandex jumpsuits. It's Indian Boogie Nights in Miami. The hats and bare skin of Coachella, the facial hair and footwear of extended travel, the linen and gold of Indians on vacation.

They sail in together—a dozen of them, a live beating mass of people bound together for the night. James has always wondered what this might feel like, belonging to the group that brings the party. He fits in fine now, he knows he does, feels eyes on them, on him, as they enter. But the difficult part about confidence, at least for James, is the blind trust the feeling requires. In a new country, in a group of strangers ignited by music he's never heard, he must pull conviction from a personal reserve. James looks out over the dancing people. He understands that the best way to project confidence— and he learns this from Riley, watches her now as she guides him forward—the simplest way to appear truly and infectiously fun, was simply to have it.

Riley taking a shot at the bar. Riley hugging the Australians. Riley jumping up and down to "Love Generation," spreading her arms and sailing in place. Riley laughing with her mouth open, pointing a finger at Remus. Riley laughing. Riley laughing. James keeps a drink cold in his hand, nodding, his right knee bending and releasing to the beat. He takes a shot with the rest of the group, feels the alcohol spread to his limbs, then a slow loosening of his head. Both his knees begin to go. The music is incredible, enormous in the warm, open air, at the top of a hill, a breeze that makes him want to throw his arms in the air and catch it. The more he moves the deeper the music digs into him. His shoulders shuffle, right and left, ever so slightly, forward and back, watching how the rest of them do it, not even on the dance floor but by the bar, bouncing to their conversations. James has always been awkward in clubs. Drinking never inspired him to dance; thirteen-dollar cocktails made him protective of his space. He long assumed he'd have to be blacked out, approaching a robot, to parade himself so ostentatiously. But here, tonight, he feels the hook sink in his chest, the weight vanish from his arms, the feeling of all his fucks fleeing his physical form. He is sober and yet he is exploding with poison. He closes his eyes and feels what it's like to step inside the music. It's just for him. It's unbelievable.

Up the stairs, into a darkness overlaid with glowing lights that look and feel like a sky of balloons. Their group spreads wide and snatches up territory. Around them the dance moves are funky as hell, a hand on an ear and a hand on a hip, men wide-legged and shimmying to the floor, sculpted fingers punching the air. Here they go: Riley winding her body around the beat, James jumping, head thrown to the ceiling. The whites of their teeth, the whites of their eyes, the whites of their straws and the tips of their fingernails. They see each other; of course they do, and the spectacle they are making with their bodies is revelatory, incendiary to them both.

The music, electronic and huge, sends waves of affection through the air, a big hollow thump that attaches beneath their skin. Riley takes off her kimono and ties it around her waist, her shoulders slicked with sweat. She throws her head forward and gathers her hair into a knot, and James tips his drink upside down, feels the last of the cold liquid slide down his throat, along his spine. He's drunk, it occurs to him, everything happening with a slight delay. He closes his eyes, feels the sound cascade over him and moves his body, doesn't care what he looks like, can feel himself smiling, sweat dripping down his temples. When he opens them, Riley is dancing with Remus, a slow beat rolling her hips as his tall, lanky body curves over her. Remus, who James likes, is touching her, just a little, fingers on her back, on her waist. But on his face is a hopefulness, a covetousness that makes James want to tear his eyes out. He closes them, opens them again, wills Riley to look his way. James keeps dancing, furiously, the Israeli girls moving around him when the beat falls out and a big airy synth comes surging from above, wrapping them in a sound that vibrates like it's trapped in a tunnel. James's heart wobbles. He feels a new density in the air. The tropical drumbeat, the soft, steady pluck of an electric guitar, then a woman's voice, scratchy and soulful, detonating across the music gives James the push to cross the room and take Riley's unsuspecting hand, to raise it in the air as a saxophone, thick and velvet, makes what he's doing feel grand and perfect. Her surprise fades almost immediately, and then it's just the two of them, slipping inside the woman's voice: *Why are we losing time?* The saxophone wails and James is suddenly nervous, his feet shuffling like the floor's on fire, when Riley puts her hands on him and slows him with a devastating gravity, holds him against her, pausing half a beat before releasing him again. The poison throbs absolutely everywhere. They feel it in their eyes, their mouths, their ears. The pulse rolls and expands, adheres to this electric womp of desire that will return, with startling force, whenever they hear this song. James takes her hands, raises them above her head and traces his fingers down her arms, looks at her like he's about to explode. Maracas sail in, the fluttering of a keyboard, their faces five inches apart when they start to laugh, their breath hot and boozy and anxious and dire.

In the auto-rickshaw, their ears ringing, emergency in the air, they tell the driver they had a wonderful evening, a lot of fun, and when he drops them at the hostel they walk quietly across the dark lawn and through the silent lobby, turn the key in the lock and collide with violence, hands against rib cages and shoulders and hips, handling each other as if trying to leave marks. James presses her against the concrete wall, kisses her as he pulls his shirt over his

BUNGALOW

The next morning, when she wakes up tangled in the tissue-paper sheets, Riley walks out of the room for a glass of water, and the way she is regarded, with quiet intrigue, makes her remember that she and James are cousins.

James sits up in the bed, rubs his fingers across his eyebrows. "Well, fuck. Okay, at least we know incest is universally frowned upon."

Riley is wearing James's soccer shorts, James's T-shirt. The word *incest* hangs in the air, threatening to upend whatever clarity they attained the night before, when they pushed the twin beds together and groaned, just before they fell asleep, that they felt a thousand pounds lighter, woozy and scrambled with a crushing, therapeutic relief. They'd come together, hard and insane, Riley touching herself until she flew off the edge, shoving a pillow into her own mouth, the boldness of it stirring a madness in James as he pressed deeper and harder and closer. But nothing changes. In the sober light of a new day, the fact that they are degenerate cousins feels more like a punch line than an allegation.

Riley flops facedown onto the bed. "I feel like I'm made of vodka and glue."

James thinks. "I'm more like a sack of slime."

"Soaked in vodka."

"Stop saying vodka."

They rock-paper-scissors. When James loses—"three papers in a row is bullshit"—Riley slips off to the car while he tallies the beers from the refrigerator pad and explains to the receptionist that they are needed, urgently and unexpectedly, somewhere he does not name. Standing there, thinking of Riley, James confronts an unmerciful fact, which is that he knew this would happen. Not necessarily in New York—when he was so myopically insecure he could barely select a sandwich from a menu—but on the plane when he reached for her hand and felt blood in his ears, in the car as they danced to that tambourine, as he gasped in the shower, as they rumbled around in the minibus, when she tied up her hair into that bun, her neck slicked with sweat, and every moment after. The jarring collision of fear and reality flusters him now, explodes a pent-up chamber of guilt and relief and chaotic joy. How hard he'd worked to deny it—assuring himself, convincing himself, that it was all a delusion of pain and grief. Karen was wrong about him, had misunderstood everything about their relationship. He and Riley were friends. The feeling would pass.

The feeling grew stronger.

James cares about this girl more than he's ever cared for anyone else—cares for her in that frightening way that makes delusion so accessible. It occurred to him the day before, as he convinced a random Indian man to give over his car, then sped away from the airport, trying to get Riley to safety. He cares about her with a reckless force that makes it difficult to care about anything else. A feeling that, for the first time in his life, has upstaged his own insecurities.

With Morgan, he was all nerves, waiting for something to collapse, the understanding that they were so mismatched, a spectacle of sorts, pumping his life with excitement. His feelings for Riley are the opposite. James wants to be steady for her, to grow in whatever direction she grows. It changes so much of what James knows about the human heart, about handing yourself over to another person. The awareness appeared like a sore throat, sobering and inconvenient, before spreading to places beyond his control.

From: "Hammir Bindal" <Hbindal@rediffmail.com>
To: "Riley Brighton" <rbrighton@gmail.com>
Subject: Invitation
Date: Tuesday, February 17, 2009 at 8:49 PM

Dear Riley,

Welcome to India—your parents tell me you're on your way. I'm writing with an invitation to Udaipur. The school for artisan children is nearly finished and I think you and James might like to see it. As we are dedicating the school to Morgan, I would love for you to give it your blessing.

I will be traveling in the coming weeks, but I hope we can arrange to meet. In any case, please come to stay as my guests at my family's hotel. I have yet to host you here, and I feel this must be remedied immediately. I imagine you both could use some peace and relaxation.

Enjoy Goa.

Yours,
Hammir

How easy it is, in a place like this, to believe you are somebody else—to ignore, then gently erase what came before. With no effort at all, the world shrinks to the one-room bungalow they've rented. Its woven walls and terra-cotta shower; its thatch roof and half a dozen geckos; the window that opens like a bamboo awning onto the graham cracker sand, the color-changing ocean. High season is over. The bungalow is cheap and they have no neighbors, no one to tell them to quiet down or share the hot water, to walk past their window and see them lying in bed in their underwear, eating masala-dusted banana chips, blowing the red powder off the sheets.

In the mornings, James goes to the lobby to call the airport and returns with flat, brown omelets speckled with chiles and the same news: the luggage-office lady is a turd, and Riley's bag remains lost. They don't care, it's all a part of the routine. Without the phone call they would not have omelets, would not sit on their small porch watching the ocean, squinting at the edge of the world. They make love like neither understood was possible, with slow, mind-shattering feeling, drained of inhibitions, learning each other's bodies until they can draw them blind. In the afternoons they fall asleep in sun-beams, wake up a little darker and go to eat in the hotel restaurant, curries with flavors that defy their appearance, chewy breads hot and crisp from the tandoor. They toggle back and forth, friends and lovers, moaning into each other's skin and then shitting on each other fondly, wondering how much fullness, how much pleasure a body can contain.

At a certain point they remember the car and James pulls on his shorts, disappears for half an hour and returns exhilarated, tells Ri-ley that he loves this country, that a man in the lobby has agreed to return the car to Mr. Manoj for twelve dollars, that Mr. Manoj says hello! When James leaves is the only time that the world stills, just long enough for Riley to imagine an existence beyond the bungalow. She thinks about Hammir, reads his email for the twentieth time; during those brief, isolated moments, she turns the knobs of the many doors of meaning behind it, all of them locked.

"What I want to know," Riley says, "is why my parents even told him." They are walking the beach in James's clothes, a nightly ritual, skipping rocks across the dark, midnight water. "They didn't want us taking this trip. And now they think we'll go see Hammir?" Riley sucks in a mouthful of air. "Do they think we're stupid?"

Riley sits in the sand and when James doesn't follow, stands there thinking out over the ocean, Riley looks up and says, "What?"

"Okay," James says, lowering himself. "I don't want to go either. I don't want to go at all. But they told Hammir that we're here, both of us. And they told him in a way that made Hammir comfortable inviting us to his hotel. Why would they do that?"

"Because my parents are *insane.*"

"Listen. That's true. But if they still wanted us to fail. If they really wanted us to fail. And you can disagree, you know them better than I do. But I don't think they'd tell Hammir at all. They don't think we have any money. They completely disapproved of this. If their goal was to get us to give up, why would they give us a free way to stay?"

Riley looks outraged. "You think we should *go?*"

James shifts closer. "What I'm saying is, imagine if we don't go. Imagine if we do what we want to do, tell them to fuck themselves. Then what happens? I just—I don't know. I think this might be an olive branch. A shitty, confusing olive branch. And as much as I don't want it, I guess what I'm saying is, what if this is it? What if there's not another one."

"Wow," Riley says. "I did not expect this from you."

"I honestly don't know why I'm saying this. I really don't want to go."

Riley tips back her head, blows a trill of air through her lips.

"My parents went," she says. "With Morgan. I guess the hotel is essentially a palace with a million staff and all that."

"Yeah." James hesitates, tries to arrange his words for a careful landing. "About that. I liked Hammir, I really did. He's cool and he's rich and I'm sure his palace is very impressive. But I guess I'm wondering," James says slowly. "Generally speaking. His relationship with your family doesn't make any sense."

"What do you mean?" Riley does not laugh the way James hoped she would.

"I mean, what's his deal? Where did he come from? Why does he like you guys so much?"

Riley nods. She shakes her head. "I don't know what you mean."

"Okay." James nods back. "See, this is what I find weird. Why will no one talk about him? Your parents. Morgan. Everyone loves him, no one wants to talk about him. Why is that?"

"We met him on the tour," Riley says, shoving her hand into the sand. "You know that. Our first trip to India, they took us to Hammir's shop. You already know this."

"That's all I know."

"There's really not much to say." She does not mean to sound so defensive. "We were bored. Hammir started dressing the travelers and we got involved. That's how the whole thing started. We put a bunch of old people in Hammir's tunics and they lost their minds."

"And Hammir just said, hey, maybe I should get into business with these strangers."

"I don't know. My parents pursued him pretty intensely. But maybe he saw a real business opportunity. And wasn't he right?" She stops, takes a minute to think. It was rare that people expected real, introspective answers to their questions, but Riley has found that James is one of them. "If I'm honest, I do think he believed in Morgan. I still suspect he paid for Parsons."

"So he *is* the investor?"

Riley is smiling, James can hear it in her voice as she tells him how, when she and Morgan were teenagers, they'd joke that they lived in Hammir's house, drove Hammir's car, ate Hammir's avocados. When Karen began getting injections, they'd called it Hammir's face. But Hammir was a joke meant just for them, an affection they nursed within the family, something that brought them strangely together. It was weird, James was right. But how could she explain that it was also normal? She thinks of Morgan, how she would not have to explain the way her parents loved Hammir, with such pure joy, it was almost filial to love him too. There are still so many things only Morgan understands, so many times Riley looks over her shoulder, looking for her. It hurts each time; slightly less each time. Then one day Riley will realize it has stopped, not the pain but the looking, because Morgan will no longer reflect her innermost life, it will just be her, and that will hurt much more.

"Okay," Riley says when it's nearly morning, when they've wound themselves up so much with talk, it's hard to find their way back down. She looks at James; their features are blunted by moonlight, flat and surreal, a strange extension of their surroundings.

Udaipur will be their pilgrimage. They will make their way to a place her sister has been, to bless a school named in her memory. If not for her parents, they'll do it for Morgan. They say her name, sit with it, and yet they do not discuss their motivation further, for fear of what they might find, here in India, sitting on the beach together.

Back in the bungalow, when James falls asleep, Riley scoots across the divide and fits herself into the curve of his abdomen. She slips her finger into the crook of his bent elbow, into the warm, yeasty crevice, and thinks it's the most intimate thing she's ever done with a man. That he doesn't even flinch.

From: "Riley Brighton" <rbrighton@gmail.com>
To: "Hammir Bindal" <Hbindal@rediffmail.com>
Subject: Re: Invitation
Date: Sunday, February 22, 2009 at 3:22 PM

Hi Hammir,

Thanks for getting in touch and sorry for the delay. We haven't been checking email, but we're safely in Goa and all is well.

Thank you also for your invitation. James and I would really like to see the school, and of course to see you. Our plan is to get a train north in a couple weeks. Is there a good time in March for us to come?

All the best,
Riley

James tells Riley he rented them something, tells her to put on her pants and come see. They walk across the sand, toward the small lobby building where, parked outside, is a red Honda motorbike.

"Hear me out," James says, standing behind it. "I'm licensed and everything. I used to have one in New York. It was a piece of shit and it kept getting knocked over, but I never had an accident. Swear to god, I'm an excellent driver, and this will make it so much easier."

Riley's grown accustomed to the smallness of her surroundings, the expanse of beach, the hotel restaurant, to washing the same pair of underwear, the same leggings and T-shirt, using her kimono as a robe as she waits for them to dry in the sun. Only recently have they realized how ridiculous it is, that she has no clothes, owns nothing of her own. Riley looks at the bike, feels a small pang of apprehension, then pulls out her ponytail and takes the helmet from James.

"If you're lying," she says, "I'll know immediately."

They bump along the dirt lane, Riley's arms slung beneath his armpits. He never asked, and so she doesn't tell him it's her first time on a motorbike. She bounces stiffly, feels the rumble of their collective weight. On the main road, smoother and wider, she begins to learn the velocity and motion. She leans with him into the turns, squeezes her ass and thighs when they accelerate. Again when they stop. Within minutes they are farther from the bungalow than she's been in over a week, and the thrill of being outside, of seeing this unfamiliar world glide by, whipping her hair, pinpricks on every inch of exposed skin, makes her want to tip back her head and howl.

They zoom beneath the jagged shade of palm trees, rush past fields being plowed by water buffalo, beautiful women in sequined saris carrying unimaginable things on their heads: gallons of liquids, kitchen cauldrons, massive bundles of vegetables they steady with upstretched arms. The buildings are small and squat; many of them lack a fourth wall and so they see shirtless men watching old TV sets on plastic stools and women picking through woven baskets and families sitting on the floor, hunched over banana leaves, fingers stained red. They pass through a town with signs entirely in Russian. For half a kilometer they ride the middle of the road because a herd of meandering, emaciated cows has overtaken the left. They point at everything. Oh my god. Holy shit. Look. Look. Look.

After twenty minutes, when Riley's face is numb from reacting, they slow in front of a big, open-air market and park among a mess of bikes. The market sprawls in endless rows, packed with stuff, everywhere piles of things to buy, and it's exciting, walking through these stalls of shoes and shirts and pants and bags and seeing everything that Riley needs. But together the stalls create a mirage, and when they look closer, item by item, the articles, stylistically at least, fall into two distinct categories: Indian, and Free Spirit Vacationer. The shirts are mostly glorified bandanas that tie closed, shredded with tassels. The dresses are long and New Agey, with psychedelic patterns and handkerchief hems. The shorts are tie-dyed. The jackets have mandalas. Riley feels something lodge at the top of her chest, in the place her throat meets her lungs. Beside her, James is making his cracks, pointing at ugly clothes that "look like her," but Riley doesn't respond. Just being here, among these things, knocks her back into her adolescence. It makes her feel like an absolute asshole. *Who*, Riley thinks, *is the real embarrassment here?* The tourists buying aspirational vacation attire, to wear and discard when they return to their lives, or the girl who's spent such tremendous energy feeling superior to her parents, then following exactly in their footsteps? That Riley must replace her things here, not just at this market but in this country, is a humiliation that stirs up the packed, muddy bottom of her soul.

"How about this?" James says, lifting a T-shirt with a big freaky daisy.

Later, when Riley feels the need to say something, looking down at the way she's dressed, trying so hard to be self-deprecatingly droll, James will tell her about that time in college his sister took him to the mall. He will tell her about the button-down and zip-front hoodie he bought to impress Morgan, the Macy's dressing room, the corrosive shame of standing before a mirror and hating yourself, and it will knock the air from Riley's brain because before this admission, Riley believed he had liked her in high school. She was positive there had been an attraction too complicated to acknowledge, especially now, after all they'd been through. It will be a warm piece of memory wiped forever away, this reckoning with reality she never wanted. But then—with focus, with effort—a second feeling will clamp down on the first, because what James is trying to say, what Riley will see in his eyes, in his posture, is that he knows her self-hatred in an intimate way. Yes, he's offered the wrong story. Yes, there must have been something else to make his point, but the point will be this, messy as it is clear: either she's not a fraud, or everyone is.

Now, Riley walks up to a woman selling sandals who is so flattered by Riley's question, she leads them ten minutes away to a shop by the road. She points to things on the wall, asks the shopkeeper to take them down, giving Riley her opinion like she's providing a professional service. With the sandals lady taking control, telling her what materials are lightest and what size she should wear, there is no opportunity to change her mind, and so Riley makes these small decisions, this over that, that over this, until she is wearing a pewter pair of big, ankle-cinched pants and a sheer lime-green tunic in a dobby weave. Without seeing herself, she can feel the change. The fabric breathes, feels like a gift after weeks in her black leggings, Morgan's T-shirt.

"Bring a mirror," the sandals lady tells the shopkeeper, who returns holding one to her chest. She stands in front of Riley, reflects her lovingly against her body, and Riley watches her face change in the mirror, that thing she hates so much, sees herself, in real time, as she is struck by her own reflection, sees something she wants to be her.

James smiles. "You look dope."

Riley does not turn away, fights against her every instinct. She lets this image cut her, so that she will not forget what it feels like, what it looks like to be uncomfortable, to contradict yourself, that it's not always ugly. For the first time in her life, Riley understands something about acquisition, about her family, about the strange alchemy of finding the right thing at the right time, and its ability to beam confidence into an anxious part of your soul. Talismans are many things. They are all the things that make you feel, for better or worse, deserving of something of which you previously felt unworthy. They make you see yourself a little differently, see yourself a little better.

Riley looks away.

Each day, James and Riley get on the motorbike and set out to find what they will. The bike becomes the force that catapults them through their days, hours swallowed by its dependable motion, adventures triggered with the turn of a key. They ride twenty kilometers south for lunch, the other direction for dinner. They drive through crumbling neighborhoods and dog-filled streets, their bike whisking them in and out, their bodies conjoined for hours. They stop at restaurants perched at the top of cliffs and built out of shacks, tumbling onto the beach. They eat Goan fish curry with pickled mango, chicken *xacuti* with roti and curd. They discover, each day, how closely their palates align. Deeply savory but partial to sour, sensitive to cinnamon. Some nights they're able to talk about Morgan, just a little, what she would like, what she would hate. They wait to get sick of each other, to feel the discomfort of too much time, no reason to be there, a sister who's meant to be there instead. Slowly, they forget what they are waiting for.

From: "Hammir Bindal" <Hbindal@rediffmail.com>
To: "Riley Brighton" <rbrighton@gmail.com>
Subject: Re: Invitation
Date: Monday, February 23, 2009 at 1:27 PM

Riley, in all your parents' time in India, I don't think they once took the train. I confess it's been some time for me as well, and it makes me happy that you will be seeing my country in this way. You are a braver traveler than all of us.

A friend recommends the overnight train called Konkan Kanya Express. You will be the most comfortable, I think, in First Class AC.

Visit any time in March. I will be in and out throughout the month, but I encourage you to come whenever you like. Just let me know and I will make the hotel arrangements.

Goa can be a hard place to leave. I hope you will.

Yours,
Hammir

Inside the travel agency, a roadside office the size of a bedroom, a woman at a desk surrounded by dogs shakes her head, tells them first-class trains to Mumbai are booked out for weeks. She uses the word *impossible* many times.

"Why not take a bus?" She hands them a card. "A luxury liner with reclining seats."

The following day, a luxury liner with reclining seats tips while rounding a corner, tumbles into a ravine, and kills eleven Russian tourists as they jolt from sleep. James and Riley see the newspaper at breakfast, the bus's nose smashed into the valley, doors flung open, glass everywhere, and a familiar trickle runs down their spines.

They've almost forgotten this feeling, which returns with knife-like precision, slitting them from head to heart. Back on the bike, they creep slowly through the dirt lanes, their bodies girdling so many pounds of liquid and tissue, to tell the travel agent they must find a way onto the train. Yes, the train derails regularly. It flies off the tracks almost every month, kills hundreds of people every year, they know this well. But they've seen the bus crash, have not seen the train crash. Hammir is proud they are taking the train. The train makes them braver travelers than Riley's parents, than Hammir himself, and fear requires so little logic.

"If you must take the train," the agent says, "the only solution is for sleeper class. But I am not liking to put tourists in sleeper class."

"That would be fine." James nods too hard. He's become super-stitious; they will not take the bus.

"I must warn you." The agent speaks slowly, carefully. "There is no air-conditioning. The quarters are very small for Westerners. They do not give out linens for the beds. And I think you will have to hold your functions for some time."

Confused, Riley looks at James, who mouths the word *toilets*. There is such hopefulness on his face, it makes Riley want to be the hero. The agent pushes her glasses up her nose, checks to see if she has scared them.

"We can hold our functions." Riley nods. "And the bed will be fine. We're not that big."

The woman examines them. "It's true," she says. "You both are very small."

James frowns and Riley suppresses her smile. She banks the burn for later, for the surprisingly vast array of situations she will find to look at James and remind him he is very small.

"Okay," the woman says. "We can try."

From: "Riley Brighton" <rbrighton@gmail.com>
To: "Hammir Bindal" <Hbindal@rediffmail.com>
Subject: Re: Invitation
Date: Monday, March 2, 2009 at 7:03 PM

Dear Hammir,

That's great. We got last-minute tickets to Mumbai. We'll come to Udaipur from there, and I'll send the details as soon as I have them.

Thanks for everything and see you soon.

Riley

TRAIN

They do not expect to be the only foreigners.

On the dusty platform, they wait beside men in jeans and collared shirts and their wives, in saris and gold, their thick hair braided down their backs. The train pulls in slowly, puffing low and steady down the track, and when it stops, everyone picks up their belongings and begins to shuffle toward their class assignment, walking forward to the upper classes or backward, like James and Riley, to the cars with SLEEPER stenciled across their flanks and short, square windows filled with horizontal bars and no glass. They find their names on a piece of paper taped to the outside of a middle car and climb aboard into the dull metal interior that is so grim and worn, with its barred windows and clean-scrubbed rust, it takes a minute to remember that they chose this option themselves, against the advice of the travel agent.

A long corridor runs down the middle of the car, dividing it in two sections. On the larger side is a row of compartments, each with two benches that face each other, no more than two feet apart, meant to seat, then sleep six passengers. The bench will double as the lowest bed, and as Riley and James look up the compartment wall, they see two more berths chained flat above the benches, later to be released as beds. The smell is metal and something stale, like a damp towel in an airless room. The seats are vinyl, the main walls a patchwork mishmash of silver and plastic panels. Where the seams meet, there are gullies of dirt and grease and mold. Humidity has made the fungus bloom. Their seat assignment is on the smaller, opposite side of the corridor, where two single seats face each other. The travel agent insisted they wait for these seats; they praise her now. They shove their bags beneath the chairs, locking them to the metal legs as she advised, and sit with their feet propped on what sticks out.

"Well," James says, nodding around him. "This is nice."

Riley adjusts herself. "It's not so bad."

Across the way passengers fill in the large compartment, sliding along the benches, and when everyone is sufficiently arranged and the chaos stills, they look across the corridor and see James, whom they stare at with big and candid interest.

James smiles at his onlookers, looks away, smiles again when he finds they're still staring. He does this half a dozen times, gazing off into random corners of the train, when the politeness barrier breaks.

Where is James from? Where is James going? What does James do? Is New York very cold? Very expensive? Full of movie stars?

Is everyone in America rich? Is James rich? Has he been to Miami? Does he like Miami?

When James answers, the passengers lean toward him. They listen as if in school, with diligent faces, duty bound to hear what the American says. No one is interested in Riley because, she will learn later, they confused her for one of their own. Riley has no beard, no white face, no Nike Airs or silver watch on a hairy wrist. In her kurta pajama, she is unremarkable, and as the train pulls out and gathers speed, she looks out the window and feels the warm, early evening air sweep across her face. She closes her eyes, hears James hamming for his audience, telling them about the time he saw Sean Connery at Dean & Deluca—*it's like a shop for fruit and expensive groceries, it's supposed to be Italian, oh, no, not Sean Connery, he's not Italian, I saw him in the Italian shop, in New York.* She tips her head back and feels thankful for this talent of hers, for once, her cloak of invisibility.

The train chugs along small, murky bodies of water and sprawling fields, fertile and barren; shacks along the track are pieced together with metal siding and corrugated plastic; half-dressed children run in and out; and in the distance, on an expanse of tilled land, a cement mansion all alone, wavering in the smoky air like a mirage.

With each stop, more passengers board. Even when the seats are full, they board and stand in the vestibule, or the corridor, or they perch on the edge of one of the benches, adding a fourth or fifth body to what's meant for three. The questions continue (Does James know *Magnum, P.I.*? Would James like to see a picture of the potbellied man's daughter?), but his fame is diminished in the swelling commotion. At the stations they gather wallahs who call out their offerings in soaring, looping chants. *Chai, chai, chai, garam chai,* like a theremin, the chai wallah hauling his silver teapot and a sleeve of paper cups. *Samosa! Cheese sandweech! Cutlet sandweech! Finger chips! Chicken loleepop! Mix fruit! Spring roll! Roti! Cold dreengs, cold dreengs!* A fat man swings a hot-water dispenser filled with tomato soup. A woman with a baby slung across her chest balances a stick weighed down with bagged lassi, dangling like pods from a tree. A cart rumbles down the aisle, pushing passengers into the compartments as the soda man performs the serving of glass-bottled beverages: the big fizzy rupture, the clink of the metal cap hitting the ground.

Riley lets her eyes drown in the moving spectacle, this supernatural cavalcade. What about the wailing old woman, a jewel sprouting from her forehead, is of this world? What part of this patched-up cylinder of tin and plastic and glue, a network that kills thousands of people every year, in which they are supposed to eat and sleep, is not insane? The feeling makes her itchy, a madcap energy she wants to amplify and capture and bottle and drink. She stands up, tells James she's going to the bathroom, closes herself into the phone-booth-size stall, and squats and pees down the metal hole. It smells acrid and rank and she does not care, which makes her feel invincible.

"Could be worse," she says, sitting down, offering the hand sanitizer. "I say we eat."

James looks at her, feels the shift in her intensity. He's come to enjoy this about her, this penchant to flex in the most impractical situations. Morgan's funeral. Moving the Chanels. Now, speeding north on this train, she has visited the toilets and decided she's hungry. James leans across the corridor and asks his new friends, a young husband and wife, what's good to eat, and immediately samosas are passed across the divide, cradled in oil-stained paper, then a metal plate of homemade pakora, a handful of spiced peanuts. When a good wallah comes through, the woman buys her and her husband a veggie cutlet or a crunchy packet of dal, then sends the vendor to James and Riley. Buying these foreign snacks, for the local price, under the tutelage of their neighbors—it overjoys them. They spread the collection across their laps, these miniature foods wrapped in newspapers and cradled in napkins, fried in someone's home, mixed by a wife's practiced hands. Morgan would never do this. It occurs to Riley as she watches James lick his fingers, then tip the last of the peanut dust into his mouth, his beard glittery with crumbs.

"Don't look at me like that," he says, wiping at his face.

"It's like you've never eaten before."

"It's so *good*," he says, with power, with passion, and it's true. The fleeting bites from these one-man restaurants taste like family, like intimacy. The Indian countryside rushing by, the wind sailing in and out, it all feels a bit like theater. Half an hour later, a uniformed man comes to take dinner orders—a choice of biryani or fried rice—and Riley asks for one of each.

"Dhanyavaad," she says, a word from the internet she has never uttered before this moment. The waiter marks his pad, carries on, and Riley is deeply moved by how unremarkable he finds her Hindi.

When the dinners arrive in their foil containers, everyone eats, heads down, plastic forks shoveling into open mouths, hundreds of oiled grains falling to the ground, smashed by feet. Within minutes, some people have finished. They fold their utensils into the foil and neatly, swiftly, push the package through the metal bars and out the windows. At the next station, the dishes spill along the railroad track, glinting softly against the moon.

The world outside slips into darkness. Fluorescent lights come on overhead and the compartment begins their nighttime routines. Women with saris to the floor disappear into the toilet stall. A man stands shaving at the sink, a boy beside him brushing his teeth. The berths are unhooked and their owners climb barefoot up the foothold-less ladders. There is unbelievable cooperation, an elaborate choreography of strangers dividing up inadequate space. A grandmother is given the bottom berth on which to lie down, and the young couple shifts to the top, where they sit crouched, peeling oranges and later, fall asleep spooned on the narrow width, ten feet in the air. The man who likes *Magnum, P.I.* sleeps across from them, and below, three boys sit up playing cards, then four, then six.

James and Riley sit in their chairs, both listening to the playlist that has grown big and surprising as they collected songs from the country's ubiquitous speakers, Atif Aslam and David Guetta, Empire of the Sun and Labh Janjua and Panjabi MC. They have faded into the dim, rustling landscape when an hour later it hits them like a missile, startling them from the lull of their headphones. With each opening of the toilet door, the deep, fecal smack of human waste sails through the car, and Riley and James snap from their thoughts, look up and lock eyes. A collective stubbornness keeps their headphones in, their eyes moving away. They play a game of chicken, competing for who is most undisturbed, who can feign the most oblivion in the heady, atmospheric shift caused by four dozen humans, four dozen dinners, one shaky target of a toilet.

Riley lowers her nose to her shirt to breathe, and below her, on the floor, she sees a young boy on his belly pulling himself with his arms, one of which holds a short-handled broom. He is sweeping the aisle and below the berths, collecting a growing pile of rice and hair and wrappers. Attached to his broom is a cloth hat with a handful of coins. He has no legs, she realizes suddenly. He is on the floor because he cannot walk. Across from her, James fumbles through his pants, scoops out his coins, and drops them into the hat. When the boy continues to the next compartment, Riley and James are left with a strange buzzing on their hearts, a thousand knee-jerk reactions held steadily away, a million neurons synapsing at once. They take out their headphones, remove a stimulus from the growing list. Riley opens her mouth and a man enters the car selling desserts, jellies rattling in a crate as he drawls, absurdly, *sweet leymooon puuudding*, and they break into a strange laugh, a sound that releases a small gust of steam, a temporary relief.

"It feels like," James says, thinking, "like I know what the devil's asshole smells like."

"I have to pee so badly." Riley presses her lips together, eyeing the door at the end of the car. "I'm worried, James. I was arrogant about my functions."

James adjusts himself. "You were so convincing."

The lights stay on all night. Riley lies on the top bunk, across the vinyl pad, trying to avert her gaze from the moldy panels above her head. She fills her mind with ambient noise, gathers static to overrun the emotions jostling up front. She does not have to pee. Her skin does not feel moist and sticky and covered in rash. She is unaffected by the bare feet dangling in the aisle, dozens of cracked and blistered pairs hanging off the ends of beds. Her mind is busy, processing her feelings, again and again until they've been sufficiently blunted. The ceiling overhead is just a ceiling. The smell flattens to merely bad. Each minute she puts between impact and reality, a distance that grows with quiet but incredible force, she can't help but marvel at this power she holds. The mind will adjust. The body will harden.

When a small shadow crawls across the ceiling, Riley flinches only internally. She glares at the cockroach like, Nice try, fuck off. Then she sits up, feels her bladder shift like a waterbed that's been violently overturned, and climbs down the ladder. James sits up in his bed and they look at each other for a moment, know what this means.

The metal door taps against its rusted frame, clicking with the motion of the train. Riley pushes it open and takes in the narrow stall, not wide enough to spread her arms. On the floor there is the metal platform she used earlier, with two raised ovals shaped like feet, and the hole that opens to the whooshing tracks below. But now the footholds and everything around them are slicked in a layer of cloudy mustard, liquids quivering. She steps in, holding her breath, spreads her feet on the footholds and latches the door.

A pipe runs vertically, from floor to ceiling, freckled black with oxidation, which Riley clutches for balance as the train bounces her softly. With her free hand she lowers her pants and squats, breathes accidentally through her mouth and tastes feces cut with warm air, rushing up through the hole. She pees. She pees far longer than she wants to, clenches her asshole so as not to accidentally shit but finds that she must, feels her stomach drop from under her, the sudden, violent relief. She wipes with the tissue in her pocket, pulls up her pants, and pushes through the door, panting quietly in the open vestibule. She shakes like a dog that's come out of the rain and feels the particles pulled into the wind.

On her return, she gives James a look that tells him everything, the quiet of the cabin forcing this telepathy that grows stronger each day they spend side by side, making decisions before an audience, attuning themselves to the other's body language. James smiles, reaches out a fist for a silent bump.

Riley thinks there is a threshold of filth, a level of tolerance, that, once passed, with time, grows gradually comfortable. She sits on her bed now, running an antibacterial wipe over her hands and across the soles of her sandals, folding it into quarters and wiping the fresh parts on her neck and behind her ears because who cares? Around her, everyone sleeps: a man flat on his back, belly high and round like he's carrying a girl, snores wet and jagged. Riley removes her shoes. She settles into her berth and closes her eyes with the sudden confidence that she will sleep.

By six o'clock everyone's awake. When Riley crawls down from her bed, James scoots over, and she fits herself into the narrow space. James looks beaten. His beard clings unevenly to his cheeks, his skin greasy, his eyes bloodshot.

"How'd you sleep?" he asks, his voice clogged from inactivity.

Riley goes slack against him, exhausted. The two of them slump into each other, the rattling soothing against two bodies, squinting into the early light. The train feels different in the morning; the smell is yeasty and the air is brisk. When breakfast comes through an hour later—omelets and chai and boxes of Milo—neither of them has any appetite.

They turn their bunks back into chairs, sit up at the window for the final stretch, and watch as the train loses speed, as the area surrounding the tracks creeps in closer and denser. The sky is the color of murky dishwater. James and Riley keep mostly quiet as beyond the metal bars, homes appear. The makeshift houses are built into one another, stacked like decrepit Legos, walls made of particleboard and metal siding and tarps. Laundry hangs from every corner and every eave. They are so close, barely five feet away, separated only by a sea of plastic bottles and trash.

From this distance they can see what's inside as well. A man washes himself with a bucket and hose, naked except for an orange cloth around his waist. A gourd-shaped woman squats over a cooking fire, frying something in oil that smells fishy and burnt. There are people everywhere, children and babies and elderly, eyeing the train, mirroring their curiosity. James feels like a trespasser, spying on these families in their intimate routines. But everyone stares. He has found, in this country, there is almost no expectation of privacy. He is not rich, he told the passengers across the way. He wants to take it back now, tell them he lied.

Riley sits across from him, sucking in the disarming feeling: lives on temporary display, strangers passing in the early morning. She thinks of how the train advances across this neighborhood, first class in their sealed-up compartments, then second class still ensconced in glass, then the rest of them, trailing behind in their legion of cars, eyes and fingers behind metal bars. At what point, she asks herself, is a person entitled to feel badly for themselves? Who gets to judge? What are the criteria for comparing heartbreak? A girl squats at the edge of the tracks, about Riley's age, sorting the trash with an infant daughter. She looks up to the sound of the train and smiles, takes her daughter's little arm and waves it in the air as if surprised by a parade.

Riley takes a deep breath. The air smells like burning plastic.

The train is crawling now, pulling car by car into a station that's under construction. The concrete platform is in shambles, as if dug up by jackhammers. Lined up across the rubble surface are what appear to be dozens of burlap sacks. As James and Riley stare, one of them moves—turns and coughs, a human body stretching inside— and something newly hardened keeps them still.

MUMBAI

They cannot pause, even for a minute, on the streets of Mumbai without someone approaching to ask for money or offer a tour or a shop or a ride. Getting anywhere proves nearly impossible. Everyone asks where they are going—calls to them from across the street, from in their cars, from behind their desks—and at first, they nod in friendly acknowledgment, say nothing, and then, when pushed, mumble their destination, careful not to break their stride. But invariably this does not end well. A response to the calls is an invitation, they realize, for the touts to cross the street, to catch up and tell them that some aspect of their plan is deeply flawed. A second man will cross the street then, too, correcting the information of the first. A third man will scold the other two, appearing as if from a secret portal. He will offer them a ride for a good price, a *very* special price, and the first two men will hear the number and encourage them to take the deal. They will not get a better price than this! Eventually, Riley follows James into the third man's auto-rickshaw, but instead of the Gateway of India, they will be taken in the opposite direction, to a shop selling suits. The driver, suddenly flustered, will refuse to take them onward until they go inside. He will plead and James will argue until finally, ten minutes later, they are forced into the suit store, where they must thwart the determined entreaties of the suit salesmen. At long last, at the Gateway of India, a man will try to sell them VIP tickets to Elephanta Island. Someone will tell them the tickets have sold out. The caves are closed. The safest boat has been set on fire. It's a national holiday, didn't they know? They must pay a fee to enter this area.

Riley has been to this city four times before, has spent months in what she thinks of as Mumbai, and yet the way she feels being here now challenges yet another volume of memory. Had she really accused her parents of boring her? The city is relentless, not just the call of touts and the hot, startling odors, but visually it has begun to infect her. She'll find herself eating a piece of fruit, still thinking about the man she saw an hour before, his body covered in golf ball–shaped boils, lying across a piece of cardboard. At night, just before she falls asleep, she'll hear a sitar, see the man in the busy intersection plucking his strings, the scarring around his eyes, the empty sockets. Since they arrived in Mumbai, their central activity has devolved, day by day, to simply going outside, looking around, trying to see how long they can last. But outside, Riley's mind has begun to betray her. Her eye follows a slender form lowering herself into a car. A honey-haired woman in a café window. She sees her sister against the city's uncontrollable chaos and wants to yell to her, to shield her from the danger she now sees everywhere. *Bored*, she thinks again and again. Had she really been so arrogant? Riley remembers lecturing her parents and Morgan, telling them to loosen up, that their fear of walking down the streets was completely ridiculous, unsubstantiated. What were they afraid of, she remembers asking them, closed up in their glass-walled hotel: seeing something *real*?

Back in this city, plagued by memories; day by day, Riley grows defensive.

From their guesthouse window, Riley watches the hordes of revelers on the street below, throwing handfuls of neon powder at one another. She knows James isn't there, but still she looks for him. It's been two hours since they had their fight, when Riley said she wasn't feeling well, that her throat was sore and she wasn't up for going outside, and James had stepped from the tiny bathroom and looked at her in disbelief. But it was Holi! James stood there, waiting for her to take it back, and in his reaction Riley saw something that flustered her instantly: James thought she was faking her sickness. And so Riley had to make him believe. She had to accuse him of being insensitive, of making her feel shitty by prioritizing a big stupid holiday over her physical well-being. But he wasn't making her feel shitty; he just thought she'd regret missing out! And maybe she would! But he couldn't guilt her into feeling better—Riley coughed, forced herself to cough—that's not how human anatomy worked! Fighting with James, feeling herself turn small and petty, made Riley feel even smaller and even pettier, and at a certain point she put her face in her hands and yelled at him to go enjoy himself. Really—she looked up, anger contorting her face—go outside and have fun, I mean it! From the window she watched him exit the guesthouse and walk down the street, hands in his pockets as he made his way through the euphoric, color-stained bodies clogging the walkways. She watched him turn a corner, disappear, and an apology pushed desperately to the top of her throat.

Two hours later, Riley's still at the window. She's thinking about

Morgan. She's thinking about how she's meant to be here, not with James but with Morgan. For the first time she lets this reality sink in. She prays, still at the window, that her sister understands what she has done.

Tomorrow they leave for Udaipur.

UDAIPUR

The driver is surprised by the name of the hotel. He's an animated man, easily surprised. He repeats the name to be sure, gets out of his auto-rickshaw to make James and Riley understand it is a very nice hotel, a very *expensive* hotel.

"A friend invited us to stay," James explains. "It's his family's hotel."

The driver nods obligingly. "Bindal family," he says.

"Yes." Riley nods, glancing sideways at James.

"Very good." The driver gestures for them to sit. "Welcome, special Bindal friends."

Backpacks balanced on their knees, heads peeking out the sides, they putter away from the train station, vehicles and motorbikes speeding past, the breeze whipping through the open rickshaw as the city reveals itself, street by street, first with shredded electrical wires and sprays of black mold, then tin-roof bazaars strung up with lanterns and elephants painted up the walls, then schoolgirls walking in blue-skirted packs, stray dogs nipping behind, and big colorful signs on white havelis with laundry swinging on the roofs and men in pastel tunics, eyes behind sunglasses, frothy beards, zipping by on vintage bikes. They cross the water, over an arched bridge, and the Udaipur of their imagination appears, tucked between the onyx lake and the chain of ravaged mountains, everywhere towers, spires, cupolas, gateways. The city is a decrepit stunner, a somber, whimsical beauty. They wind their way past restaurants and temples, until the streets grow clean and manicured, the buildings larger and farther apart, and pull into the porte cochere of a lemon meringue palace with two silver Mercedes parked in the shade, an Audi, an Aston Martin, and no other rickshaws. With the engine idling, they crawl out and pay the driver his eighty rupees. He's smiling now, amused by the sight of them before this palace hotel, their backpacks and sneakers, his beard, her bun and glasses, their genuine, escalating disbelief.

Inside, entering through a grand archway, they step into a room lined with gold-framed oil paintings, each a four-foot portrait of a mustached man sitting on a throne or leaning on a jeweled cane. The walls are painted in bright reds and mint greens, with delicate hand-drawn flowers that swirl around the portraits. The checkered floor is blindingly waxed, the ceiling dripping with chandeliers. They are greeted by a uniformed staff of six, one of whom drapes a white flower garland around each of their necks; another serves them a glass of ice-cold juice from a silver tray. It is disorienting, after Mumbai, this perfect onslaught of formality. It makes them feel like children, like wartime children sent to stay with a rich relative they barely know. They introduce themselves as guests of Hammir. Of course, the pretty receptionist says, the friends of Hammir! She calls over a shrunken man in a bellhop uniform to take their backpacks ahead to their suite. The receptionist refers to the old man as a boy, their room as a suite. James and Riley stand in their garlands, sipping their juice. What an incredible hotel, Riley says, and the receptionist agrees. Construction took sixteen years.

She leads them in and out of a gold elevator and down a hallway wrapped in twelve-foot frescos. When she opens the door of their room, it is indeed a suite—easily two thousand square feet—an entrance chamber connected to a sitting room, opening to a bedroom they could lead horses through, with a walk-in closet and a cavernous bathroom seemingly carved from a slab of marble. There is not a single unpainted wall. Murals of bright blue Rama and his golden bow are trimmed with swirling foliage; Mewari horses ride across the ceiling; tigers chase elephants; vines crawl up pillars. It's a Rajasthani Sistine Chapel, a miniature Mewari Michelangelo. From their height and vantage, they can see rivers and hills, the tops of the city's whitewashed buildings.

"Who will stay in this room?" The receptionist holds the key in her hand, and Riley and James return briefly to reality. "The second room is just next door."

When the receptionist leaves, they open the door between their rooms and careen through the space, calling to each other and waving from its endless nooks and altitudes, popping out from curtains and behind wardrobes, sitting fully clothed in the jetted tub, balancing along the window seats. They are filled with the frenzied desire to use everything, to soak in the warmth of luxury because soon the war will be over and they will be sent back to where they belong. They lie starfished across the dozens of floor pillows, drinking in the sun like champagne.

Dressed in their swimsuits, they take the elevator to the top and find themselves the only guests on the palatial roof, an expanse of bright and marble, dotted with little pavilions topped with domes like dollops of cream. The staff knows who they are. They place chilled flutes of beer at the water's edge as they swim, gliding through the crisp emerald water, the glasses topped off and effervescing each time they return to shore.

James watches Riley beneath the water, his eye drawn to her glistening back, her tanned shoulders. He's barely thought about sex since Goa, and James feels the desire flood back in, after so many days away, feels enough space in his mind to roam frivolously again. He feels nearly drugged, swimming atop the lemon meringue palace. He floats on his back and closes his eyes, feels the sun blasting him with vitamins, this girl he adores doing handstands beside him. Tomorrow, when Hammir arrives, they will put on their sadder selves, the ones they tried so hard to leave in New York, in that basement. They will bring those people out again, confront their reality. But today, which takes James entirely by surprise, he feels wiped clean. He feels thankful to Hammir, for this complimentary reset. Tomorrow they will see the school, pay their respects to the Morgan-shaped hole in their lives. But today no one is there to keep track of who is behaving as they should, and so they eat finger sandwiches by the side of the pool, wipe their hands on starched and ironed napkins, fall asleep in the fat-cushioned loungers and wake up in the late afternoon, their hearts warm and easy and quiet.

Riley turns on her side, shifting the soft weight of her breasts and stomach.

"How are you?" she asks, her voice low and kind.

"I'm good." James smiles. "I'm really good."

Showered and shaved, blow-dried and moisturized, dressed in clothes that feel, suddenly, like crusty misshapen sacks, they step out onto the roof for dinner and pause in the soft, lambent light. In the three hours since they left, the light has diffused across the walls, sunken into the delicate carvings, and the roof has become a new type of dreamscape. The shadows of long-torsoed humans and infinite pillars reach across the pearl-lit glow. They are standing by the elevator, overwhelmed, when a man greets them like dignitaries, like wealthy honeymooners, and leads them to a table under a chhatri—their own cloistered gazebo—where he inquires after their preferences. For friends of Hammir there is no menu, just a man in a bleach-bright kurta and cherry turban, insisting they try the lamb shank, the tandoori fish, getting worked up and exclaiming he will take care of everything! Just relax and enjoy, Chuni will bring the wine. He refers to himself as Chuni, affectionately in the third person, as if he is a beloved miscreant who must be scolded often and given clear instruction.

Alone, their faces lift and widen suspiciously. From his side of the tablecloth landscape, the silver and crystal terrain, James says, "Jesus."

Riley laughs. She lifts her chin and the light spreads velvet across her throat, her clavicle and her open mouth. It is challenging to see her this way, with this filter of elegance. They have lived a month in the same musty clothes, their meals scooped from vats and served hand to mouth. Before that they barely showered, sat in the basement waiting for the world to end. Now here she is, looking more like her sister than James has ever noticed. It's Morgan across the table, cheekbones and lips, making him think about all the times he sat across from her, holding a topic in his head in case the conversation lulled. He understands, in this moment, why he and Morgan invited Riley everywhere. She gave their togetherness a warm center of gravity, a place to focus.

"What?" Riley asks.

"Nothing." James shakes his head.

The wine arrives, uncorked and decanted at the table, and they raise their glasses to Chuni. Then to Hammir. Then to a country that feels like being shot from a cannon every goddamn day. A country that has delivered them relentless, resplendent nonsense.

"To nothing making any sense."

Riley takes the stem of her wineglass, extends it across the table, and smiles at the thought of her sister, sitting at this very table, drinking this Chuni-poured wine.

"And to rolling with it anyway." James lifts his glass.

The taste is cold; berries and smoke.

"Here's to doing things that make us uncomfortable."

"You're welcome," James says, nodding in acceptance.

"Oh, you're taking credit for this now?"

"You didn't want to come," James says. "So yes. I am."

Riley groans.

"Go ahead, you can say it."

"You're so annoying."

"And?"

"And you're the reason we're here. Obviously. Thank god you're so close with Hammir."

James smiles. "I can wait."

Riley rolls her eyes. "I'm happy we came. You were right. I thought it would be weird. I thought we'd hate it. What else do you want from me? You're a genius savant; I'd be completely lost without your brilliant insight."

"Perfect." James reaches to refill their wine, grinning like a dumbass, and Riley shakes her head, wrapped around a feeling she's finding impossible to reconcile. She had said it, so there it was. She feels happy. She is happy. Impossibly, confoundingly, distressingly happy to be exactly where she is right now, here with James, this man who makes her bones feel lighter smiling at her from across the table, making everything a little glittery. The feeling stings her, this nostalgia for this very moment, exactly this and exactly now, the universe tilting in a way she knows it may never tilt again. Riley is acutely, achingly present. She understands this in real time, how fucking good it feels, that it will not get better with time or remembrance.

"You look nice tonight." When she looks up, James is examining her. "By the way." Already, he is a little drunk; they both are. The sun has zapped their moisture and the alcohol slips easily into their veins, their blood absorbing the molecules happily, greedily. Never before has he looked at her like this, complimented her appearance, and it drags her focus through a sea of milk. She feels his attention on her skin, in her posture.

"What if we just told him?" As it slips from her mouth, Riley wonders what she's doing.

"What if we just told him what?"

"Hammir, I mean. What if we just told him? Wait," she says, puts down her glass. "I'm serious. What's the worst that could happen? I don't care if he tells my parents; I'd rather just be straight with him. He wanted to see us. He wants to be a part of this family? Well, here's what's happening."

"Could we," James says slowly, "tell him at the end?"

Riley looks to her left, an amused smile contained in a frustrated one.

"Okay, okay," James says. "I know what you mean."

"Do you?"

"Yes. I do. And if you want to tell him, fine, let's tell him. But more than Hammir." James looks around drunkenly. "I mean, this is grand, but fuck Hammir. When we go to that school, who we need to tell is Morgan."

Riley tilts her head, squints at him like he's messing with her. James, who does not believe in astrological forecasts or winking from the universe. The same James who has given her talks, plenty of talks dismantling the coincidences she takes as signs, Morgan's day of death in particular. Riley stares at him, tries to confirm what he is suggesting, which is that they stand in a building Morgan has never entered, a would-be school funded by rich people's doors, to tell her sister what they have done. It is the kind of esoteric gesture Riley craves but assumed he wouldn't understand. It stalls her thoughts, makes her feel like jumping across the table and squeezing his face in her hands.

Chuni arrives then, carrying a silver tray the size of a bassinet, his smile cartoonish, his teeth lit up. A boy trails behind him and runs to set up a stand, where the tray is lowered and the dishes presented one by one. Chuni waves his arms like a showboating magician forced into modesty, each reveal at once fantastic and demure. Naan glistens with butter, studded with garlic; a lamb shank sits in a pool of tomato, handle erect; blistered chicken thighs form a triangular stack, sticky with cilantro; a whole pomfret lies on a bed of foliage, rubbed orange, stuffed with shallots and mango; a silver gravy boat holds green chutney; liquid tamarind shimmers oily and crimson.

"A first course." Chuni winks, refilling their wine. "Maybe after you will be hungry."

When Chuni leaves, James digs in immediately, with a relish Riley now expects and loves, tasting with sound, remarking upon everything. Watching him, Riley puts down her fork and reaches to pinch meat from the fish and tear off lengths of fluffy, crackling naan. They eat. They eat like they are five years old, like it is their first time in a restaurant. Was there always this much pleasure in pleasure? Did things taste differently, smell differently, feel differently, depending on who else was there? Food is a lifeline for Riley, which is why she takes such pleasure in eating alone. How many people had she shared a meal with, who took a first bite and continued with their sentences, chewed through any visceral response? James is a clown. He takes it too far, mixing sauces, everything dripping in something else. But look at him. Riley drinks her wine. She listens to him talk, about a lamb shank he bought at a butcher in Harlem that he stewed all day and still tasted like hay. About the polemic of cilantro, and how tasting the flavor of soap is all genetics. Has she tried the chutney? Did she eat the fish together with the mango? Chuni writes his email address on the back of a business card. He wants a picture with the two of them, wants a postcard when they return to USA. By the end they are stupid with excess, bloated and wilting, yelling at Chuni when he brings a third bottle of wine. They laugh with the maniacal despair of people grossly over-fed. When Chuni turns his back, they fling their gulab jamun over the balcony and nearly die from their ingenuity.

Back in the room, they are too full for sex, too full even for pants. They change into their sleeping shirts and elastic shorts and lie atop the bedspread, their bodies hot and beating with wine, looking up at the Mewari horses. James, unable to lie still, tells Riley he's going to walk around the rooms, and five minutes later, when Riley hears a knock, she thinks it's James messing around, tapping a wall from the opposite side. "Cut it out," she says, "I'm dying."

Voices from across the suite, at the door, filtering through the entrance chamber, the sitting room. Riley sits up in bed and adjusts her ear to the muffled frequency. One of the voices is James's, the sound of him animated, caught off guard, and the other, she realizes suddenly, is Hammir's.

"Riley," James calls loudly. "Hammir's here."

Riley scrambles to her feet, runs to the bathroom off the back of the room and shuts the door, feels her stomach flip. "Wonderful!" she yells through it. "Be right there."

In the mirror, Riley searches herself for she doesn't know what, scanning her face for signs of betrayal or happiness or agitation. Her face is oily from dinner; she wipes a tissue beneath her eyes, fingers her hair. She looks at herself in Morgan's shirt, a faded black thing with the thin gold outline of a star, and knows that Hammir has seen much worse. Just after the accident, he'd stayed in the small hotel off Broadway for a week, maybe longer, who can remember, dropping by with pizzas and beers he handed to her bathrobed father, her nightgowned mother, Riley in her sister's clothes. Aloud, Riley tells herself to stop being an idiot.

Outside in the sitting room, Hammir stands up from his chair. He smiles at her with a loving sadness, the way everyone had the summer before.

"Riley," he says. "Look at you." He opens his arms and squeezes her warmly.

"It's so nice to be here," Riley says and feels how much she means it. Seeing Hammir, it cradles her like a familial safety net, the network of kin compelled to care when your parents have had enough. She sits next to James, on a couch opposite Hammir. "We had the most amazing day," she tells him. "This place is a dream. We swam in the pool and had a mind-blowing dinner. That garlic naan, my god, honestly, I can't even talk about it I'm so full. But Chuni is amazing. He said he's worked here for thirty-three years?"

"Mm," Hammir says, smiling faintly. "And how was everything?"

"Good," Riley says, glancing briefly at James. "Really good."

They sit in silence for a moment, then James says, "Hammir was at a skeet-shooting competition."

"Wow," Riley says. "How did it go?"

"Oh." Hammir looks up and scratches his neck. "Badly, I guess. Anyway, I don't understand this tradition. Shooting at clay and pretending they are birds. What is the point? Already there is so much violence everywhere. My family thinks it preserves a tradition. We were hunters once, centuries ago. Our ancestors went on long hunts to catch boar, riding on horseback. But now we have more food than we can eat in a month, so we do not need to hunt boars to feed our families. We do not need to shoot at clay, pretending we are hunters."

"Yeah." Riley nods. "We didn't eat any boar."

"All the time I'm thinking to myself, why destroy things that don't need to be destroyed? Why make something with the only purpose to shoot it down? Naturally no one in my family understands. They think I've gone strange. You see, I have attended this competition since I was a boy. But tell me—what is more strange? The desire to shoot a gun for no useful reason at all? Or to not have such a desire?"

They are so full, the sheer effort of being vertical makes it hard to concentrate.

"And it's not only the guns." Hammir uncrosses his arms, relaxes backward. "It's all the playacting. The performance of being men. I'm not interested in this kind of spectacle. At least not anymore." He says this firmly, as if scolding himself, before brightening with his next thought. "But tomorrow you will see the school. They painted the murals while I was away and I haven't seen them yet. We'll go tomorrow, first thing! I've already alerted the driver. Can you be ready in the morning? I don't sleep much. I can be ready first thing.

"Ah," Hammir interrupts himself. "I'm making something. I forgot to tell you. It's a kind of memorial to put up in the school. I have pictures and a few things of my own, but do you have anything with you? Anything we could add would be so wonderful." Hammir looks up, shakes his head. "I'm sorry. I'm being very rude. How are you both? Are you enjoying your time in India?"

"Yes." Riley nods. "Yes, it's been unbelievable. The train to Mumbai was wild. I didn't want to tell you until we got here, but we ended up taking sleeper class."

"Good." Hammir nods. "Very good. I'm thinking we could go straight to the school, maybe even before breakfast, to see the walls. I just want to make sure they've done them properly."

"Okay," Riley says.

"Anything you have would be great," Hammir says. "Really anything at all."

"Sure." Riley nods, wine swirling in her brain. How badly she wants to lie down.

"It turns out I am a sentimental man." Hammir leans forward in his chair. "I keep everything. My sister calls me a customs officer. She told me once— That's my shirt," he says, his eyes moving to the star on Riley's chest. "Can it be?" He leans in closer, across the table, and blinks at the shirt like a photograph of a forgotten friend. "I gave it to her. I completely forgot." He shakes his head, overcome. "We ate at the most beautiful restaurant. It had a fish tank in the wall."

For the first time since he arrived, Hammir grows quiet.

"Okay," he says, standing up.

James stands and looks at Riley, who doesn't say anything, remains in her chair.

"Pardon my interruption." Hammir looks at his hands. "I think it must be getting late."

The year Morgan graduated from high school, the year she went away to Parsons, she came home for winter break with this shirt. This shirt she wore every night to bed, this shirt that Riley saved until last, knowing it was threadbare with love, saturated with her. The same shirt Riley's been dragging around India, handwashing in sinks, inhaling to be closer to Morgan. She opens her mouth. Closes it. Feels her bottom lip, her jaw, begin to tremble. Riley stands, motioning at James to let her do this alone, and runs out behind him.

"Hammir," she calls in the hallway, his name blooming in the long empty space. He turns around but stays where he is. He lets her close the space between them, visibly distraught.

"Your shirt." Riley looks down at the star on her chest. "She slept in it every night. Did you know that?" Hammir looks like he might cry.

He shakes his head. "I don't think so. As I said, I had forgotten completely."

"Yeah." Riley's voice is shaking, gently, like an overused muscle. She breathes, doesn't know what it is she's doing. "She had it for a while."

"I really don't remember."

"I do. The rest of us were still in Oregon. She brought it home from New York."

"I guess I was in New York. On business. So we must have had dinner. I think she had a spill or something. My hotel was nearby, so that's probably how she ended up with it. I can't recall."

"It sounds as if you do recall."

232

Hammir shifts his weight. "That's what I recall."

Riley nods, feels like she might puke. But she holds herself steady. Riley can see he's tempted. She can see how badly he wants to talk, which is why she's still standing there, waiting for an answer she's not sure she wants. When she left the room, she hadn't intended for this to happen, not at all. But here they are, Hammir weighing what Riley knows, how badly he wants to speak, deciding how much he will say.

"She told me everything," Riley says, and the way she delivers it, it's as much a statement of fact as of disbelief. The sentence astonishes her, to realize that it isn't true.

Hammir cries then. A glassiness overwhelms his eyes and he lowers his head, shoves his sleeves into his face. The sight of him weeping beneath the chandeliers—his hunched silhouette against his family's ancient murals—soaks Riley in regret, then insanity.

"I barely got to say goodbye." As he cries, Hammir looks too big in his body, like a boy halfway through puberty, his balled fists and long arms stripping him of authority. "If I had known, I would have—"

"Hammir." Riley cuts him off, suddenly no longer willing to watch him cry, a strange, sickening feeling wrapping her heart. "What did you do?"

Hammir stops, looks like he's about to have a stroke.

"Holy shit," Riley whispers. "What did you do?"

"What?" Hammir is taken aback. "Riley, no. I didn't do anything! I *loved* her. I was in love with her, yes! But she was the one who did everything to me. She was the one who wouldn't stop. I tried to end it, a thousand times. Even the last time, after the gala, she just showed up at my hotel!" Hammir yanks at his beard. "Riley, I know it was bad. I know it was wrong. But it was like a disease, do you understand? I was sick about it." Hammir looks at her, pale and miserable. He shakes his head. "I'm sorry, Riley. I didn't mean to upset you."

"After the *gala*?" Riley drags a brick of air into her lungs, fights the urge to slam her fists into the wall. It floors her, cuts her in two, how absolutely wrong this makes her.

"I loved her."

Riley's hands go up, silencing him. She can't take any more.

She stands there a minute, dumbstruck and speechless, feels a vital string cut between her and her sister. Riley closes her eyes, unable to look at him, and feels that string drop her into a pit of her own.

"You're wrong." Riley looks at him, teeth shaking as she stares him down. "Don't you dare tell yourself you loved her, you fucking coward."

She turns around and walks back to the room, hands in her hair, where James looks as alarmed as she feels and has already begun to pack their things.

TEMPLE

Twelve hours later, it's pouring rain and velvet black. Just outside the Ajmer train station, the only light comes off the sparse street stalls, bulbs dampened beneath plastic sheets that shield them from the downpour. A group of men swarm the covered area by the train station exit, where all the passengers have congregated, yelling numbers over other numbers until a deal is struck and a small group, including James and Riley, pile into the back of a damp SUV. By the time they get to Pushkar, Riley can feel her organs on her skin: heart, lungs, stomach. Everything inside out. They check into a guesthouse, tell each other to get some sleep. Riley waits for the shift in James's breathing and slips quietly out.

In the morning James wakes to a smoky desert, squinting out the window before turning to Riley's empty side. He stares at it a moment, still waking up. The bathroom door is open, the room vacant. When he steps outside there is nothing but light. Her backpack is gone; sneakers too. James stands in his boxers, barefoot on the ceramic floor, unsure of what he's supposed to do.

At the reception desk, they haven't seen her. The morning attendant juggles his tasks as he assures James his friend is fine, calling harried orders to a languid team of boys before apologizing and running off himself. It's barely eight o'clock. *Where are you?* James sends this text in vain. They use their phones as alarm clocks, flashlights, music players, calculators, but never as phones, rarely as cameras. A month in India and between them, they've taken fewer than a dozen pictures, appearing in the same frame just once, separated by a blushing Chuni. For now, the lack of documentation feels principled. Later—on the nights they spend wringing out their memories for details and texture, for one another—they will feel differently.

In her headscarf, her sunglasses, Riley picks her way along the torn-up roads, sweat gathering along her hairline and beneath her backpack, but also down her chest, between her breasts, sliding into the slit of her navel.

The night before, flattened beneath the silvery universe, Riley struck a deal with the electric moon. A promise caught in the sprawling membrane of her exhaustion. If she could just find her sister, she could ask. Riley could ask how and why and when and what else— how many things had Riley missed? How many times had she looked away, blinded herself, never willing to acknowledge that her sister had demons too? The questions kept her awake all night, spiraling and morphing into something so heavy, she couldn't put it down for fear of never finding the same grip.

In the town center it happens quickly; the buildings multiply and condense and suddenly Riley must pay attention. Without James, there is a surprising anonymity to the streets. Most of the tourists are still in bed; Riley passes and the shopkeepers nod, arrange their silver and sweep their entries. She slips through, street by street, regarded then disregarded, lost and found. At first she follows her intuition: the feel of streets, the pull of turns. Then she's caught by a sound like a hundred books being blown wide open, their pages fluttering in the wind. She tracks it to a wall and follows its gradual curve. The flapping intensifies. She picks up her pace, heels kicking until she sees the massive archway to her left, with its scalloped edge, framing a frenzy of pigeons rushing beneath, stampeding across the sky. When they clear a lake appears, flat and expansive. An oasis dropped into a desert city. Already there are people bathing, bright saris blooming like jellyfish in the water. An old woman bends forward and brushes her wet hair, stark white against the mineral brown of her skin. Beside her, a cow stands watch like a lover.

A thin voice sails from a crackling speaker and a holy man climbs the steps to greet her.

Here I am, she thinks, hard into the universe, and feels tidal waves of sound coming off her body.

The legend goes that Brahma, god of creation, dropped a lotus flower and a lake appeared in the Rajasthani desert, spreading in the jagged shadow of the tall and spindly Snake Mountain. A village grew around the lake, rising from the fifty-two ghats, buildings to withstand a thousand years of pilgrimage: shops slathered in milky yellows and pinks, translucent blues, hand-painted signs advertising beads and gems and leather, then slowly chips and tahini and internet. Monkeys scale the tin roofs above and below, rose petals everywhere, trampled by feet, scenting the air. James weaves through obstruction after obstruction: children on motorbikes, stumbling hippies, packs of street goats. He stands beside a cow at a busy intersection, noses pushed into the juncture, timing their entrance.

He's not surprised by Riley's behavior, and the feeling further complicates his task. In no way does he think Riley is in trouble, or even lost, but yet here he is climbing the stairs of a dozen restaurants, hunting for her in the tourist bazaar, removing his shoes before Brahma Temple, unable to stop. Between the two of them, it's difficult to know who has the lead, who even wants it. When they left Udaipur, Riley had seemed okay, disturbed but fine. As they settled onto the seven-hour train, she told James she did not want to talk about it, and James had wrestled with all the things he wanted to say and ask. She didn't need his anxiety on hers, James told himself, waiting for her to take out her headphones and open her eyes. When she finally did, the sun half-dipped behind the mountains, she looked right past him, out the window.

Seven things to drop in the lake. The first things is a red color, give you good luck for your body self. Yellow color to drop in the lake give you good life in your family people. Third is the rice to drop in the lake and give you good food and a future life. Fourth is a sugar, one you drop in the lake, give sweet mother, father, sister, brother, friend, wife, children, life. Five is a flower for everyone is a happy and a good smile. Six is a holy ribbon, when you travel the world any problem will far away because you come to the Pushkar Lake. Last coconut for stomach food, and the women get children, the good children. Do you understand everything?

Riley nods. One after the other, she tosses the flower petals, the sugar, the coconut, into the lake below. The man ties a piece of string around her wrist.

Repeat after me.

Riley steadies herself, tries to clear her mind, but the words come at her chaotic and fast. She is deeply self-conscious mimicking his Hindi. Still, she doesn't miss a sound, tries to wrap her tongue, her heart, around this prayer with as much of herself as she can. After a few minutes, the man switches to English and instructs her to fill in his blanks.

Mother, he says, to which Riley says *Karen*.

Father, he says, and Riley says *Hank*.

Brother; no.

Sister; Morgan.

Luck, good luck, no bad luck, happy luck.

He smears red paint vertically between her eyebrows. She hears voices behind her, English voices whispering commentary, waiting their turn. *Look*, they say, *he's going to paint our forehead.* A knot hardens in her stomach. All of a sudden, she wants to take it back.

Now to give the donation for the blessing and also for the food.

The man nudges a silver plate and, startled, Riley removes a bill from her backpack.

Please. You can give more.

It takes her by surprise. She puts a second bill on his tray. The man looks up gravely, and for the first time, she sees the puka-shell necklace. She realizes he is wearing cargo shorts.

American people pay American money. For you it's not so much to give.

She asks how much he wants, feels humiliated by this question.

Some give fifty dollars, some people one hundred, two hundred. Up to you.

Morgan. How good it felt to say her name. She says it now, says it again. *Morgan!* The man raises a palm, careful now.

Twenty dollars, okay.

Morgan. She yells it like she's calling for her attention, like it's time to go.

She gets up, shaking her head or perhaps just shaking. *Morgan.* She's laughing now, walking past the gathering crowd, the sound exploding like shrapnel in her lungs. She says her sister's name, holds it against her fear like a bandage. She carries it away from this place.

He spots her then, climbing the ghat, red backpack fleeing up the stairs.

To see her there, alive and moving, is such a profound and startling relief that James drops his argument with the sadhu—the fourth man trying to hustle him toward the water—and falls silent mid-sentence, feels only joy to be in pursuit, trailing ten seconds behind, pushing through a tangle of bodies only to lose her on the other side.

It's late morning now; two-thirds of the pedestrians are tourists. The Brahmans swarm, corralling them toward their holy lake. James stands on tiptoe. He is close to yelling her name in the crowd when there she is, squatting under the shade of a canopy, leaned against a pee-stained building. Her arms are folded and pressed to her chest. James takes a step toward her, then back again. He moves closer to a nearby wall. Is she talking to herself? Riley tilts her head up, her fingers strumming listlessly on her bent knees, her bent knees bobbing softly, everything busy. If there was music, if techno blasted from ten-foot speakers and feet pounced and stomped around her, her movement might look perfectly ordinary. But seeing her like this—eleven a.m., dripping like a junkie—disarranges James entirely. He looks, he looks away. Every impulse feels somehow mistaken, every presumption entirely unfounded. But showing himself now, exposing her like this, seems to James an unforgivable intrusion.

Up. Away. Out of this alley. Away from this ungodly place. She commands her legs until finally they move, down the lane, carrying her from the throngs of people. She will not break, Riley demands of herself, because some fraud made her feel like a fool. It means nothing; she'll walk it off, laugh about it, laugh so hard she won't remember why. She looks up and squints at the mountains, bites down on her lip, and a cascade of sweat falls down her nostrils, along the sides of her mouth. The air moves like oil, drips translucent in the heat. Never before has she felt this sensation of merging with the atmosphere, being punished by it.

What was the worst thing that could happen? Hadn't it already happened? Or was it still happening, the avalanche of things unknown as ceaseless in death as it was in life?

There, in the distance—at the crown of the mountain that rises highest above the city—Riley sees the temple, tiny and white. It is far away until slowly, with each forward, impulsive step, it is not. She arrives at a set of concrete steps, tilts her head, and takes in the elevation. The magnitude surprises her, extends a challenge coupled with a promise. If she can make it to the top, there will be something for her. She doesn't name it, doesn't ask that of the universe, but she feels it with an aching certainty. A voice, a feeling, an answer tucked in the sky. She throws herself at this intuition and begins to climb.

Nine months. Long enough to conceive a baby, grow a life, produce a child. Was it long enough to become a new person herself? Since last summer, it was simpler to count the things that hadn't changed. Riley hovers just outside her body, shuffles step by step, feels her brain leaking a noxious gas. Before the accident Riley knew things about herself. But it was all relative. She knew herself only in relation to Morgan. Now, Morgan slipping from her grasp, Riley isn't sure what kind of person she is. So much of herself was lost in the crash, has been erased each day since the accident, and Riley is faced with how much this vacancy has freed her.

The concrete stairs are suddenly gone, swallowed by the mountain, replaced by steps cut from the rock face, jagged and zigzagging. Up ahead Riley spots the first other people, leans into the mountain and pushes to get a better look. Two grandmothers pick their way up the mountain, barefoot and wrapped in saris, their shrunken bodies hunched over, hands grasping from rock to rock. She is startled by the sound of hooves, turns around and sees a boy in slacks coaxing half a dozen donkeys up the slope, bags of cement hanging at their flanks. She lets them pass, looks up and locks eyes with a monkey in a spindly tree, its branches like petrified shocks of lightning. None of her senses are exempt from this onslaught. She climbs, blistering wet, circling her own throbbing mortality. She has reached an altitude that is half mirage, half lucid dream. She isn't positive where she is, if she'll even remember any of this. She muscles her focus back to the temple, fills it with color and noise. It shakes her awake.

Morgan is gone and so she and James are together. This is the unshakable foundation of her reality, what has looped largest and loudest, messiest in her heart. But now Morgan had secrets too, and it is less the secret than the act of believing, all these years, that her sister had none that makes Riley feel insane. And so she pushes herself up this mountain, ready to take her sister by the face and tell her how terrifying it feels to have her disappear like this, how angry she is to be left with this, and how sorry she is for disappearing herself, when they were alive and there were things to say, things her sister might have said if there were someone there to listen.

Morgan, she thinks. *Morgan, I'm coming! Morgan, please, don't stop talking now.*

Shanti! A man appears above her, old and lean, descending in a white lungi. His bare chest is the color and texture of jerky. *Shanti!* he cries jubilantly, shaking a walking stick as he passes Riley, down the mountain. For the first time she turns and takes in her progress, the trail extending like a sleeping dragon, running along its curved, pitched spine. In the distance, a pale cluster of roofs encircle Pushkar Lake. She marvels at how far she's come, her breath short, punching quickly in her chest. The sight emboldens her. She is nearly there.

Now Riley is using her hands. Now her fingers grip the rocks. Her body pitches forward, dividing her weight among four limbs, scaling the mountain with brutal urgency. People are gaining on her. She feels bodies behind her, can hear their voices. She fears seeing them, fears being seen; it's a superstition she has created on the spot, keeps her from turning around and looking, breaking the thrall that has carried her here. The pathway narrows and steepens, then the progression reverses: footholds, rock steps, concrete stairs. When she reaches the top she is panting and dripping wet, her vision pounding in her ears.

This is the temple of Savitri, the first wife of Brahma, a fact that Riley will never know. Here is a trick of the universe: even when it cannot be seen, there is grace, handfuls of invisible mercy, dampening the flames.

Potted plants and a garden hose. Worn pillars and whitewashed walls. Flat and open, what Riley sees looks less like a temple than the patio of a Hindu grandmother. The building is small, unremarkable in every way. As she crosses the space, her breath mirrors her steps in weight, in despair. The austerity of the place dismantles her. She blinks, twice and hard, and it occurs to her that she is exhausted, wilting, sliding from herself. She hasn't slept since Mumbai.

The goddess Savitri was Brahma's first wife. One day, they planned to meet at the bank of Pushkar Lake to perform a ritual arranged for a precise, auspicious window of time. Vishnu and Shiva were in attendance with Brahma, along with a gathering of townspeople. A wife was required for the ceremony, and the crowd grew nervous as the time approached and Savitri did not appear. At the last minute, Brahma was offered a replacement wife, a shepherdess of the untouchable caste named Gayatri. Brahma married her quickly, in the presence of the gods, and they performed the ritual without Savitri.

Riley stands before a room the size of a child's bedroom, arranged with packaged snacks and cold drinks, scanning desperately for her sister. She moves on to a room with three walls and a tree growing in the middle and tries again; a plastic broom leans against a wall, beside it an orange mop and a cardboard box of trash bags. She's running out of chances, she knows this; there is only so much stubborn faith. The last room is a mahogany color, the tiles nauseatingly polished. Three female figurines are displayed like porcelain dolls, wrapped in identical triangles of gauze with bright embroidered marigolds. Two women kneel before the figurines. Riley lowers herself behind them, closes her eyes, and hears a slow puncturing of her sanity, a whistle growing higher and louder from the part of her that knows her sister will not appear just because she needs her to. That she literally cannot. That death is a place as real and distant as where she is now, at the top of this desert mountain, praying to a god she does not know. She lowers her head to the floor, her forehead on the cold, hard tile, and closes her eyes, begging in spite of herself. *Please*, she hears, *please please please please.*

When Savitri arrived at the lake and found another woman in her place, the ceremony was over. Brahma had a second wife. Savitri was furious, cursing her husband, cursing his accomplices Vishnu and Shiva. She vanished into the hills, refusing their appeals for many days. Eventually, the wounded goddess would agree to a treaty. The people of Pushkar, the holy city, would build her a temple on the tallest mountaintop. It would tower high above Gayatri's temple, across the lake. It would be superior in every way. They promised Savitri that pilgrims would visit her first, worship her first, always before Brahma's second wife.

Nothing. Nothing comes, nothing leaves. The room smells like antiseptic and mothballs; her knees press defiantly against the floor. What is the meaning of this place? What here is meant to be sacred? Riley is dizzy, the lack of sleep, the dehydration, the blistering climb, the disorienting feeling of being exactly the same when she expected the opposite—it hits her like an open palm. What was the point? She needs to aim her madness somewhere. If there is nothing at the top, what was the fucking point? It rips at the seams of her lucidity, this feeling of being cheated by something she can't explain. It was the promise or the exertion or the profanity of it all. Of course she can't feel the weight of time, how the tide turns over and over, that within ten years, the temple will have cable cars that run between the base and the peak, packing the space like an amusement park. That soon enough, visitors will mourn the empty hovel. They will lament the holiness they have been cheated of, just as she does now, as if the concept is a guarantee, an absolute.

Riley rises to her feet and walks from the room with a body that weighs a thousand pounds. She wonders how she will find her way back. For the first time, she wants to go home; truly, she longs to be someplace she understands. Her brain buzzes with flat, dry activity, telling her to start down the mountain, to ask for help. She pushes herself slowly forward, and the grace of the universe is this: when Riley thinks of this moment—which she will, countless times throughout her years—she will remember only being drawn in by the wind. She will remember the feeling of being inflated, overinflated, barely holding herself closed as she walks to the edge of the courtyard, clutching the railing with the trembling belief that if she let go, she would be blown off and burst into a shower of latex and gas. She will remember the air in her throat, the sweeping vertigo, the wind whipping at her tangled hair. She will recall the rickety, lonely feeling of being stuck in her body, in this point in time, and when she turns around, still clutching the railing, she will remember how it feels to rupture. The pop, then the heat, caught in her throat then up to her nose, her eyes, everything flushed and leaking. She will remember the uncontrollable curl of her face when she sees him standing there, realizes it's him, hands in his pockets, body stiff against the wind. She will store this memory, this vital moment, in stinging, visceral detail, without ever knowing the folklore of this place. The ending will alter the beginning; more than anything, she will remember how it ends.

BANGKOK

The hotel is modern, a forty-three-dollar-a-night extravagance, with plush towels and robes and a small rooftop pool. Walking in, the effect is strange. It smells like lemongrass and eucalyptus; the halls are wide, the ceilings tall; staff push carts of fresh linens and bottled water. It is the perfect place to shelter them from the world, to recover from six punishing weeks in India, but when the door shuts behind them, gliding with ease, they find themselves in a new predicament. In the room with them is the new strangeness, the distant politeness. What once was small has grown monkey limbs—their minds swinging endlessly, quietly. In the time since Hammir left their room, since James chased Riley up a mountain, their fears have turned simian, making them doubtful, keeping them moving from Pushkar to New Delhi, from New Delhi to Bangkok, trying to outrun the feeling that they have not outrun anything at all.

They drop their bags, peel the shoes from their feet, and follow a clanging noise to the window. Below, two women in train conductors' hats are setting up tables and chairs, erecting a kitchen on the narrow sidewalk.

"Can I ask you something?" James says, keeping his eyes on the street, and Riley feels the relief of someone who has waited too long for a bus, who sees it coming in the distance.

She watches the women move in and out of her faint reflection. "Sure," she says.

"I've been thinking about that night at the gala. How Hammir was with me. I remember thinking even then. Why was this guy being so fucking nice? I kept catching him looking at me, smiling. And now, I guess I know. But I can't get it out of my head. He wasn't jealous. He was *nice*, which means I wasn't in his way." James pauses. "She was using me."

"Mm," Riley says, the sound vibrating through her body. She doesn't know what to do with her hands, which feel wild and slippery, like fish pulled from the ocean.

"Chances are she didn't even like me." He looks up now, squinting at Riley in the sun, so deeply vulnerable, and it pushes a long, thin nail into her chest. "She probably needed a date to the gala, right? A decoy. And I just happened to call."

Everything James is saying, Riley has thought over the last few days. But always from her perspective, never from his. Indeed, Morgan had not been straight with James, with either of them, but for Riley this meant that James was uncontested all along. What she'd won, finally won, her sister never even wanted. It meant Riley hadn't won at all; she was once again existing in an alternate reality, a construction of her own where she mistakenly believed she was the principal character, that she mattered. And now, to see James feeling the same way, searching for reassurance, still hung up on her sister, it pushes the nail into a lung, punctures something newly fragile.

"It was crazy to see Hammir like that. Kind of sad, actually. I know your sister was lonely that year, which probably makes it even worse. But my god. The look on his face. I think he must have actually loved her."

Riley rubs the hem of her shirt. "And what about you?"

"What about me?"

"Did you love her?"

It catches them both off guard, the way James hesitates, then finds himself unable to answer.

"Okay," she says. She turns to a wall, turns the other way, starts to walk to the door.

"Riley. Come on."

She looks at him, smiles as she shakes her head. "I am such a moron."

"Of all people, *Riley*. You should understand it's complicated."

"Yes, James, it's complicated. But it's also pretty fucking simple. You chose Morgan. Morgan chose Hammir. And here we are, you and your second choice."

"Riley." James blinks. "You can't actually think that."

"What am I supposed to think?" She throws up her hands, explodes from across the room. "Look at you! All you can think of is Morgan. Was she cheating on you? Was she using you? She was lying to all of us! Do you get that? Stop falling apart!"

"I'm sorry—*I'm* falling apart? Do you not remember what happened in Pushkar?"

Her outrage walks her back to him.

"Are you any different than Hammir? Are you forgetting that you were obsessed with her too? Did you forget that you gave yourself a fucking makeover? For someone who never even talked to you? You were the biggest creep of all!"

"You know what?" James says, the intensity in his voice startling her. "Fuck it, you're right. I was obsessed with her too."

Riley tilts her head back, face bulging with disbelief, feels the horrible, torrential weight of something veering irreparably off course.

"Since yearbook." James looks at her, looks away—speaks with hard, uneven momentum. "I was obsessed with her. Morgan was the girl I could never have. She was everything I wanted. All the things I hated about myself."

"Holy shit, why are you telling me this?!"

"Because I got her."

"What the fuck."

"Riley! Jesus, let me finish."

Riley crosses her arms and James takes a minute to refocus.

"Dating Morgan, it was validating, okay? Not because I loved her. Because being with her proved that I'd done it, you know? That I wasn't the same fucking loser I was in Oregon."

"Great." Riley drops her hands into fists, feels herself shaking. "What a feat."

"I was lonely, Riley. I was so depressed. And being with Morgan, it was easy to feel like someone else. I'm not an idiot. Obviously, I wasn't her *type*. Obviously, she didn't usually date guys like me. But your sister was in a weird place too. She was running from herself too, and I just hoped it wasn't as obvious to everyone else as it was to me." James frowns. "Sometimes it gets confusing, okay? We're not all like you. We can't all be totally clear on who we are or what we want."

Riley glares at him.

"Do you know why your parents hate me?"

"Yes," she says.

"Well, you don't. Because you weren't there. You left the funeral

and someone decided I should speak in your place. And I did, appar-
ently. Because according to your mother, although I don't remember
any of it, absolutely fucking zero, I talked about you for twenty
minutes."

Riley's jaw tightens, her arms rigid beside her.

"So yes, I went for Morgan first. I thought it would make me feel
good, and for a while it did. But then Morgan died and I lost *you*. Do
you understand what I'm saying? You were the one that I missed
most. *You* were the one I couldn't stop thinking about." He stares at
her, distress dripping from his veins. "Your mom asked me to keep
my distance because she knew I was in love with you."

"Bullshit," Riley says, spooked by the word *love*. James's face falls.
He punches the wall.

"Riley! Are you even *listening*?"

Riley inhales through her nose, begging herself to stop. The
temptation to say something awful is enormous: she teeters at the
edge, feels that old defensive itch to douse herself in starter fluid and
flare up in her own intensity. She thinks of her sister, of all the one-
sided victories Morgan conceded; then of her mother, how she never
learned to extinguish her rage; and Riley understands, for the first
time in her life, that if she does not try to do this now, she risks hard-
ening into this person.

"Look." Riley glares at him, part focused and part defiant, the
only way she knows how. "I've hated every boyfriend she's ever
had. Every single one. So when Morgan started dating you, it was the
only time"—Riley pauses, frustrated—"it was the only time I've ever
been jealous of her. Really and truly fucking jealous. It was the first
time I looked at her and thought, you will never understand me. She
didn't even have to try; all her life she'd gotten what she wanted and
I dealt with it. But with you, it was the first time she took something

from me." They are shocking her, every single one of these words. As she says them, she feels the excruciating liberty of releasing this information, too late and to the wrong person. "And you don't need to explain yourself. I get it. Everyone loved her. I've lived with it my entire life."

"No," James says.

"No what?"

"You missed the point."

"Don't be a dipshit. Quit while you're ahead."

"How do I say this?" James pauses, hopelessly, pulls in his lips. "Your sister was perfect," he says, but he intones the word like it's a stand-in for something else. "She was really, really perfect. She was kind and generous and fun to be around and I genuinely don't have anything bad to say about her. But for someone like me." His face creases. "For someone who's spent most of his life feeling weird and messy and not good enough for people like her. It's difficult not to resent that."

The air kicks on. The sound of traffic presses against the window. Below, the tables and chairs are filled with diners drinking beer, smoke lifting off the woks in big white plumes.

"Riley," James says and she looks up. His eyes remind her of that night he came to her parents' house, the spill of red near the iris. "You are the least perfect, most real person I have ever known, and it frightens me every day, every fucking day, how in love I am with you. It's distressing, actually. I don't know how else to explain it. The last few weeks have been mind-blowing, delirious pain because I had *no idea* this feeling existed, and now that I do, there's no going back. There's no way to forget what it's like to be with someone who slips into your brain so completely, who makes you think about everything differently, who makes you laugh a hundred times a day and doesn't take your shit, who makes you feel like the best fucking version of a self you never even knew you could be, it's *you*, Riley. You do whatever the hell you want. You don't care what anyone else thinks. You eat like a monster and you dance like a teenager, but watching you dance makes me want to dance, and eating with you makes me never want to eat without you. You're the truest friend I've ever had. You have no idea how sexy you are. You're a smartass with a smart mouth and I am so lucky to be here, to be here with you, and I'm sorry if I ever made you feel otherwise."

Riley realizes she is crying. "I care what you think," she says.

"I'm not sure you do."

"I do."

James shakes his head. "Then you hide it really well."

Riley wipes her face with her right arm.

"I shouldn't have said you were the biggest creep of all."

"Is that an apology?"

"Yes," she says. "I'm sorry I say mean things when I'm angry."

"It's okay. I was creepy in college."

When Riley laughs, the sound is clogged with snot. James wraps his arms around her and she gives in, feeling herself, the two of them, having reached the other side of the abyss.

The last six weeks, since they left New York, have felt like being jolted by a bungee cord, plummeting them deep into the crypts of their souls and then so high they felt like dying, like to die, right then and there, might not be so bad at all. The last six weeks they've been bungeed alive. More alive than they imagined real. And now, knowing what they know, understanding what they do, there's no question in their mind: everything ahead, they've earned.

· · ·

If everyone else was allowed to have secrets, why not them?

What kept them from doing the very thing they wanted most?

And if the answer was nothing, then why would they not?

In their hotel room, scheming on their white duvet, they expose a recklessness that feels revelatory. This trip is for them, a gift from the universe that will expire by the end of the year. The hourglass helps. They feel the sand shifting, their narrowing window to see and do as much as their money will allow. They have settled something between them, wrapped a tourniquet around their skittish hearts. For three days they sweat furiously on the hotel's treadmill, baptize themselves in the bright white tub. They recalibrate their silences, find that pocket of safety they almost lost.

Then they cut the cord, fall together into the void.

RUBBER BAND

Ninety-five degrees and cloudless, six o'clock in the morning, the ocean still and clean as they have ever seen, like liquid glass. The sand seeps between their toes like silt, feels almost fuzzy beneath the water. Riley stands at the shoreline, squinting in sleeping shorts and glasses, then runs back to their yurt-shaped bungalow. Five minutes later she is in the water, floating on her back, absorbed into the scenery like she's been there all her life.

On an island they must reach by cargo ferry, a young man named Bong becomes their tour guide. He wears a Kobe Bryant jersey, a thin gold chain, carries a picture of his dog. In his souped-up tricycle, Bong takes them to every pocket of the island, dropping them at isolated beaches that appear private, with locked cabanas and polished outdoor showers, giving them the names of the families whose guests they are and leaving, despite their protests, telling them to enjoy themselves. He comes back when he wishes, often hours late, smoking a cigarette, blasting hip-hop through the sparkling silence. Bong has a swagger they come to associate with his nation, flashy and macho and yet charmingly childish. He takes them snorkeling at a fish sanctuary, to a cave with a phosphorescent lake, to the newly opened Jollibee in the center of town where everyone Bong knows is gathered in the air-conditioning, Bong's basketball friends and Bong's auntie and uncle, Bong's little niece in a too-big school uniform, the guys outside leaning on tricycles who call Bong over for a cigarette, and the rest of them: girls in spandex dresses and families licking purple ice cream cones and men dark from the fields, staring up at the menu, brows rumpled with hands clasped behind their backs.

When they bathe, when they remove grit from their ears and fingernails, they feel pieces of India still clinging to their bodies. Sometimes it happens when they open their backpacks, when they pull out a shirt and the air blooms with something sentimental. How strange it feels: particles from one place deposited into another, scents that have leapt across oceans and continents, no one who can feel this transference but them and perhaps, they like to believe, the things that saw it with them. The soles of their shoes, their sunglasses, their socks, each piece of plastic and rubber a kind of confidant, a time capsule.

They stand on a sidewalk, looking up at a city smoldering in lights, clutching their backpacks like safety harnesses, pummeled by the acute, bodily alarm that comes from two months spent in the developing world, learning its logic and chaos, only to be spit out in a place like this. That the world is a place that can accommodate a city like Mumbai and a city like Tokyo. Simultaneously. It blows their fucking minds.

. . .

They zip beneath the city, looking for food at the surface. Never have they been hungrier. Even when they are not eating—not cruising convenience stores and food courts and shopping center grocery stores, gaping at sea urchins like tiny velvet livers, quivering tarts of Hokkaido cheese, bento boxes with hot dogs cut to resemble octopus and shrines to tofu, shrines to hand-cut soba and fancy cookies shaped like fish and bananas—they stop at the glass cases that line the streets, filled with plastic reenactments of conical omelets and paint-charred eels and jewel-toned sashimi on pearly grains of rice, the way someone else might enjoy cherry blossoms, or a gallery exhibit.

They are people who eat their feelings, who wake up each morning and go to bed at night thinking of what they will eat next, and having found themselves here, in this madhouse of uncharted edibles, they find one appetite ignites the other, that every day they are hungry is reason enough.

They spend their evenings with strangers, eat yakitori beside a group of businessmen who explain the parts of a chicken with their own bodies, helping with the menu. It's hard to explain how these nights develop, first with the gifting of sake, poured shot by shot from businessman to Riley, James to businessman, each of them drinking the overflow from the small wooden dish that holds the shot glass—an excess the businessmen call *omake*, a phrase they decide to take together on a tour of the Golden Gai, entering shoebox-size bars to a man on a stool playing Simon and Garfunkel on the harmonica, at each stop James or Riley leaning across the bar to say *omake kudasai* with increasing flair, confusing the bartender, who scolds the businessmen, then pours them all a little extra.

It's tremendously easy, unlike any other relationship they've had in their lives. Being together, bouncing from place to place, waking up in the middle of the night with just the faintest recollection of where they are—the presence of the other the only center of constant gravity. They aren't homesick, not at all. The repetition and thrill of finding themselves in a new place, letting the dislocation instruct and mold them, their instincts growing, their patience deepening—it's the best education of Riley's life. The truth is neither she nor James has had many friends, and they are taken by how easy it is, how enjoyable, to make them together. People enter and exit their world, making the days longer and shorter. Time is a rubber band. It's a phrase they say almost every day, a phrase that explains to them how strange it feels to be profoundly lost with nowhere to be, nothing to do but what they are doing. Five months has stretched to hold their entire world. Some days they see every stretched rib of time, feel minutes like hours, like time is being pulled to its thinnest point and they live on that infinite line. For the first five months, they are lousy with time, and then slowly, suddenly, the band begins its release, like summer to fall, making the days end before they're done, one rolling into the next, concealing that thing they know time can do.

In their Taipei hostel, they meet a Canadian on break from teaching English in South Korea, who invites them to his small country town. They trail him a week behind, arriving by bus to a sleepy industrial village, and meet his classroom of fifth graders, who call them James and Riley Teacher, like it's their last name. They eat barbecue with the teachers, then sing karaoke until well past midnight, belting and beating on tambourines before heading together to the bathhouse to sleep on the communal floor, for nine dollars, side by side in matching pajamas. Five days they spend together; two in Taipei, three in Korea, and yet they will attend the Canadian's wedding, four years later, to a girl he meets in Burma while setting up a chicken farm. He'll be exactly the same, almost exactly as they remember him—warm and playful, emotionally confessional—and it will make their lives feel off-balance somehow. Neither good nor bad, just the acute, disorienting feeling of the past blown across the future.

Everywhere they go, they dance to their own music, converse with strangers in their own language. It's disgraceful, how the entire world must learn their language, while they must learn nothing at all. But this year, at least, it is good to be American. Obama is president and the world looks at them, a young mixed-race couple mouthing the words of a Brooklyn rapper, like ambassadors of what's possible in America, the land of the rich, the impossible, the free.

Stout middle-aged Bunna takes them around Siem Reap in his tuktuk, down ancient avenues lined by thousand-year-old trees, the putter of his motor like they're being pulled behind a lawn mower. Bunna plans everything, knows everything, drops them off at ruins where there is no one but them, where they can climb and teeter, crouch in the gullies and trace engravings older than the Western world, run their fingers along columns and tombs and arcades while growing sunburnt and dehydrated and small against the universe.

They sit beneath a thatch-roofed cabana at the edge of a lake, mist suspended just above it, and talk about that experiment in elementary school, the one with a cup of water on a string that's spinning so fast no liquid escapes. James turns to Riley, says the world is such an insane place that they are literally suctioned to the planet, spinning around so fast it glues the oceans to its surface. Why should they not feel crazy? There they were, riding on a spherical vacuum moving a thousand miles an hour, trying to find meaning in their lives.

In June, Riley drinks so much that James must hold her upright as they bump along in the back of a tuk-tuk, telling her they're almost there, just a few more minutes and they'll be back. She's already puked in the bar's bathroom, been comforted by two Australian girls who rubbed her back because it's her birthday. It's her birthday; she's twenty-two. The sentence excuses all her behavior, how she's poisoned herself into ugly oblivion. Back at the hostel, Riley laughs in the elevator and then cries in the shower, in the lukewarm downpour, balled up in the tub. She can't believe it's been a year.

The world stills for nearly six weeks, in a newly built condo in a neighborhood filled with the nomads of the digital age, poking at laptops in coffee shops, trying to sell cheap crap online. They arrive in Chiang Mai heavy and tired, in need of a break from packing and moving, from the ritual of rising each day to a blank page they must design and fill themselves. In this easy, beautiful place they find equal parts wonder and plain life itself. They climb a waterfall; they get haircuts; they ride a motorbike along a sixteenth-century moat. They grow accustomed to the city, learn its roads, its foods, its greetings and numbers and temples and markets. This becomes life. Hiding out from life becomes their lives, feels very nearly lifelike. The shopping list on their fridge reads: toilet paper, rambutan.

. . .

Five thousand dollars left. They sit down with pen and paper, August sun high above the mountains, filtering through a gauze of clouds. People do this their whole lives; they see them here, previously lost, beginning to sprout roots. But roots make little sense to them. Movement, they believe, is what's given them balance, and so they press forward, tilting the viewfinder every day, tumbling the kaleidoscope of place and feeling, energized by the heat in their bones and the oxygen in their blood they won't know is missing until it's gone.

In Istanbul, they meet a street vendor selling mussels on Istiklal Avenue, who calls out to them every night as they leave their apartment, calls them over to speak English into a cell phone to his son, who lives near Cappadocia. Everywhere they go, the vendor finds them: drinking raki in alley cafés, walking in the bazaar, and feeds them so many mussels stuffed with rice, squeezing lemon on them one by one, always offended when they've had enough, that they begin to hide from the mussel vendor, taking roundabout routes in hoods and headscarves, walking quickly.

They take a picture at the top of Delphi, their tanned faces squinting into the sun, that will become an iconic image in their lives, chosen for seminal birthdays and invitations, the kind of photo you take out over and over just to marvel at when you looked like that, when you *felt* like that, to wonder where the time has gone.

In a small farmhouse, at the end of a road near Castellina, they sleep above a family's wine cellar, where unmarked bottles of Sangiovese sit in the dark, listening to Vivaldi twenty-four hours a day. When they taste the wine, piano soft, they believe—once again, for the hundredth time in an astonishing year—in something that defies explanation.

They watch the sun rise from their tiny Chinatown balcony, a baguette on the table between them, open jars of jam with knives propped sideways in their mouths. They've stayed up all night, trying to cram an impossible set of desires into the remaining hours. They walked along the Seine, ran into a carnival, rode a Ferris wheel high above the Place de la Concord. As they got hungry, they ate: a crepe, a kebab. But mostly they walked, taking in the closed-up shops and boats left to sleep, the softly lit cathedrals rawboned and exposed. The night was fully shed of summer, a new chill bringing their arms to their bodies. They walked, street after street, past menus they couldn't read outside cafés they would never eat in, walked up the small hill and crossed the street to their pension, rode the elevator in silence, turned the key in the lock and made love across the unmade bed with the gravity of people whose lives are ending, like after this, they might disappear. They lay there beating on each other's skin, in the early morning of their final day, an hour responsible for more than any hour ever should. An hour stretched to the ribs before time snaps back. They say it, as they sit on their balcony watching the sun creep slowly, then quickly, up the stone fronts of the buildings, across the windows and their white shutters, illuminating the wrought iron, the sidewalks, the unstoppable new day. Time is a rubber band.

PART FIVE

November 2009—June 2010, New York City

FEEL THE TIDE

Karen stands in a mess of boxes, overwhelmed. The sheer amount of stuff she owns makes her want to give up. Put on a coat. Walk out the door and start a new life. The temptation grows stronger with each new box she must pack and label and lift. What keeps her here? Why does she care about this shit? She packs a box, wraps her crap in newspaper that makes her hands feel powdery and her cuticles inflamed, and thinks about the meaning of life, how hard we try to manufacture purpose that we swaddle our clutter like newborn babies, making its footprint five times what it should be, so that when we move it feels consequential, the size of our accumulation representative of what we have done with our time.

In the living room, the boxes have formed a wall that reaches above the windows, a cardboard barricade that traps the light, turns what passes into thin, fractured beams. Seeing her life like this, growing beyond her control, with no sense of when it will stop, Karen is floored by each frustrating discovery: the never-been-opened water flosser, the barbells, the gallon bag of nuts and bolts, the cruddy fish tank filled with pebbles. At first, when the boxes made two neat rows, Karen would yell to Hank and tell him to deal with the fish tank he never used, the records he never played, the endless bottles of vitamins and supplements he never took. But now Karen says nothing, quietly throws it all away. In each drawer and shelf and neglected closet, what Karen finds disturbs and exhausts her, the infinite crap a reminder of her husband's long-winded failure. Most days her marriage feels like quicksand, like the more she fights it, the deeper she's swallowed. Even if she had the energy, which she does not, Karen no longer sees the point of fighting. She packs the boxes, grows resentful as quietly, as separately as possible.

They'd sold the house two months before. For not enough money. Against the advice of their real estate agent. The money had disappeared in a way Karen hadn't understood possible—that is, quickly and without warning. Seven months before, when Hank had revealed the extent of their problems in actual dollars, the quicksand made its first appearance. By then, Karen was getting dressed in the mornings, showering most days, occasionally cooking; Hammir had called to say he'd made contact with Riley, that she and James were safely in India; and Karen had begun listening to a song about a turning tide, believing it true for the first time since her daughter died. Right when Karen was beginning to accept the realities of her new existence, the stock market swallowed so much of their savings, Riley disappeared from Udaipur in the middle of the night, and Karen was drowning once again.

Kaleidoscope was not doing well. Despite her efforts, the odds were against her—a trifecta, she felt, of monstrous fortune. Without Morgan, the year's designs had fallen flat; she and Hank were barely communicating; and the recession cared not at all that her life was in shambles, that Karen needed time to figure things out. So here they were, downsizing their dreams, everything going in the wrong direction. She and Hank were moving to a two-bedroom rental. Three of seven Kaleidoscopes were slated to close. Karen pushes a stack of boxes marked "Books," cursing with effort, against the stripped-bare basement wall. She leans against the tower and takes a difficult breath, knows that she must tell Riley soon.

When Karen was a girl, her mother used to say that life was short, that if she wasn't careful, it would zoom right past. But Karen has learned that life is long. Life can feel so long—so deeply, ceaselessly long—that recently, she's had trouble piecing together the various lives she's already lived. In this life, the same one she's in now, she once had two daughters, once slept in a rental car while driving the length of California, once worked entirely with her hands. The act of moving unearths an avalanche of memories that Karen arranges any way she can to keep herself moving, lingering in the past for long, hypothetical stretches of time that lead her to a different present. Oregon is where her mind likes best. In memory, Karen gifts herself a happiness, a wholeness she can now inject from where she stands, having seen the future. They'd gone to Oregon to build something of their own. What she remembers now is hard and honest work. A grocery store they built with sweat. A small loving family that rarely fought. An uphill climb turned downhill joyride she had engineered, executed, and delivered to that family.

But since they sold the house and Karen became fixated on the past, there is one piece of the narrative that her husband insists on bringing up, over and again, which is that Karen was not happy in Oregon. She and Hank fought all the time, pressed under the restraints of being poor—or, as Hank loved to say, of pretending to be poor. Until they sold the Hawaii house, opened the vault of Karen's trust, she and Hank were miserable, too strapped to buy their daughters jeans, ready to jump on each other over the slightest hiccup, a missing glove, a broken dishwasher. It's true their lives got easier with money, when the tedium of exhaustion, of endless bickering, finally overtook Karen's pride. Hank found purpose. Morgan became a star. Riley got to go to New York. But it was Karen who had given them all this! Karen who used what she had to enlarge her family's lives, and now that it was gone, everything was being rewritten, taken away.

It was not Karen who saved them; this is what she obsesses over, her husband's shattering appraisal. They'd ridden a wave that had risen and crashed, no one's fault, no way to divvy up credit for the good and the bad. In response, Karen worked harder, to show how wrong he was, how necessary she was to keep their lives from falling off the rails. But Hank could never see what she wanted, always something else. Wake up, he'd told her, because this was his point. She'd placed her ego in the wrong place. She was protecting the wrong thing. How could she care so much about Kaleidoscope, about the *money*, when Morgan was gone and Riley was missing? She takes his point and yet she resents it. How easy it was for Hank to say, when the money had been hers, when she had watched over it so vigilantly all those years, and when she had finally loosened her grip, handed it over for Hank to invest, it was gone.

Karen walks upstairs to the kitchen, brings her laptop to the counter, and pours herself a glass of wine. When she finds it empty, she pours another. She thinks of Riley. With effort, she pushes her daughter to the front of the mess, feels herself shrink. What about Riley makes Karen feel this way? When she thinks of the time after Morgan died, before Riley left, it's all a blur. She remembers fighting, but of course there was fighting. They had to forgive themselves for that. And yet no matter how hard she tries to forgive herself, a thick, guilty fog emerges when she thinks of her daughter: Was Karen supposed to have done something differently?

She opens the email Riley sent the week before, the email announcing her return to New York, asking if she could stay until she found a job. She reads her and Hank's flushed acceptance, the sentences padded with exuberant excuses. So much about Riley demoralizes her, spreads through her body like a sedative. First it was days, then weeks, then months in which Karen had wondered what she should be doing, all the while doing nothing. The inaction became the action, the act of thinking, worrying, growing depressed, all part of the action. What else could she do? This was the question she liked to ask, the one that led reliably to nothing. She'd tried to write, received no response. Karen was up to her ears in problems of her own. If Riley didn't want to speak to her, how many times was she supposed to try?

The difficulty with Riley was that she did not need her—a fact that has cut Karen down, humbled and wounded her on a hundred occasions. All Riley's life, Karen couldn't help but feel cheated of something, of some facet of motherhood she'd assumed guaranteed. Because what was motherhood, if not a showcase of selflessness, a way to prove yourself worthy of unconditional admiration? The act of growing a human, sacrificing your body, claiming responsibility over whatever came out, for the rest of your life, willfully loving a difficult child the same as a brilliant one—it was an everlasting, mind-altering act of insanity. Was it so wrong to want this acknowledged, to be appreciated for this tremendous exertion?

With Riley, Karen has so rarely felt her worth.

Riley needed food and shelter, some scolding, a few pep talks, money, generic things, nothing that pushed against that motherly satisfaction, that wholeness of being urgently, singularly needed. Riley had never come to Karen with a real problem. Karen had never helped her daughter get over a heartbreak, never taught her something formative, never felt like a genius the way she had, all the time, with Morgan. Morgan, who spilled herself so easily, who never could see herself quite right, whose desire to be valued, to be of value, filled Karen with purpose. Morgan needed constant tending, while Riley needed practically nothing—all her life—had easily, blithely denied Karen that reverent gaze she desired. And so Karen had looked to where she could find it. She'd looked to Morgan. She'd looked to Kaleidoscope.

Karen opens her laptop and plugs in her headphones, listens to the song about the turning tide, finishes the second glass of wine.

One daughter is dead. One daughter she has distanced so immensely, they have not spoken for nearly a year. But now Riley is coming back. In one week, Riley will walk through the door from who knows where, from traveling with James, another barbed fact that Karen must swallow. Whether or not Karen is ready, Riley will soon enter this reality, see the house in its boxed upheaval—the sad state of affairs she has put off sharing.

Karen opens her email and begins to write. By the time she's finished it's nearly dark, early November, the boxes blocking the outside world. She reads the three paragraphs seven times, writing new sentences she promptly deletes, then hits the button that delivers her words to the other side of the world. She takes the wine bottle by the neck and tips it into her mouth, lets the cool, minerally liquid overtake her teeth. She has seven days to clean up her act. Now is not the time for pretending she is something she's not.

AN EERIE, PERFECT TIME MACHINE

Riley stands outside her front door, shivering in her cheap canvas coat, her too-thin jeans, the bright yellow sneakers she's worn since Japan. She tries the knob quietly, once reliably unlocked—finds it cold and stiff, which she can't help but take as a sign—then lifts her hand to ring the bell, when she hears movement on the other side, the sliding of locks, and the door opens.

Her mother looks good. Jarringly good. Her hair has grown out, falls below her shoulders like the grocery store days, and there are freckles across her nose and her cheekbones, which means she's seen the sun. Riley steps forward and hugs her, and her mother pulls her in with a warm and manic energy, disappointed and overjoyed, like Riley is four years old and has wandered away at the mall.

"Come inside," her mother says. "You must be freezing in that coat."

Though she was warned, Riley is not prepared for the baldness of the walls, the curtainless windows big and exposed, the boxes gaping with open mouths. It reminds Riley of moving in, that first New York summer, the memory offering a perfectly identical but reversed reflection. It stings her immediately, the way her sister appears absolutely everywhere.

"You didn't have to take a taxi," Riley hears as she walks into the living room. "We wanted to pick you up." She stands in the middle, her backpack still on, thankful suddenly for its familiar weight.

"Wow," Riley says.

"Yep." Her mother sighs. "Your father has a lot of crap."

Riley looks up, surprised by the tone—not the words, but the honesty. Little digs, cheap shots, vaguely bitchy asides, these were all a part of her mother's speech pattern. But this did not come off as an insult, rather the reality of a tired woman who had packed these boxes for a man who owned a lot of crap. Riley opens her mouth to say she doesn't know what, to extend something honest back, when her father comes down the stairs and Riley is surprised once again, after seeing her mother, by how beaten he looks, his drooping jowl, his shaggy hair too thin to wear the way he always has. It pains her to see his big theatrics, his waving arms. "There she is!" He leans down to scoop her toward him. "Take off that backpack! Oh my god. Did you bring back all of India?" He drops her backpack to the floor, leaving it exactly where it falls, and guides Riley to the kitchen table, where he fills the air with questions. Her mother follows, listening as she busies herself at the stove.

"Paris, huh?" Hank whistles and Riley laughs, unexpectedly, because her father is exactly the same, despite everything, still ready to whistle at the word *Paris* like some kind of townie, sitting in his multimillion-dollar home.

"Paris." Riley nods and it's astounding. A bodily sensation, the way she's falling backward in time. "I ate so much cheese I had to buy new pants."

Her father chuckles. "You look great."

The house, for all its eerie emptiness, smells like her mother's cooking—an aroma that swaddles her, for the first time she can remember, in homesickness. A pot of rice sits lidded and resting on a dish towel. A saucepan of gravy bubbles on the stove. Riley smells again, this time deeper, with purpose, and a foreign word appears in her mind: meat loaf. Her mother has made a meat loaf, a packet of brown gravy, cooked rice on the stove the way Riley liked it as a kid, steamed and buttered a bowl of broccoli. Naturally, the food is ready and waiting; her mother has executed with her signature precision, fills the table as Riley and her father carry on about the French and their cheese and soon they are in their typical spots around the table, scooping rice onto their plates and slicing meat loaf, pouring gravy over everything in that familial way, an eerie, perfect time machine except, of course, that there is no Morgan.

Her father opens a bottle of Oregon pinot noir and they talk about Japan, about the vending machines that line the streets, but also about the buyers of the house, a young banker named Andrew and his wife, Alice, their two-year-old son, Felix. Their conversation forms a natural relay, one topic easily handed off to the next, orbiting around a central bank of so much experience and memory. They recall her parents' trip to Japan, how they brought back a tea set for Riley and Morgan, which her mother has recently packed in a box. The Realtor, Beverly, Riley is told, has a son who recently went to Japan, and Riley asks if Beverly still cuts her hair like it's 1985. Hank asks what's wrong with that, fingering his own locks, and Riley assures him his hair is at least a decade older, more 1975 than Beverly the Realtor. It is a brand-new exercise, just the three of them, performing for one another. There is life in the air, an eagerness that buoys them all. Riley can't remember the last time this happened, if it ever happened at all. How happy her parents are to be in her company, looking at her like they've been starving, like between the two of them, they couldn't figure out how to eat. So much has changed since she left, in all of them. Her mother does not mention her sister. Her father gets up to clear the table. Riley lingers, does not whisk herself away with the dishes.

When her mother asks about James—her father dealing with dessert, staring into empty drawers, thwarted by the ice cream scoop that's been packed away—Riley tells her he's in Oregon, doing the same thing she is, staying with his mom until he finds a job. It's the first time the atmosphere swings. Riley and her mother fumble between *that's good* and *how nice* until the well dries up, and Riley is quick behind with a change of subject, a question about the new apartment, how they found it, what it's like, which they discuss until the ice cream is finished and Riley's mother tells her to go get some sleep, that her room is ready and they'll see her in the morning.

Upstairs, Riley's bed is made with linens that smell like a previous life. She sits down, inhales deeply through her nose, and pulls out her phone for the first time that night. There's a message from James. *Hope it's going okay. So fucking weird to be back in Eugene. Call me whenever, I love you.* She sets her phone down on the bed and thinks. She wants to call, is desperate to unpack the millions of conflicting currents of feeling, but she doesn't know how, from this bedroom in her parents' house, across a bathroom from her sister's room, hearing the sounds of her mother washing dishes, her father watching TV. How can she explain what's happened tonight? It is their first night apart in nearly a year. Just hours before, they were making promises at the Paris airport, and yet it feels like she never left this house, like she might never leave again. Riley stands and walks across the bathroom, turns on the light in her sister's room, and gasps aloud in the gutted space. The mattress leans against the wall; boxes are labeled "Morgan Room." Riley pulls in her lips with a sharp inhale, willing herself not to cry. Standing there, letting the scene soak into the crevices of her heart, she understands this emotion is not for her sister, for the dismantling of what was once a sacred and contested shrine. She's trembling because her mother left her own room intact, her things exactly where she'd left them, as if to say, You are alive, this is your home, and perhaps, Riley thinks, that she is sorry.

Over the next few weeks, the moving keeps them busy, dealing with their own trucks and movers and Andrew and Alice's designers and painters, all while running around like idiots, with no idea where anything is, reminding one another what is staying and what is going. Some of the furniture is too big, too flashy, for the modest dimensions of their new apartment, and so they sold Andrew and Alice their dining room table and chairs, the teak sideboard, the massive wardrobe. Everything they offered, Alice took; the person buying their house is, of all people, a devoted Kaleidoscope shopper. Alice's interest in their lives and where they are moving, her penchant for wearing Kaleidoscope pieces, makes this process simultaneously more dignified and profoundly demeaning. The store closings are not yet public, and so they tell Alice the house is too big, Kaleidoscope is doing fine. Karen and Hank are masters of abating reality, have offered this phrase so often, to so many people—fine! they are just fine—it becomes a salve they apply as often as possible. Karen at the helm, their days are structured by a list, on which she focuses and which she praises above all else. Thank god for this list. What would we do without this list? It's a good thing I put it on the list! Over breakfast, Karen consulting her list, Riley is told what they'll be eating for dinner—a habit of her mother's she now remembers and hates. The bell of her memory rings again and again, the off-kilter anxiety of adolescence compressed in her lungs. How easily her parents push the past to the surface, by simply being themselves, spreading an English muffin with apricot jam, wearing the same house slippers, listening to talk radio on a dark winter morning. Riley finds she can't wait to leave this house behind. The big, opulent edifice no longer makes sense in their Morganless life, has become something of a monument to their family's missteps.

On Saturdays, her mother still goes for regular pampering—massages, facials, salt soaks, blowouts—which is why she still looks so good, while her father goes to the bar on Seventy-Ninth and comes home with three slices of pizza. And while Riley would much rather be drunk, she accompanies her mother, fills her sister's spot in those big leather chairs, if only to prove she is willing. They sit in the Chinese spa on Amsterdam, reading magazines as women knead their feet. This is the only way her mother knows how to relax: with applied force. It reminds Riley of her first pedicure, watching the gloved technician hold Karen's feet by the ankles, shredding her heels as her mom closed her eyes, almost fell asleep. They talk, prodding along, using the magazines for guidance. Neither of them has ever maintained a relationship of this sort—based on the shallow passing of subjects, based on nothing. They are learning, perhaps for the first time, that relationships can be forged from the sheer act of willfulness, of sitting in the same chair Saturday after Saturday, showing up even when there's nothing to say, creating something out of nothing.

"He's good-looking." From her leather massage chair, Karen extends her magazine to Riley.

"Yes." Riley nods at the picture.

"And he lives in New York." Her mother shrugs. "Something to think about."

Riley wrinkles her face. "Something to think about? Are you under the impression that Jake Gyllenhaal is hoping I'll call?"

"I know, I know. You're not on the market." Riley hadn't told her about James; her mother had simply looked at her one day and said: You think I don't know you two are together? It was disconcerting, how she'd dropped this bomb and swiftly moved on, so different from how Riley had imagined it. Somehow, they'd crossed this massive hurdle—this subject for which Riley has been preparing—by simply kicking it down, pretending they had leapt over it. Beyond these minor allusions to her off-stage relationship, she and her mother didn't talk about James, and Riley can think of no other plan but to pretend like this is completely natural. "Just keep an open mind. He lives in New York."

"So does Robert De Niro. Do you think I have a shot with him?"

"Robert De Niro! Robert De Niro is old enough to date me."

"That's a good point. I mean, I know you're married to Dad and all, but why not Robert De Niro? I hear he lives in New York."

This is the closest they get to subjects of consequence. Back-of-the-magazine horoscopes. A profile of Jake Gyllenhaal. Twelve ways to look like money without spending any. Riley finds a surprising new aptitude for deflecting her mother, for sharpening her words without drawing blood. She extracts the humor and patience she picked up over the last year, the composure she built while smoothing out misunderstandings, eluding the people trying to sell her things, dodging scams and listening to the narcissistic ramblings of the lonely and drunk. For the first time, Riley studies her mother with the interest and care of an anthropologist, and what she sees has begun to frighten her. Her mother is like a piece of petrified wood—for better or for worse, she is a person frozen in time, unwilling or unable to be anything else. It's as if the light turned red and instead of waiting, her mother got out of the car, set up her life. Karen picks the same nail color, requests the same masseuse, tells the same stories over and over with full knowledge of her repetition. In many ways, it's difficult to look this closely, to understand that her mother has been drained of her power. Before the accident, Karen was capable of everything, took pleasure in showing Riley, in showing all of them, what she could do. For all her overbearing preaching, Karen at least was learning then, the sponge of her brain ready to absorb and squirt. But now Karen's vision is stubbornly cloudy. She's seen enough, has only the strength to preserve what she has. One daughter, a weekend routine, a relationship that involves sitting side by side in these worn leather chairs. It surprises Riley, how Karen shows no interest in diving any deeper, in probing what happened while they were estranged, in talking about James, in forging a truer path to being mother and daughter. Instead, she's asking Riley to revise, to take erasers to the page and rub out the errors that came before, so that they might pretend to be these people; and Riley finds she is willing to do it. It's a stubborn collaboration unique in families, this instinctual resilience to keep trying, against reason, in the face of mistakes and humiliations not meant to be spoken of ever again. And so they bash their heads against the wall, paint their nails, think of how nice it feels to be here, wherever this is, getting along.

Then there is the other part of Riley's day. After she's eaten dinner with her parents and helped clean up, wished them good night and climbed the stairs, Riley gets on the phone with James and feels the crashing of her internal pieces, the bright shards of glass, as she turns herself back into the person James thinks he's speaking to. Hearing his voice sets off a sore, duplicitous unraveling of her day. Sharing it makes it feel worse: she ate Thai food, applied for two jobs, went for a run, hadn't said anything to either of her parents. *How*, James wants to know, sincerely. How can she avoid this subject for so long? How was it possible Riley could spend all day with them without ever mentioning the life she spent the last year erecting, the plans she's made for the future? Riley doesn't want to return to school until she can pay for it on her own. She wants a job, to continue on the track of independence; but no one asks her any of this. Her parents don't question what she is doing with her life, if she is planning to return to Barnard or look for work. For now, at least, they want nothing but the present—so Riley says nothing, plays along. She can't explain what happens in the vortex that is her parents' house, living among the things that remind her, with every turn, how much she owes them. When James says she was once better at this, once easily able to stand up to her parents, Riley says it's not like before. Morgan is gone. Her parents have nothing left. You should see them, she says. I would like to, he says.

Despite what James says to her—that she's making it harder, that she's messing with her parents' expectations—what Riley finds most disconcerting is how readily she slides into these competing worlds. The way she inhabits both these people, as if the other doesn't exist, is simpler than the alternative, which is pushing them together, making the person who can exist simultaneously. Even worse, she isn't sure who or how she wants to be. The Riley she likes most, the one she is with James, is so much harder to be than the Riley she likes less, the one she's been all her life, who has a home and a family and a resigned but easy sense of belonging. The first Riley is challenged every night, made to think hard and long about the choices she's making, about what she wants out of the next week, the next year, the rest of her life. The second Riley is asked no questions, made to

BAG OF CRAP IN THE CRAWL SPACE

The week of the move, Hank stands outside the kitchen, telling himself to fucking do it. That he must do it here, in this house, if only to spare him the shame of hiding what he holds in their new apartment—a thousand square feet of open concept—where he knows it will not go undetected. Even his reasoning is cowardly, but none of this is new. Since the accident, since they lost that money, Hank lives on the defense, considering the worst-case scenario, then trying to prevent that from happening.

Before he changes his mind, Hank walks into the room with a clumsy, nervous step and his daughter looks up from her phone.

"Hey," she says, puts her phone down. "What's up?"

Hanks hesitates. "I . . ." he says, then lifts the backpack onto the table and watches his daughter's face turn surprised, then confused, then alarmed.

"What." Riley stands. She touches the backpack, leaves her hand there.

"I never opened it," Hank says. "I promise." He raises a palm, as if not opening it makes the difference. The way his daughter gapes at him, Hank feels like he has let down every single person he loves.

"Are you going to explain?"

"I'm going to explain."

Hank walks to the fridge and takes two beers from the wiped-clean shelf that contains just the beer, bought for this occasion. He pulls a lighter from his pocket, pries off the tops, and hands his daughter a bottle. He wipes his forehead, does not sit.

"Your mother doesn't know, okay? That's the first thing. And not that it's my choice, but I don't want her to know."

"Okay," Riley says. It occurs to Hank that he has never been in a confrontation with his daughter. Not really. Fighting with the girls was Karen's job. Long ago they'd accepted their roles, and it takes him by surprise, how this dynamic is so strange and confusing that it does not escalate as he assumed it would. Hank sits. When Riley sits too, he drains half the bottle and sets it back on the table.

"You know your mom and I were fighting. A lot. After the accident, it got really bad between us and things were pretty miserable. We were making each other miserable. I didn't know what would happen with us. I mean that. Some days would be fine and then some days, I thought she might kill me if I breathed the wrong way." His daughter nods, and her expression isn't shocked or intrigued or any of the reactions a child might make upon hearing one parent talk badly about another. Riley's expression is open—like she knows exactly what he's talking about, like she is pulling empathy from her own personal experience—and Hank understands that in the last nine months, while he and Karen were at each other's throats, his youngest daughter has grown up.

"I don't know if James told you," Hank says, and to this, he knows there will be a reaction. He watches his daughter turn vigilant, her whole body attuned. "Before you two left, he came to talk to me. He explained a lot of things to me, actually. How you felt trapped. That you needed some space to get yourselves together, to leave the place where everything had happened. It made a lot of sense to me. In fact, it was all I could think about for a while."

Hank waits for his daughter to tell him to hurry up, to get to the point the way Karen did when she felt wronged, but Riley says nothing. Her patience makes him want to hurry.

"The point is, I was lost. And I was probably also a little jealous. Here your mom and I were, drowning in our anger, and you and James had found a way out. I just kept thinking how smart you were, to go disappear for a while. And the more I thought about it, the more I wanted to go too. And I knew what flight you were on and it just seemed like, I don't know, it sounds absolutely insane now, out loud. It was a much better plan when it was just in my head."

Now Riley is shocked. "You followed us to *India*?"

"No." Hank is relieved to have something to refuse. He shakes his head as if following them to India was absolutely not what happened. "I mean, I wanted to. That was the plan. I tried."

"What do you mean you tried?" There it was, finally, a spark of her mother's indignation.

"I got to the airport. I had the ticket. But I couldn't get on the plane."

"Oh my god."

"I know. And to tell the truth I didn't want you to ever know. That was such a bad, dark time for me, and it's embarrassing. I'm supposed to be your father, for god's sake. I'm supposed to know what to do, and there I was following you, because you had a better plan than I did. But then I couldn't get on the plane. They had to pull my bag from the cargo, and"—Hank nods at the backpack between them—"they must have been in a hurry. They got the wrong Brighton."

They sit there in silence, the backpack enormous between them. For the first time, Riley picks up her beer and tips it back. She squints from the cold, wipes her mouth. "So why are you telling me?"

That this is his daughter's question makes Hank want to laugh. Whose daughter is this, so logical, so devoid of drama? He thinks of Morgan and her endless ambition, her desire to please, and the regret Hank feels having never once told her to slow down, that there was nothing left to prove. Riley had always been the straight shooter—sure-footed, sanctimonious—more like her mother. But Riley's shot has grown gentle, and it is a beautiful, alarming phenomenon to see his daughter echo something of his wife, but made her own. At first, Hank's not sure how to answer Riley's question. He's not sure if he has a point beyond coming clean, passing this polyurethane bag of guilt back to her. But then, it comes.

"I don't have a problem with James," he says. "I like him, actually. I think he's a good guy. I always have."

Riley looks like she might cry, and Hank understands she thought he didn't know—that this giant worry of hers was invisible. Once, Hank thinks, she might have been right. But now, there is nothing but time to repent, to look.

"I can't speak for your mother," Hank says. "She's got her own hang-ups when it comes to your relationship. But I think the two of you found something pretty cool."

"Pretty *cool*?" Riley repeats, amused.

"Hey. You got me to buy a thousand-dollar ticket I never used and hide this bag of crap in the crawl space all this time, because even I thought you two had it figured out. You're good for each other. It's clear to me."

"So why does Mom hate him so much?"

"It's confusing for her. You know she likes things clean. I think, I don't know, but he must remind her of the accident."

"Did she say that?"

Hank shakes his head, finishes the last inch of his beer. "To be honest with you, your mom and I don't talk about that stuff much. Not anymore. Having you back has been such a shake-up for us. It's been nice. I haven't seen her like this in ages."

"What do you mean?"

"I mean she's been depressed."

"This is her *happy*?" Riley blows out a mouthful of air.

"Yeah." Hank laughs, despite himself. He looks his daughter in the eye and feels proud of her. Of both of them. Communicating on their own like this, still evolving. "But that's not for you to worry about. Everything's going to be what it is. That's something I've learned, and the earlier you learn it, the better. You only get to control so much."

Hank puts his hands on the table and stands, opens his arms and embraces his daughter in the gutted kitchen, says, "Now, go hide that backpack before your mom gets home."

WALKING IN CIRCLES, NEARLY BLIND

The apartment on Eighty-Sixth is smaller than they're used to, with two bedrooms that share a wall through which Karen can hear her daughter on the phone. Each night she falls asleep to murmuring, wakes up occasionally to spontaneous laughter. Riley displays a discipline that stuns her, able to hold her two worlds so far, so neatly apart. She exerts a capacity for disassociation that alarms Karen, in multiple and complicated ways, because Karen knows what it's like to live two lives, to keep them apart, and it's nice to see something of her own reflected, finally, in her youngest daughter. Of course Karen knows what's happening with James; it was apparent even before they left, when Karen took him out for coffee to tell him her daughters were not his personal playground. She still remembers the look on his face, the genuine alarm, when she brought up the funeral.

James had looked at her, and the blankness made them both unsteady. "I'm sorry. I have no idea what you're talking about."

"You don't remember standing there? Telling everyone to check their phones?"

James opened his mouth. Closed it. "Why would I do that?"

"Because you thought Riley texted someone where she'd gone."
James nodded. "She went missing."

"So you remember."

"That she went missing, yes. But I didn't give a *speech*."

"James." Karen didn't know what to do. "Are you serious?"

"Swear to god." He shook his head.

"You went on and on. You'd looked in the bike racks. All along Fourteenth. In the bathrooms. Then you just stood there, looking at everyone like they knew where she was but they wouldn't tell you. James, it was incredibly embarrassing! I'd just introduced you as *Morgan's* boyfriend and you stood there for twenty minutes harping about how worried you were about Riley. I see the way you are with her and I'm telling you, for all of our sakes, let Riley be. You're *Morgan's* boyfriend. Riley doesn't need this confusion; none of us do."

James had taken a moment, looked at Karen with that alarm she still remembers. At the time, she had believed she'd finally broken through.

"Okay," James had said. "All right." He nodded. "Look, I apologize for making you uncomfortable. Genuinely. I was not trying to make that day any harder. That was the last thing I wanted to do." James closed his mouth, took a breath through his nose. "But I can't be sorry about caring for Riley. I know you don't want me in your house. At this point, I don't want me in your house. But Riley deserves an ally right now." He touched the handle of his coffee cup, looked up, and returned her gaze. "And if not me, Karen, then who?"

Seven weeks have passed since Riley returned, a month since they moved into the new apartment, and the phone conversations are growing longer, more frequent, Riley excusing herself from the room to take calls during the middle of the day. Having her daughter back has felt like a small earthquake—mild enough to keep the paintings on the wall, but large enough to make Karen pay attention. She is awake, alert to her surroundings in a way she's missed, buried in her troubles all these months. There is life in the house again, a structure and energy to her days. Yet a few things have fallen from the shelves, evidence of the tremor on the ground. And instead of picking them up, inspecting the damage, she and her daughter have decided to step around them. They have rerouted themselves, forged new paths around the obstructions until here they are, walking in circles, nearly blind.

The truth is Karen had assumed things between her daughter and James would unravel on their trip. It was almost aspirational, the way she waited for her phone to ring at some inconvenient hour, imagined her daughter's voice, strained and sorry. Travel was not easy. Karen learned this over and over throughout her years—patience ran short, expectations ran high, nothing ever went as planned—and Riley and James were young, troubled, and had no money. How many nights had Karen stayed up thinking through the scenarios, imagined flying to Asia, checking her and Riley into a nice hotel before making the long journey home? At a certain point, she'd spent so much time flying to Asia in her mind, rescuing her daughter, that her prophecy seemed inevitable. What did it matter that they hadn't heard a peep from Riley since she left, weeks before? They'd recovered from worse. Kaleidoscope, her marriage—both had survived. Everything would fall into place. By Karen's reckoning, Riley had to call. She had to be humbled as they all were, to ask for help, and so when the first post-card arrived in April—a golden temple in Thailand, *Mom and Dad* in her daughter's hand above their address—Karen was not prepared. She had held it up to the light, squinted at the empty message box as if that might reveal something, but it remained blank. She'd immedi-ately written her daughter an email leaden with her own unreality, telling Riley it wasn't too late to ask for help. When a reply came instantly back, just seeing her daughter's name in her inbox made Karen's heart leap. Then she read the words, the single line: *I am away and not checking email.*

The postcards continued to arrive: palm trees in the Philippines, Mount Fuji, Taipei 101, a Korean flag, Angkor Wat, a red tuk-tuk, a table full of meze, the Acropolis, a cartoon woman on a Vespa smiling into the breeze. By the time she pulled the Acropolis from the mailbox, Karen understood she would not be saving her daughter. As usual, Riley was fine. She'd left for nine months, asked for no money, sent her parents regular signs of life, and came home so balanced and at peace, so clearly in love, that she felt no need to explain herself. And hadn't it always been this way? Riley never explained herself. She accepted herself in a way Karen had never managed, right or wrong, in a way her oldest daughter had never managed. It was this mutual need for reassurance that brought her and Morgan strangely, sometimes painfully, together.

When Riley's phone rings, she picks up her second life and walks it into another room. It frightens Karen. That's the closest thing to the truth. Watching her get this close to James, carving out this path—it scares the shit out of her, makes her feel entirely out of control. Still, they sidestep what's happening, lifting their feet a little less each time. But the new apartment is too small, their worlds growing close enough to touch.

"Guess what," Riley says, sitting at the counter with a cup of coffee.

"What?"

"You're supposed to guess."

"You won the lottery and you're going to retire your tired parents in luxury."

"Close. I got an interview."

"What?" Karen stops what she's doing at the sink, turns around. "What do you mean an interview?"

"For a job. You know, that thing people do to make money."

"You're applying to jobs? But what about school?"

"I'm going to finish school. Don't worry about that. I'll go back when I'm ready. But I want to pay for it myself."

"But we pay for school," Karen says. "We'll give you the money for school."

"I know. And I really appreciate that. But I don't want you to. I want to do it myself."

"I don't understand," Karen says, shaking her head, understanding perfectly. She trusts what Riley says, that she will finish school on her own terms, and feels once again entirely impotent.

"I want to be independent, Mom. I want my own place. I don't think you want me living here forever."

"Not forever." Karen leans against the sink, wipes her hands on the front of her pants. "But I thought it would be for a bit longer."

"It's been two months."

"And that feels so long?"

"That's not what I said."

"What's the job?"

"It's this small company downtown. They import food, mostly from Asia but Europe too. It's actually perfect for me—"

"So are you trying to move out now?"

Riley looks into her coffee. "I mean, yes, eventually. That's the idea."

The silence is tangled up in their stubbornness, both of them thinking what they have not yet said. Finally, Riley looks up at her mother. "With James," she says, and Karen swallows. Her daughter's voice is thin with nerves, but still, she looks her in the eye. "I've been waiting for you to ask about him. I figured you would ask when you were ready."

"Riley." Karen sighs. "I'm still not ready. I'm sorry, it's just too weird for me. He was your sister's boyfriend. He was her boyfriend when she—" Karen shakes away the rest of the sentence. "There are so many men in this world, in this city. Why does it have to be James?"

"Because it's James."

"What does that mean?"

"It means no one else is *James*. I get that it's weird, I do. And it is. But James and I are so good for each other. If you would give it a chance, I think you'd see that he and I make so much sense. And if you're worried about Morgan, I really think she would give her blessing."

"Oh!" Her mother jumps. "Now you're speaking for Morgan?"

Riley can feel the delicate whirring of her body, the warm blood rushing at the surface.

"No," she says. "I'm not speaking for Morgan."

They go silent again in that old way, before they learned to sit in leather chairs.

"Mom," Riley says. "Why not? Why can't you just let me have this?"

"Let you?" Karen looks at her, incredulous. "Riley, you've never asked permission for anything. Do you really think I have a say?"

Riley takes a breath, forces herself to say it, even if it feels terrible. "I think that Morgan got everything she wanted," Riley says, clears her throat when it comes out scratched. "I think I should be able to be with James, without you resenting me."

"Oh, Riley, don't be so dramatic. You want to be with James— fine. Okay, you have my blessing, is that what you want? But I want to say something. All your life, you always thought you got such a bad deal. You think your sister had it so easy. But it's not true. All your life, everything *you* wanted, you got it. New York. James. This yearlong vacation! So don't give me this woe-is-me stuff. You were the one who got everything, not Morgan. And look. You'll get your way again now."

Riley blinks at her mother. "Are you *kidding* me?"

Karen holds steady.

"Are we talking about different Morgans? Because I'm talking about Morgan my perfect gazelle-looking sister who charmed the fucking eyeballs out of every person she ever met. Is that the Morgan you're talking about? The prom queen. The famous fashion designer. The one who James asked out first?"

"Yes, Riley, but it's far more complicated than that!"

"Then, please, enlighten me!"

Karen is flustered, feeling suddenly cornered, not sure what to say.

"Tell me. I want to know what was so complicated, so hard about being Morgan."

"She was miserable, Riley! Since she followed you to New York, she was so unhappy, she just never wanted to tell you. She didn't want you to know."

Riley shakes her head. "Okay, let me get this straight. Morgan went to New York of her own will. Sometimes she felt sad. And now she's gone and I'm the winner who got it all?"

"Riley, what I'm trying to say to you is that James came into your sister's life during a very fragile moment. You were busy, Riley. And I'm not blaming you. Let's not get into that again. I'm saying your sister was going through some things of her own. Maybe even things you didn't know about. And James was so good for her. He was so

good for her, and I think they would have been happy. I want to remember my daughter happy! Is that so terrible? She was happy with
James!"

Riley opens her mouth. She stares at her mother.

"You knew about Hammir," Riley whispers, and everything Karen
fears about her youngest daughter comes true. "You fucking knew."

"No!"

"Holy shit."

In the dampness that's collected at her hairline, in the impulse
she must fight to turn the questioning around, to ask her daughter
what *she* knows, Karen is confronted by what has always frightened
her about her daughter. Since she was a girl, Riley had an eye for
what Karen was doing wrong. When Karen was spending too much
time with the Emporium's general manager, seven-year-old Riley
brought it up at dinner, told her father a man named Nick had taken
them to lunch, had bought her a Shirley Temple, and she and Hank
had nearly divorced. Riley had a stubborn habit of paying attention
to everything Karen wished she wouldn't, and so Karen had developed a habit of her own: holding her daughter just far enough away
that she couldn't look so goddamn closely.

"She was in a terrible place, Riley." Her daughter stares at her like
there's a tree sprouting from her neck. "From what I understand it
was consensual."

"She was a *teenager*! He was like fucking forty."

"I know, Riley. But please." She lowers her voice.

"Oh my god," Riley says. "Dad doesn't know."

Karen wants to pick up the dish rack and throw it across the
room. Instead, motioning for her daughter to follow, she walks from
the small kitchen into the attached living room, where she slides the
pocket doors closed, turns on the TV, and sits on the couch. She

looks at Riley, waiting for her to sit, as if this is something they've done before.

"Your dad does not know," Karen says quietly. "And I think it should stay that way, because it's over now, and your father would never forgive him."

"And you *do?*"

"No!"

"You don't think your husband should know *why* Hammir's been bankrolling his life? You don't see any problem with that?" Riley's outrage slices through her mother, that confident, bombastic way about her that makes Karen want to set her straight. What she wants to say next is purely from a desire to shock her daughter, to tell her something, anything, Riley can't throw in her face first.

"Hammir has never given us a penny! If he had anything to do with our finances, if we owed him money—I'm not a monster, Riley. Life isn't so black and white."

"And I'm supposed to believe that?"

"*Yes,*" Karen hisses, steadies herself. A commercial for life insurance fills the room as they stare each other down. "Yes, you are. Because it's true. Everything we have is ours."

"Bullshit."

"I'm telling you, I never took any money from Hammir."

"Wow. This is an interesting tactic."

"We never needed it," Karen says too loud. "Your grandparents. My parents left me some money. They helped with the house in Hawaii. We got help, okay? We didn't start with nothing. But I never took a cent from Hammir. That's the truth. When I found out something was happening between them." Karen shakes her head violently, in a way that makes Riley uneasy. "I could have killed him. But what was I supposed to do? He was so much a part of our life and Morgan *loved* him. She made some threats. She said if I stopped it, she might do something to hurt herself. She never left the house, Riley! Unless it was with you, she was always in the basement. So when James came along I thought, finally. Finally, we are going to get past this."

To Karen's surprise, Riley is crying.

"This whole time," Riley says. "You didn't do anything."

"I did what I could, Riley! It was only *me*. I did the best I could do."

Riley freezes, neon flashes of TV swirling in the dampness of her eyes.

"Riley. Say something."

Riley looks up at her mother. Her entire life, she assumed her mom was looking after Morgan, loving her, mothering her best. But here she is, telling Riley that Morgan was sacrificed long ago, and it was Riley, kept at a distance, who had been accidentally spared. Riley whispers, shakes her head. "Best for who?"

"For all of us!" Karen reaches for her daughter's hand, thinks better of it. "Your sister was so talented, Riley, but she never believed in herself, not the way you do. But Hammir believed in her. He made Morgan believe in herself. They were such a brilliant team, you know that. If I had broken them up—if that was even possible—everything would have been destroyed! Morgan would have quit; she would have *hated* me." Riley is holding her breath, trying to listen, trying not to explode. "All I wanted was for her to succeed. Your sister deserved to *succeed*. Of all people, hard as she worked, did she not deserve a shot at greatness?" As Riley listens, the words get mixed up, sound as if her mother is talking about herself, defending herself. Her life, her ambition, the vast well of confusion and regret that has become her mother's life. She is transposing herself onto Morgan, thinly and sloppily tying them together, and the depth of her delusion, the sincerity of her mother's delusion, tears a brand-new hole in Riley's consciousness.

Riley stops crying, feels her awareness lift from her body, the room swelling big and strange around her. She's confronted with the anger she's been carrying for Morgan. That she had held this from her, had so easily managed this double life—it made Riley feel like a foolish child. But Morgan had told their mother. She'd done the thing of last resort and confided in their mother. Yet again Riley is faced with the magnitude of what she's gotten wrong, how in the end, she and her sister were so stupidly similar. They both had weaknesses and fears and the compulsion to preserve themselves in the eyes of the other. To hide their mess, so that they might remain absolutely knowable. Riley thinks of how different it might have looked, had they understood what she does now—that this very preservation is what made them lonely and estranged, that the darkest, weirdest parts are the ones that might have drawn them closest. And what a tiny, terrible miracle it was that in losing Morgan, in the course of grieving her sister, Riley had learned to be knowable to someone else.

Back in the living room, her mother looks at her expectantly. Riley's heart is heavy, lodged someplace low in her chest. And while she doesn't know what her mother will say next, she braces herself, knows that it will be wrong.

"What?" Riley says, realizing her mother is waiting for an answer.

"I just—" Karen flicks her eyes away and back. "I didn't think she told you. I was under the impression. When did she tell you?" Her mother looks so uncertain—her attempt to be flippant landing in that starving way. "About Hammir," she says, her clarification making it even sadder. The way she says it, with no concept of how obvious she's being, how badly she needs the reassurance, for the first time in so many years, it makes Riley want to feed her.

"She didn't," Riley says, her eyes shining wetly, her mouth contorted by sadness and a strange, heartbreaking kind of love. "She never told me, Mom. I figured it out myself. She never told me. Only you."

ALMOST HOME

"Do you ever fear you're turning into Mom?"

"No. Not really."

"Well, that's because you aren't." Morgan sighs in the back of the cab. She's still wearing her gold headpiece, which glints as they glide beneath the streetlights. "Sometimes I hear myself, or I see myself doing something and I think, Whoa. That's no good. That's Mom crazy, that intensity's in my blood."

"Yeah," Riley says, hears her dryness. "Well, we all got something."

"What did you get?"

Riley looks out the window. "Her appetite."

"I'm being serious."

"It's late, Morgan. It's been a shitty night."

"I know. But come on, you're barely around anymore. Just talk to me, we're almost home."

Riley unwinds the dopatta from her neck and shifts it to her shoulders like a shawl. They're approaching Seventieth, still on the east side. As they left the gala in the cab, James was still there, wearing his tunic, keeping watch like some irritating knight. How was Morgan making this about her?

"Why are you turning into Mom?"

"Never mind."

"Morgan, you're *fine*. Everyone loves you. It's frustrating that this is even a real concern for you."

"But that's exactly it. Why do I need everyone to love me? Why am I like this? I get so fucking stupid for approval, and Mom is the same way. *Dad* is the same way. You don't seem to understand how lucky you are to not care about any of this. Why don't you care?"

Riley rests her head on the window. They're crossing the park, winding between the stone walls. "I do care."

"You know what I mean."

Riley can't think about her sister's problems right now, can't explain that she cares less not because she's lucky, not because she doesn't desire approval—she's twenty, for Christ's sake—but because she's unable to be anything different, not even secure enough to say this now.

"I really don't."

Morgan looks at her, frowns tenderly.

"I love you," she says.

"I love you too. Everyone loves you, you needy animal."

It doesn't always happen exactly like this. Sometimes, through the force of Riley's subconscious will, the cab ride lasts all night and Riley asks the things she's supposed to ask, doesn't walk into Morgan's room an hour later to find her gone, doesn't wake up two years later, panicked in a studio apartment, a new life, her sister's voice cracking in her bones. Are the dead ever really dead? Riley's learning, day by day, that grief is something you grow with, that grows with you, that ebbs and flows just like other feelings, like happiness, like fear, like love. She's getting better at talking about these things, at asking questions, of herself and others—learning that question asking is not an ability gifted to some and withheld from others, that the ability to ask grows from the capacity to be present, to step beyond yourself, to care. The day her mother told her father, the afternoon they all fought in the living room, the night her father called Hammir, Riley felt something expand between them: both a chasm and a bridge, a terrible depth beneath them, but which they had crossed. Her parents will never be exactly who Riley hopes, but for the first time, she feels that they are hers, and she theirs.

On the mornings Riley wakes up disoriented, shaken by a visit from her sister, it takes her a minute to remember where she is. The tiny studio apartment is a fourth-floor walk-up, has a small window facing Second Avenue. She's learned to walk to the window, to look out at the world, to stand in the morning light and feel how different it is to be here, in a space of her own. How far she's come since those cold showers at dawn, standing in her sister's clothes, trying not to cry because her mother was listening. Was that really her? Time remains a strange magician. She looks back on that summer and marvels—looking at her thrift-store dishes, her drooping ficus, her mismatched set of kitchen towels, the three-quarters-size fridge that holds whatever she puts inside, the Kaleidoscope sofa from her parents beneath the picture of her and James at the top of Delphi, smiling into the sun, and James in the bed, sitting up and rubbing his eyebrows, asking if she's okay, seeing her at the window wearing her blue kimono, knowing what it means—because all of this belongs to her. She did it. She pushed her worlds together, can see them all in this small room.

Acknowledgments

Thank you to Meredith Kaffel Simonoff, the smartest reader on the planet, who showed up at every critical moment and rotated me toward the light. To Maya Ziv, deeply generous editor and first-class human: thank you for taking the long way with me, it was so worth it.

Endless gratitude to Julia Pierpont, Julie Buntin, and Yelena Akhtiorskaya—the sharpest, funniest, most nourishing writing group. Long live the Kweens.

To the exceptional team at Dutton: John Parsley, Christine Ball, Lexy Cassola, Eileen Chetti, LeeAnn Pemberton, Susan Schwartz, Ryan Richardson, Dora Mak, Katy Riegel, and Tiffany Estriecher. Vi-An Nguyen, for the cover of my dreams. To the talented people at Defiore: Jacey Mitziga, Dana Bryan, Adam Schear, Linda Kaplan, and Emma Haviland-Blunk.

Thanks to Gavin McKee, for the best advice, for 2014. To my parents, for their patience and encouragement as I roamed far from home.

To Stephanie Sisco Luccarelli, Emily Anne Hathaway, Sauyeh Hadjatry, Maddalena Fiorini, Tao Tao Holmes, Allison Chamot,

ACKNOWLEDGMENTS

Tyler McCormick, Galen Fairbanks, Allegra Sachs, Andrew Underberg, and Lindsey Wong, for the kind of friendship that enriches both my writing and my life.

Thank you to Zoe, for sleeping on a pillow in my lap as I finished this book. And as always, to Read, who is definitely not James—thank you for being my perfect companion, for bringing joy and heart to everything you do, and for an absolute firecracker of a decade.

About the Author

Cecily Wong is the author of the novel *Diamond Head*, which was a Barnes & Noble Discover Great New Writers selection, the recipient of an *Elle* Readers' Prize, and voted a best debut of the Brooklyn Book Festival. Her work has appeared in *The Wall Street Journal*, *Los Angeles Review of Books*, *Self* magazine, *Bustle*, and elsewhere. She is a graduate of Barnard College and lives in New York, where she is a writer at *Atlas Obscura*.